"The author is brilliant in not only writing character portrayals, but in creating a mystery complete with twists and turns that will keep the reader trying to figure it all out. . . . I absolutely could not put it down."

—Socrates' Book Reviews

Cat Trick

"Match two magical kitties with an extremely inquisitive librarian and a murder or two and you have all the makings of an extraordinary mystery series . . . a captivating cozy!" —Escape with Dollycas into a Good Book

"The characters are likable and the cats are darling."

—Socrates' Book Reviews

"Small-town charm and a charming cat duo make this every cat fancier's dream." —The Mystery Reader

Copycat Killing

"I've been a huge fan of this series from the very start, and I am delighted that this new book meets my expectations and then some. . . . Cats with magic powers, a library, good friends who look out for each other and small-town coziness come together in perfect unison. If you are a fan of Miranda James's Cat in the Stacks mysteries, you will want to read [this series]."

—MyShelf.com

"This is a really fun series, and I've read them all. Each book improves on the last one. Being a cat lover myself, I'm looking at my cat in a whole new light."

—Once Upon a Romance

"A fun whodunit. . . . Fans will appreciate this entertaining amateur sleuth." —Genre Go Round Reviews

"This charming series continues on a steady course as the intrepid Kathleen has two mysteries to snoop into. . . . Readers who are fans of cats and cozies will want to add this series to their must-read lists."
—*RT Book Reviews*

Sleight of Paw

"Kelly's appealing cozy features likable, relatable characters set in an amiable location. The author continues to build on the promise of her debut novel, carefully developing her characters and their relationships."
—*RT Book Reviews*

Curiosity Thrilled the Cat

"A great cozy that will quickly have you anxiously waiting for the next release so you can spend more time with the people of Mayville Heights."
—Mysteries and My Musings

"If you love mystery and magic, this is the book for you!" —Debbie's Book Bag

"This start of a new series offers an engaging cast of human characters and two appealing, magically inclined felines. Kathleen is a likable, believable heroine, and the magical cats are amusing." —*RT Book Reviews*

Also Available from Sofie Kelly

Curiosity Thrilled the Cat
Sleight of Paw
Copycat Killing
Cat Trick
Final Catcall
A Midwinter's Tail

FAUX PAW

A MAGICAL CATS MYSTERY

SOFIE KELLY

AN OBSIDIAN MYSTERY

OBSIDIAN
Published by New American Library,
an imprint of Penguin Random House LLC
375 Hudson Street, New York, New York 10014

This book is an original publication of New American Library.

First Printing, October 2015

For more information about Penguin Random House, visit penguin.com.

ISBN 978-0-451-47215-1

33614056426140

Printed in the United States of America
10 9 8 7 6 5 4 3 2 1

Penguin
Random
House

To all the readers who have embraced Kathleen,
Owen and Hercules, my heartfelt thanks.
This one's for you.

ACKNOWLEDGMENTS

My deepest thanks:

To my editor, Jessica Wade, and the production team at Penguin Random House for all of their hard work on this book and the entire Magical Cats series.

To my agent, Kim Lionetti, for helping turn writing dreams into reality.

To retired police chief Tim Sletten for his patience and good humor.

And to Patrick and Lauren, just because.

I couldn't do this without you!

1

There was a severed head on the blue patterned quilt folded at the bottom of the bed. I turned my head slowly and looked into the eyes of a killer. He stared unblinkingly at me. It would have been terrifying if the head hadn't been from a yellow catnip Fred the Funky Chicken and the eyes hadn't belonged to my little black-and-white cat, Hercules.

"What did you do?" I asked, frowning at him.

"Merow," he said, looking from the disembodied chicken head to me. If the cat had been a person I would have said that there was a touch of righteous indignation in his tone.

Hercules's brother, Owen, had a thing for catnip chickens. My neighbor Rebecca and my best friend, Maggie, were always buying them for Owen, much to his delight.

Hercules didn't see the appeal of catnip at all, and he especially didn't like dried bits of it in his things. For the past few months Owen's chickens had been turning up in his brother's territory: upside down in Hercules's dinner dish, making a lump in the middle of his favorite blanket and sitting in what he considered to be his spot on the bench in the sun porch. As far-fetched as it seemed, I knew something was going on. It was almost as if Hercules was doing this on purpose, although I didn't quite see why.

I stretched, slid my feet into my slippers and stood up. "Owen is not going to take this well," I said to Hercules.

"Murp," he replied, dropping back to the floor. He looked up at me, green eyes narrowed, furry chin jutting out.

"This isn't going to fix anything," I said, heading for the bathroom. Hercules trailed me, making little noises as though he were trying to justify swiping the catnip toy and decapitating it.

Just then I heard a loud, furious yowl from downstairs. Herc's furry head swiveled at the sound. I leaned down and gave the top of his head a quick scratch. "You're on your own," I said. Then I darted into the bathroom and closed the door.

Of course that was pointless. If Hercules had been an ordinary cat he would have stayed on the other side of the door, in the hallway. But he wasn't. So he didn't.

Hercules had a . . . unique ability. He could walk through walls—and closed bathroom doors. Which he did. An area on the wood panel door seemed to shimmer for a moment and then the cat was standing at my feet. I had no idea how he did it. And it wasn't like I could ask anyone. Walking though walls defied the laws of physics, not to mention logic. I didn't want Hercules to end up in a research lab with electrodes stuck to his head—or worse. And I didn't really want to end up there myself, either.

"You can't hide in here forever," I told him.

He half turned to look at the bathroom door he'd just come through. Then he began to wash his face. Translation: "I can for now."

Unlike his brother, Owen didn't have the walking-through-walls skill, but he did have the ability to become invisible, which meant he could lurk in wait for Hercules anywhere in the house. And he would.

"I'm having a shower," I warned, leaning over to turn on the water.

Hercules took several steps backward. Among his many little quirks was an intense aversion to getting his feet wet, more so than the average cat. A heavy dew on the lawn in the backyard would make him hold up a paw and give me his best pathetic look in a calculated scheme to get me to carry him—which most of the time I did.

The first week of April had been rainy in Mayville Heights and there were only a few patches of snow left on the grass behind the house, but the ground was still soggy, which meant that for the last week I'd been carrying Hercules though our yard into Rebecca's so he could have coffee with Everett Henderson, Rebecca's new husband. Everett had funded the renovations to the Mayville Heights Free Public Library for its centennial and had hired me to oversee everything as head librarian. In eighteen months I'd fallen in love with the town, and when Everett offered me a permanent job I'd said yes.

When I got out of the shower Hercules was gone. I

dressed, dried my hair and went downstairs to see what returning salvo Owen was going to fire in this little war.

Owen was in the kitchen, sitting next to the refrigerator, the picture of innocence, with a little smug thrown in. The headless body of Fred the Funky Chicken was dumped in his bowl. Why wasn't he yowling his frustration at me or prowling around the house looking for his brother?

I leaned over to stroke the top of his gray head. "You're taking this very well," I said, narrowing my eyes at him. "Don't think I don't know you're up to something."

He gave me his best "Who, me?," which didn't fool me for a minute. I started the coffee, put my bowl of oatmeal in the microwave and then got the cats' breakfast.

Hercules appeared in the living room doorway. He looked warily toward Owen. The small gray tabby already had his head bent over his bowl. Herc started for his dish, moving slowly, his eyes locked on his brother. Owen gave no sign that he was interested; in fact, he shifted his body sideways a bit so Hercules was out of his line of sight.

I gave a sigh of relief. Maybe Owen didn't care about the decapitated chicken. Maybe he'd finally had his fill of them. Maybe he had no retaliation planned.

Maybe by now I'd know better.

Owen shifted again. I saw a flash of gray paw. Then his water dish upended and a puddle of water spread across the floor . . . in front of Hercules's food bowl. Owen shook his foot and continued to eat. Damp feet were not an issue for him.

Hercules howled in anger. Then he looked at me.

I shook my head. "You knew when you went all Ozzy Osbourne on the chicken that it would be a declaration of war as far as Owen is concerned." I reached for the coffeepot. "I'm staying out of it."

Hercules's green eyes narrowed to two slits. He moved around the pool of water, looking for some way to get to his dish. There wasn't one. Somehow, Owen had managed to tip his water bowl in just the right spot so that Hercules's breakfast was marooned.

Had he planned it that way? Was he capable of planning it?

Oh yes.

Hercules made a noise that sounded a lot like a sigh. The only indication Owen gave that he'd heard anything was a slight twitch of his left ear.

Herc dipped his head and sniffed the floor. It was clean. I'd scrubbed it on my hands and knees with a scrub brush just the night before, my way of working off a frustrating day at the library. The cat's pink tongue darted out and he began to lap at the water. Owen's head came up.

"Touché," I said, holding up my coffee cup.

He made grumbling sound low in his throat. I didn't need to speak cat to know that he was probably telling me where I could go.

I ate my oatmeal while Hercules lapped his way to his dish. As soon as he could reach, he stretched out one white-tipped paw and pulled the bowl closer. He made a dramatic show of shaking both paws before bending his head to eat.

Owen had finished breakfast by then. He made an equally dramatic exit, picking up the remains of the yellow catnip chicken and making a wide circle around his brother before disappearing—literally—into the living room.

I finished breakfast and cleaned up the kitchen. By then Hercules had eaten his breakfast. He started a meticulous face-washing routine while I wiped up the last of the spilled water. I moved his dishes over by the coat hooks on the wall by the back door and left Owen's beside the refrigerator, giving both cats some fresh water and a tiny pile of sardine cat crackers.

By the time I was ready for work there was still no sign of Owen. "I'm leaving," I called. After a moment there was an answering meow.

Hercules was in "his" spot on the bench in the porch. He went ahead of me out the door—waiting for me to open it this time—and waited at the edge of the lawn.

I looked across into Rebecca's backyard. I still thought of the small blue house as Rebecca's, even though she and Everett were married now. Rebecca was one of the first people I'd met when I'd arrived in Mayville Heights, and I admit I'd been happy when she'd told me that she and Everett had decided to live in her little house after the wedding.

I could see Everett in the gazebo, seated at the table with his coffee and the newspaper. I knew there would be a treat for Hercules as well.

"Merow," the cat said, winding around my ankles.

I bent down and scooped him up. He nuzzled my chin.

"You're such a suck-up," I said.

He licked my chin and looked up at me as if to say, "Is it working?"

"You're spoiled," I told him as we headed across the grass.

Everett smiled and got to his feet. "Good morning, Kathleen. Good morning, Hercules." He was wearing a crisp white shirt with a navy-and-red-striped tie, along with the trousers and vest of a gray suit. His beard and what little white hair he had were closely cropped and he looked every inch the successful—and self-made—businessman that he was, with a bit of the sex appeal of actor Sean Connery thrown in.

Hercules jumped up onto the wide railing of the gazebo. Everett took a tiny container of cat kibble from the table and set it next to Herc. "All-natural ingredients," he said to me.

"You've been talking to Roma," I said with a grin.

Roma Davidson was the town veterinarian as well as one of my closest friends. She'd decided that the boys had been eating way too much people food and she'd made it her mission to get people to stop sneaking them toast and peanut butter (me) or pie (Rebecca).

He nodded. "I have my orders." He gestured at the stainless steel coffee carafe on the round metal table. There was a second stoneware mug next to it. "Do you have time to join me for a cup of coffee? I'd like to discuss something."

I glanced at my watch. "I have a few minutes."

"Good," he said. "Have a seat." He indicated the other chair at the table and reached for the carafe. Hercules already had his head in the little dish.

I gestured in the cat's direction. "If he becomes a bother, let me know."

Hercules turned his head to look at me, his green eyes wide.

Everett set the mug of coffee in front of me. "Hercules is good company. He has some interesting insights on what the town council has been up to." A smile pulled at the corners of his mouth and was reflected in his dark eyes.

The cat made a soft murp of self-satisfaction and went back to his treat.

I reached for the small pitcher of cream. "I'll be sure to get his input before the next council elections," I said with a completely straight face.

Everett leaned back in his seat and straightened the crease in his trousers. "You could do worse," he said. He regarded me over the top of his cup. "How are things going at the library?"

I knew he didn't mean in general. Patron visits were up, so was borrowing, and Lita—Everett's executive assistant—and I had just recently secured a grant to add more books to the children's department. In recent months we'd hosted several workshops and talks that had brought people all the way from Minneapolis. The most recent special event at the library was a traveling exhibit of museum art from the 1800s. I knew that's what Everett was referring to.

"We've had some . . ." I hesitated, searching for the right word ". . . challenges."

Everett gave a snort of laughter. "In less politically correct terms, Margo Walsh is a pain in the ass."

"She's not that bad," I said with a smile.

He shook his head. "You're probably the only person who's worked with the woman who would say that."

Margo Walsh was the curator of the exhibit. Its focal point was a detailed drawing of a Dakota encampment by military artist Sam Weston, who had lived in Minnesota early in his career. The drawing belonged to Marshall and Diana Holmes. The brother and sister had inherited it, along with other artwork, after the recent death of their father. The Weston sketch, as well as several other pieces in the show, were on long-term loan to the museum, but somehow the siblings were very involved in every aspect of the exhibit, probably because their late father's money was funding it.

I'd watched Margo with both of them and I got the feeling from her body language that she would have been happier if they'd been a lot less involved. According to my friend Maggie, who was an artist herself, when someone loaned a piece from their collection to a museum, that was generally the end of their involvement. Marshall and Diana Holmes didn't seem to know that.

At each stop on the exhibit's tour Margo was featuring artwork from local artists. Maggie, who had two pieces of her art in the show, had been impressed with how much the curator had known about the local art scene and how positive she'd been.

Margo might have been enthusiastic about the artists who were part of the Mayville Heights artists' co-op, but she was decidedly unenthusiastic and vocal about the exhibit's delicate paintings and sketches, some of which were more than two hundred years old, being out of a climate-controlled museum setting.

I took another sip of my coffee as I tried to think of the best way to explain Margo Walsh to Everett. "Margo is very, very good at what she does," I said. "She and Maggie have spent hours finding just the right frames and mats for the local pieces that are in the show. She's studied the way the light comes in through the windows at different times of day just to make sure they're shown at their best."

One of Everett's eyebrows went up, but he didn't say anything.

"She's picky," I admitted, fingering the rim of my cup. I could have used a less diplomatic word. Or told Everett that more than once I'd had the urge to brain the woman with my briefcase. But I didn't. I set down my coffee and leaned forward. "Everett, this exhibit is going to bring a lot of people into the library, into Mayville Heights. It's going to showcase some very talented people—Maggie, Ruby, Nic Sutton. I can handle Margo Walsh. Don't worry about it."

He studied my face for a moment and seemed to be satisfied with my response. "If there's anything I can do—" he began.

"I know—call Lita," I said. The exhibit had come with grant money to install a temporary security system at the library. I was already talking to Lita several times a day. "You could give her a bonus when this is over," I added with a smile. "I couldn't do it without her."

That was true. Lita was related to at least half the town and it seemed as if she'd gone to school with or babysat pretty much everyone else.

Everett took half a piece of bacon from his plate, turned and offered it to Hercules. The cat took it from him, bobbed his head in thanks and dropped it into his now-empty dish. I refrained from pointing out that bacon was not on Roma's list of approved cat treats.

"Thank you for the coffee," I said, getting to my feet, "and for your support."

Everett stood up as well. "I'm very glad I hired you," he said.

"I told you Kathleen was the best choice," a voice said behind us. It was Rebecca, carrying the coffeepot in one hand and a small waxed-paper-wrapped package in the other.

Hercules leaned around one of the gazebo uprights.

"Good morning, Hercules," she said with a smile. The cat seemed to smile back at her.

She looked at me. "Your hair looks beautiful. Are you still happy with it?"

Rebecca had been a hairdresser before she retired and she'd been cutting my hair since I'd arrived in Mayville Heights while I grew out a pixie cut that I'd gotten on impulse and immediately regretted. Unlike Maggie, whose close-cropped blond curls hugged her head and showed off her neck and gorgeous cheekbones, my hair when it was that short poked out in every direction. I looked like the scarecrow from *The Wizard of Oz*. Rebecca had layered my bangs and evened the ends of my hair on the weekend and I still felt a bit like a shampoo model when I tossed my head.

I took the coffeepot from her and set it on the table. "I love it," I said, leaning over to give her a hug.

"I'm glad," she said. She held out the paper-wrapped package. "This is for you."

I could smell cinnamon. I pulled out of the hug and narrowed my gaze at her. "Coffee cake?" I asked.

"Cinnamon streusel muffins," she said. "I know how hard you've been working. I thought you might like them for a break a little later this morning."

"You're an angel," I said.

She gestured at the package. "There are two in case you wanted to share with anyone who might drop by the library." Her expression was all innocence, but I knew she was talking about Detective Marcus Gordon. Ever since Rebecca and Everett had gotten their happy ending, she'd been gently nudging Marcus and me even closer together. At the wedding she'd even broken with tradition and handed me her bouquet of daisies, gently telling us not to wait too long for our happily ever after. Given how long it had taken the two of us to get past our differences, a few gentle nudges probably weren't a bad idea.

"I'll keep that in mind," I said. I looked over at Hercules. "Are you coming?"

He gave a soft "murp" then stretched and began to wash his face.

"He's fine, Kathleen," Everett said.

"They like to talk politics," Rebecca said as though Hercules was a person and not a cat. She touched my arm. "I'll see you this afternoon. Margo Walsh invited the board at two to see how the installation of the exhibit is going." She frowned slightly. "It is all right, isn't it?"

"Of course," I said. It would have been better if Margo had told *me* she'd invited the board for a look-see, but it wasn't the first time she'd blindsided me like this.

The day after the layout for the exhibit had finally

been settled, Margo had decided to add an artist from Red Wing, Rena Adler, who worked with egg tempera. Larry Taylor, the electrician who had been wiring the new lights Margo felt she needed, had just laughed and shaken his head when I'd told him the final lighting plan was now the former lighting plan because the way the artwork was being displayed had changed. On the other hand, my parents were both actors, so Margo wasn't the first temperamental person I'd had to deal with.

"Have a good day," I said to Everett. I turned to Rebecca. "I'll see you this afternoon." I took my muffins and started back to my own yard.

Mary Lowe was waiting by the library steps when I pulled into the parking lot. She was wearing a soft green sweater with yellow chickens dancing across the front. She had a big collection of sweaters to match the seasons, including a Christmas sweater with flashing lights and a Halloween cardigan with moaning sound effects. With her tiny stature, soft gray hair and sweet expression, she looked like someone's cookie-baking grandmother—which she was. And as state kickboxing champion for her age and gender, she could also kick your kidneys up behind your ears, as she liked to put it.

I looked around as I walked over to Mary. There was no sign of Margo Walsh's car, or of the woman herself. More than once in the past two weeks I'd arrived at the library to find her waiting at the top of the steps by the front door, impatiently tapping one elegant high-heeled foot on the landing.

"No Margo?" I asked Mary, raising one eyebrow at her.

"No sign of her," she said, following me up the stairs to the entrance. "Thank heavens for small mercies."

I looked at her over my shoulder.

She rolled her eyes. "Or in the case of Lady Margo, large mercies."

"She's not that bad," I chided as I stepped through the first set of doors and punched in the alarm code. Margo had gotten off on the wrong foot with Mary the day she'd arrived when she'd tried to send the older woman for coffee.

Mary laughed and reached up to pat my cheek. "Do you ever say a negative word about anyone, Kathleen?" She moved ahead of me into the library and flipped on the overhead lights. "You don't have to say anything because I already know the answer."

I held up one hand, fingers spread apart. "Five days, Mary. That's it. If everything goes well—and it will—Margo will be finished on Friday. All we have to do is make it to the end of the week and things will get back to normal."

Mary shook her head and laughed. "Oh, Kathleen," she said. "Just because you get the monkey off your back doesn't mean the circus has left town."

2

Abigail arrived about five minutes later, carrying a Sweet Thing box and a square stainless steel tin. She held them out to me. "One dozen of Georgia's maple crème cupcakes and some Earl Grey tea bags," she said with a smile.

"You're a lifesaver. Thank you," I said. After I'd left Rebecca and Everett I'd called Abigail and asked her if she could bring some tea bags so we could at least offer the library board a cup after their tour. Abigail was friends with Georgia Tepper, who ran Sweet Thing, the cupcake bakery. She'd offered to stop in and bring a dozen of whatever cupcakes Georgia had on hand. I'd been happy to take her up on the offer.

"Do we have enough cups in the lunchroom to give tea to the entire library board?" Abigail asked as she followed me up the stairs.

"I brought cups and saucers from home," I said.

Mary had made coffee. The aroma drew me toward the small second-floor lunchroom.

Mary had set two mugs on the counter. When she

saw Abigail she grabbed a third. Once we all had coffee we sat around the small table and I went over the day's activities.

The art exhibit was using the open space overlooking the water that normally held our computers. The computers had taken over the magazine and reading area, which was now temporarily in the larger of our two meeting rooms. It wasn't an ideal situation, but it was the only way to keep the computers in sight of the main desk so users could be supervised.

We hadn't really had much of a problem with our public-access computers—aside from the occasional teenage boy trying to access certain sites that our security software prevented him from getting to. Still, it didn't hurt to have Mary, who knew all the kids' parents and grandparents, at the circulation desk while they tried to work their way around the latest firewall I'd installed.

"Larry should be here about nine thirty to do a test of the window alarms," I reminded Mary and Abigail. They both made faces. The temporary security system that Larry Taylor was helping to install had an alarm that sounded like an air horn. "The board will be here at two for an update. And the quilters are using our meeting room because there's water in the church basement."

Mary took off her glasses and began cleaning them with the end of her sweater. "Kathleen, where are we going to entertain the board if the quilters are in our only meeting room?"

"I already thought of that," I said. I held up a finger. "The quilters finish at one thirty. Give them fifteen minutes to gather their stuff." I held up a second finger. "At one forty-five I give the room a quick vacuum and toss a cloth on the table. Mia will be here by then." The teenager had started out as a co-op placement from the high school and now worked part-time for me. The little ones loved her Kool-Aid-colored hair and the seniors were charmed by her lovely manners.

I added a third finger to the first two. "Mia sets the table while I run back upstairs to make the tea, and at five to two I will be waiting, graciously, by the front desk." I extended both hands with a flourish. "Ta-da!"

Abigail laughed. "All you need is one long-winded quilter and your whole plan falls apart."

I narrowed my gaze at her. "O ye of little faith," I said. "Do you remember those boxes of books that Pete Simmons brought us when he cleared out his mother's house?"

She nodded.

"Eva was a quilter. There were several books about quilting in one of the cartons. Mary is going to ask the ladies to come out to the desk and take a look at them so we can decide if we should add any of them to our collection." I raised one eyebrow at her in classic Mr. Spock–from–*Star Trek* style. "As I said, ta and da."

"Very crafty of you," Abigail countered with a grin.

I made a face at her pun and got to my feet. "Let's get started, then," I said.

It was a busy day. Rena Adler showed up just after we opened.

"Hi, Kathleen," she said. "Is Margo here?" She was carrying a blue file folder and she tapped one edge of it with her fingers.

I shook my head. "Not yet."

Rena made a face. She was a bit shorter than me, maybe five-five, in her black Dr. Martens, with her black hair in a twist. "She asked for my bio." She held up the folder. "Would you mind giving it to her for me? I'm meeting Ruby at the co-op store in a few minutes."

Rena had been staying in Mayville Heights all month. After they'd met, Ruby had recruited her for a painting workshop she was doing with a couple of art classes at the high school.

"I don't mind at all," I said. "Does Margo have a number for you in case she wants to talk to you about it?"

Rena smiled. Like Marcus, she had deep blue eyes and incredibly long eyelashes. "Yes, she does. She's probably called me ten times just about the frames for my paintings."

"Margo is very . . . exacting. But she cares about every piece in the show."

She nodded. "You're right about that." She handed over the folder. "Thanks, Kathleen."

"You're welcome," I said.

Rena left and I took the papers she'd given me upstairs. I'd meant what I'd said to her: Margo did care about every single painting and drawing in the exhibit. She wanted the local artwork to be seen at its best and she worried about what the change in conditions would do to the museum pieces. I felt certain that if the decision had been up to her, the library would never have been chosen as a venue.

Margo Walsh walked in at nine thirty with Larry Taylor. I caught enough of their conversation to know she wanted to move some of the new lights he'd installed.

Again.

Luckily, Larry, the younger of Harrison Taylor's sons, was one of the most laid-back people I'd ever met. He smiled at me over the top of Margo's head.

Margo Walsh was a tiny woman, five foot four or so only because of her four-inch heels. She wore her blond hair in a sleek bob with side-swept bangs.

"Good morning, Kathleen," she said as she passed me, her head bent over her phone.

"Good morning," I replied, but she was already past me, heels clicking on the mosaic tile floor. I walked over to Larry. "She wants to move those spotlights again," I said.

He pulled off his ball cap and smoothed a hand over his blond hair. "That she does."

I shook my head. "I'm sorry. I know working with Margo has been a bit of a challenge."

Larry laughed. "The old man when he gets his shorts in a bunch over something—excuse my language—now, that's a challenge." He gestured toward the steps with one large hand. "Her, not so much."

Larry's father, Harrison Taylor Senior, was one of my favorite people in town. He was also, to use an expression from his other son, Harry Junior, as stubborn as a bear with a closed picnic basket.

I laid a hand on Larry's arm. "How about a cup of Mary's coffee in about half an hour?"

"I wouldn't say no to that," he said. He had the same warm smile as his father and brother. He headed toward the exhibit area, and I went upstairs to talk to Margo.

She was in the workroom that she'd taken over as a temporary office. She was dressed in slim black pants and one of her ubiquitous white shirts, the sleeves rolled back to her elbows. She turned when she heard me in the doorway. "Kathleen, I need a favor," she said.

That was a change. Usually Margo left out the word "favor."

"What is it?" I asked.

"Do you know Oren Kenyon?"

I nodded. "Yes, I do. Oren did a lot of work on the restoration of this building."

Margo leaned back against the worktable that she was using as a desk. "Maggie Adams told me he made the sun that's over the entrance."

"Yes, he did."

Our library, like many others of its vintage, was a Carnegie library, built with funds donated by Scottish American industrialist Andrew Carnegie. The carved wooden sun Oren had made for the entrance was a nod to the first Carnegie library in Dunfermline, Scotland.

"The detail is incredible," Margo said.

I wondered how she knew that. The sun was twelve feet in the air over the main doors.

She must have read the question on my face. "Lorenzo let me use his ladder."

Lorenzo? Did she mean Larry Taylor? Why didn't I know his full name was Lorenzo?

Margo was still talking. "I've heard that Mr. Kenyon has created a replica of this town's seal done in the same way as the sunburst over your door."

I'd heard that rumor, too, although I wasn't sure if it

was true or not. Oren didn't talk a lot about what was going on in his life.

"It seems that he doesn't have a cell phone." She glanced over at her own smartphone, lying on the table next to her briefcase. "And I haven't had any luck getting his home phone number, either. I asked Mary and somehow the conversation turned to how many third cousins she has in town."

I bit the inside of my cheek so I wouldn't laugh. If Mary didn't want to tell you something, she could lead you into a conversational labyrinth.

Margo's eyes flicked to the heavy, stainless steel watch on her left arm. "If the seal does exist and it's as good as that sun, I'd love to have it in the exhibit. It fits with the overall theme of the other artwork: the history of this part of Minnesota."

Oren was a very private person. His father, Karl Kenyon, was a frustrated artist, a metal sculptor who'd spent his whole life working as a laborer, dreaming of a different life. Oren had inherited his father's artistic streak, but unlike Karl, Oren enjoyed his quiet, small-town life in Mayville Heights. He liked working on the old buildings, extending their lives or giving them new ones. He was an incredibly talented pianist as well as a skilled woodworker and he had no desire to do anything differently.

"I'll talk to him," I said. "I can't promise he'll say yes. But I will ask." I knew that Oren was doing some work for Roma out at Wisteria Hill, her new home.

"Thank you." Margo glanced at her phone again. Most of her focus was clearly somewhere else.

"I'll be in my office if you need me," I said.

She nodded without even looking in my direction and reached for a file folder on the table. I headed for my office, but before I got there I caught sight of Larry Taylor coming up the stairs.

"Kathleen, do you have a minute?" he asked.

"Of course," I said. "Is something wrong?"

He shook his head. "It just struck me that it might make more sense to put in a permanent fixture for the little spotlights Margo is talking about rather than doing something temporary. Cost-wise it'll actually save you money, and Oren won't have to patch the ceiling when this show is over."

"Exactly how little are these spotlights?" I had a mental image of the computer room looking like the stage at the Stratton Theatre.

"That's what I wanted to show you," Larry said.

We started down to the main floor. I darted a quick sideways glance at Larry. "Lorenzo?" I asked, keeping my voice low.

His face flushed with color. "It's a long story, Kathleen," he said, ducking his head.

I held up one hand and smiled at him. "I love long stories."

At that moment, behind me, I heard Margo Walsh call my name. At the same time Abigail came around the corner of the circulation desk. She raised a hand. "Kathleen, the reference computers have gone catawampus again."

I blew out a long breath. I had a feeling it was going to be a long day.

And it was.

The spotlights Larry was proposing to install permanently were small and could be rotated 360 degrees, so I told him to go ahead and put them in, making a mental note to call Lita and tell her what I'd agreed to.

Margo had final (final, final) confirmation that the exhibit would be arriving Friday afternoon, which meant the library would be closed from one o'clock on Thursday until Saturday morning. Mary started making signs so our patrons would know what was going on, while Abigail dealt with a pile of books from the book drop and I tried to persuade the aging reference software on our even older computers to boot up for another day. I found myself thinking longingly of Rebecca's muffins sitting on my desk.

In the end, one of those muffins and a large cup of coffee were all I had time to grab all day—I gave the other muffin to Larry, who worked through his own lunch—and that wasn't until after the library board had left, all of them happy with the way the work for the exhibit was shaping up, and charmed by Margo and her genuine praise for the library and the town. She could certainly turn on the charm and tone down the nitpicking when it mattered.

I was very happy that Marcus had offered to cook supper for me. He'd also stopped in at my house to check on Owen and Hercules so I could drive directly out to his house when I left the library.

Micah met me at the door. The small marmalade tabby had appeared one day out at Wisteria Hill, the former Henderson estate that was now Roma's home. She hadn't been part of the feral colony of cats that called the old carriage house home. They had all been neutered as part of Roma's trap-neuter-release pro-

gram and were cared for by Roma and a group of vol-
unteers that included Marcus and me. Roma's best
guess was that someone had simply dumped the little
tabby near Wisteria Hill, maybe believing she could
just join the other cats.

For months Roma had put out food for Micah; she
had named her for the way the sunlight glinted off her
ginger fur. She'd also erroneously said that Micah was
a he. Marcus was the one who had first noticed that the
very cautious cat was in fact a she, something he'd
gently teased Roma about.

Just as Owen and Hercules, who were also from
Wisteria Hill, had bonded with me, Micah had bonded
with Marcus. Roma was certain she had had a home
somewhere before Wisteria Hill. She was happy to let
other people stroke her fur or scratch under her chin. If
anyone other than me tried that with Owen or Hercules
they would go from charming house cats to Tasmanian
devils in about a second and a half.

There was no sign of Marcus, but something smelled
wonderful. Micah wound around my legs and I bent
and picked her up.

"Lasagna?" I asked.

"Merow," she said.

The cat tipped her head to one side and looked at
me, whiskers twitching. Her sense of smell was as good
as Owen's.

"I brought you something," I said quietly. I pulled a
small bag of the same sardine kitty treats I made for my
own cats out of my pocket. I took two out and held out
my hand.

Micah made a soft thank-you meow before leaning over to eat one of the small crackers.

"You're spoiling my cat," Marcus said behind me.

I turned around to face him. "Look who's talking," I said with a laugh. Marcus had snuck so many "treats" to Owen and Hercules, Roma had finally given him a stern lecture about what constituted "cat food" and what didn't.

Micah took the other cracker from my hand and I reached over and stroked the top of her head. "And she's not spoiled. She's an angel cat."

As if she'd understood every word I'd just said, Micah leaned her furry face against my cheek. We both looked up at Marcus.

He laughed and shook his head. Then he leaned down and gave me a quick kiss and ran his hand over the little cat's fur.

I handed him the bag of fish crackers and put Micah down on the floor. She licked crumbs off her whiskers and looked up at Marcus.

"One," he said, his voice edged with warning.

The cat bobbed her head as if in agreement. I knew he'd give her more than that and so did she.

Marcus opened the bag and fished out two crackers. He bent down and held them out to the cat, who took them both in her mouth and then set them on the floor.

He brushed his hands on his jeans, straightened up and pulled me into his arms for another, longer kiss. I still felt the same rush of giddiness I'd felt the first time he'd kissed me, standing out in the driveway next to my old truck.

"How was your day?" he asked.

"Long," I said, pulling off my jacket and hanging it and my purse over the back of one of the kitchen chairs.

Marcus turned to look at the timer on the stove. "Are you hungry?" he asked.

My stomach growled loudly then, as if in answer to his question.

"You skipped lunch again," he said, reaching for an oversize pair of oven mitts. I noticed that he hadn't phrased his comment in the form of a question.

"No, I didn't," I said, just a little defensively, as I pulled out a chair and sat down. "I had one of Rebecca's muffins."

"A muffin is not lunch," Marcus countered. He opened the oven door, mumbled something and closed it again.

"It was a big muffin."

He turned to look at me then, and I gave him my best innocent expression. It was the same kind of look Owen gave me, generally when I'd caught him doing something he shouldn't have been. It worked about as well on Marcus as it did when Owen used it on me.

"Kathleen, this is the third time in the last week and a half that you've missed lunch."

Actually, it was the fourth, but I wasn't stupid enough to correct him. Micah was at my feet, looking from one to the other of us as though she was following the conversation. For all I knew, maybe she was.

Marcus waved an oven mitt at me. "I'm bringing you lunch tomorrow."

"Leftover lasagna?" I asked. That was assuming there was any left over by the time I'd finished my supper.

"How did you know I made lasagna?"

"Merow," Micah said then. She had the same uncanny sense of timing that both Owen and Hercules seemed to possess.

"She told me," I said, gesturing at the little cat and trying to keep a straight face.

Marcus set a multicolored pottery bowl of salad on the table. "The cat told you that we're having lasagna?"

I shrugged. "I asked. She confirmed."

Once again, the "meow" was perfectly timed.

"See?" I said.

He laughed.

I gestured at the little marmalade tabby. "She seems happy here."

He nodded. "I actually took her over to Roma today. She's gained a little weight." He smiled. "I mean the cat, not Roma." He went back to the refrigerator for the salad dressing, his own secret concoction. I'd been trying for months to wheedle the recipe out of him.

I watched Marcus move around the kitchen for a moment, just enjoying the view, so to speak. "Does she still think that Micah was abandoned?" I asked. The little cat leaned against my leg and I bent forward to pet her, wondering how anyone could have left her out at Wisteria Hill to fend for herself.

"Uh-huh," Marcus said. "And it makes sense. All the carriage house cats have been neutered. And she's definitely socialized." He gestured at Micah, still leaning against my leg, eyes half closed, purring as I stroked her ginger-colored fur.

"I'm glad you decided to take her," I said.

He smiled. "I think it was more like you and Roma decided I should take her."

I smiled back at him. "Potato, potahto."

He grinned as he turned back to the stove.

"There's no way I could have taken her," I said. "As it is, Owen and Hercules are squabbling over—" I exhaled loudly and shook my head. "I don't know what. Bacon, possibly."

Marcus took the lasagna out of the oven and set it on a tile trivet on the countertop. "Bacon?" he asked, glancing back over his shoulder at me.

I thought about Hercules eating Everett's treat with what had seemed to me to be a somewhat smug expression on his furry black-and-white face. "Maybe," I said. "Hercules has been eating bacon nearly every morning with Everett, and Owen loves bacon almost as much as he loves Maggie. But he's slow in the morning. I think it's just sibling jealousy, although you may be called in at some point to investigate the decapitation of one Fred the Funky Chicken."

"You know, Micah may not be a true Wisteria Hill cat, but I think she's one in spirit," he said.

"What do you mean?" I asked. The lasagna smelled wonderful and my stomach growled audibly again. It had been a long time since Rebecca's muffin.

"You know how Owen is always sneaking into your truck?" Marcus reached for the plates on the counter.

"Uh-huh," I said slowly. Marcus didn't know about the boys' "superpowers," so he didn't know that Owen was able to "sneak" into my truck by making himself invisible.

He tipped his head in Micah's direction. "She's done the same thing to me. Twice I was halfway to work before I realized that she was sitting on the backseat."

I felt the hairs rise on the back of my neck. "Really?" I said slowly. "You didn't see her jump in the back?"

"I didn't even see her follow me out of the house." He set a steaming plate in front of me and leaned down to give the top of Micah's head a little scratch. "I guess she shares that stealth-ninja gene with Owen."

"I guess she does." I stared down at the cat, who looked up innocently at me and then began to wash her face.

It wasn't possible. Micah didn't share Owen's ability. I was overreacting, I told myself sternly as I unfolded my napkin. Over. Re. Acting.

If I repeated the words enough times, maybe I'd start to believe them.

3

Mia was waiting by the main entrance when I pulled into the parking lot in the morning. She had convinced both her history and art teachers to let her shadow Margo, which meant that she'd been Margo's unpaid grunt on Tuesday and Thursday mornings for the previous two weeks.

I pulled up the hood of my raincoat and sprinted across the pavement, dodging the puddles, grateful for my new red rubber boots. Once we were inside, Mia pushed back her own hood and I got a good look at her hair, which was now lime Jell-O green.

"I like your hair," I said.

She smiled shyly. "Thank you." Then she took her coat out into the entryway and shook it over the rubber mat. Mia was a study in contrasts. Her hair was always some neon crayon color, but she dressed conservatively. Today she was wearing a black pencil skirt with black tights and a pale blue shirt.

I smoothed a hand over my own hair, which I had

pulled back into a low ponytail. "Maybe I'll go green," I said.

Mia tipped her head to one side and studied me. "I think blue would suit you better," she said. "Or orange." She headed for the stairs.

Orange? I was never quite sure when Mia was kidding and when she was serious.

Harry Taylor and his sister, Elizabeth, came into the library just after ten o'clock. Elizabeth was carrying a large mason jar. I walked over to meet them. She held the jar out to me.

"I made a new batch of yogurt," she said. "And I added the rest of last year's rhubarb."

Harry and Elizabeth had different mothers but they'd both gotten the Taylor stubborn streak from Harrison. Elizabeth had been placed for adoption when she was born and had gotten to know her birth family only in the past year, but she was already in league with her brother to make their father's diet healthier, hence the yogurt making. This would be the third batch I'd gotten to try, and while I had no idea if Harry Senior liked it, I certainly did.

"Thank you," I said. Marcus was bringing lunch and now I had something to enjoy with my late-afternoon coffee.

"You're welcome," she said, and I caught a look pass between the siblings.

"Kathleen, do you have a minute?" Harry asked.

I glanced over my shoulder. Margo was standing in the exhibit area talking and gesturing. Mia was beside her, silently making notes.

I held up three fingers. "I probably have about three. What do you need?"

Before he could say anything, Elizabeth spoke.

"Harrison met a woman online." She folded her arms over her chest. "He's going to meet her."

I'd seen the same determined expression on her father's face more than once.

"What do you want me to do?"

Harry swiped a hand over his chin. "Talk to him. He isn't listening to either one of us."

"He could be meeting a con artist, someone who could hit him over the head and take his money," Elizabeth interjected.

"Your father is very . . . stubborn."

Harry gave a snort of agreement. Elizabeth opened her mouth to say something else, but I held up a hand to stop her. "He's also one of the savviest people I've ever met. If some woman thinks she can take advantage of him, well . . ." I shook my head and tried not to smile too broadly. "I feel sorry for her."

Elizabeth sighed softly.

"But I will talk to him."

"Really?" she said.

I nodded.

"Thank you," Harry said. He took off his hat, ran one hand over his balding head and put the cap back on again.

"I can't promise that I'll have any more success than you two did," I said.

Elizabeth made a face and her mouth pulled to one side. "He gets an idea in his head and he's so"—she made a growl of frustration that sounded so like her father I had to bite my cheek so I wouldn't laugh—"unreasonable."

I held the container of yogurt to my chest with one hand and touched her arm with the other. "Let me see what I can do." I shot a look back over my shoulder. Margo caught my eye and lifted a hand. "I need to get back to work," I said. "But I'll give Harrison a call at lunchtime."

"I appreciate that," Harry said.

I smiled at them both and then walked over to Margo. "I talked to Oren last night," I said.

Her eyebrows went up and she gave me an expectant smile. "And?"

I turned to Mia before I answered. "Would you take this upstairs and put it in the refrigerator for me, please?" I knew that Margo could easily work Mia all morning without a break.

"Of course," she said, taking the glass jar from me. "Is that homemade yogurt?"

"And the fruit on the top is rhubarb." I smiled at her. "You're welcome to try it."

"Thank you," she said.

I saw her glance at Margo, who was waiting not so patiently for my answer to her question. She'd crossed her arms over her chest and looked like she was about to start tapping one gray snakeskin high heel on the mosaic tile floor.

Mia headed for the stairs and I turned back to Margo. "As long as the town council agrees, yes, you can display the town seal Oren has been working on."

"Oh, Kathleen, thank you," she said, a genuine smile of pleasure spreading across her face.

I smiled back at her. "You're welcome," I said. "I'm happy that Oren's talent is going to be recognized." I knew that the only reason he'd agreed to let the seal be part of the exhibit was that it might bring some attention to the town.

I didn't get a chance to call Harrison until quarter to one.

"How are things going with the museum people?" he asked.

I exhaled softly. "Busy."

"You haven't coldcocked Margo Walsh with the *Encyclopaedia Britannica* yet, have you?"

"Of course not," I retorted. I paused for a moment for effect. "The encyclopedia is all digital now."

He laughed. "That is a tightly wound woman, Kathleen, but if anyone can deal with her, it's you."

"Good to have your vote of confidence."

"I didn't expect to hear from you until tonight," he said, his deep voice rumbling through the phone. "Looks like my daughter was on her horse this morning."

I turned in my chair so I could look out over the water. "You knew," I said.

"Course I knew," he said with a snort. "My children aren't exactly subtle. I'm guessing Harry came to see you as well."

"He did."

"You know, Elizabeth's just as stubborn as her mother was."

"She is stubborn," I agreed. "But the jury's out on who she got that particular trait from."

"I'm not stubborn, girl," he said. "I'm persistent. Big difference."

This time I was the one who gave a snort of laughter.

"My personal life is none of their damn business," he grumbled. "You don't see me meddling in either one of theirs."

"I'm putting the phone down now," I said, "because I don't want to get any kind of a shock through the line when you get hit with a bolt of lightning."

That made him laugh again. We set a date for tea on Friday afternoon, agreeing to continue the conversation then.

After I said good-bye to Harrison I headed downstairs to see what was going on.

Susan was at the circulation desk, wearing her black cat's-eye glasses and a big smile. She reached below the counter and handed me a small red picnic cooler. "Marcus left this for you," she said. "He has a meeting. He said to tell you, 'Eat.'" She tipped her head to one side and studied me. "I think it's so cute the way he made you lunch. He even put in a napkin and a little note." She held up a hand. "I wasn't snooping. He was giving me instructions on what needs to be reheated and what doesn't."

Before I could say anything, Gavin Solomon walked through the main doors. The security consultant smiled and raised a hand when he caught sight of me and started toward the desk.

Having such valuable art in the library meant that we'd needed a temporary upgrade to our security system. Gavin had been hired by the museum. Even though he'd never worked with Margo Walsh before, they seemed sometimes to have a kind of secret code or verbal shorthand that left me confused.

Gavin was handsome and personable, and he flirted, just a little, with every female over the age of fifteen. He had thick red-gold hair and a close-cropped beard. I wasn't sure if he actually needed his dark-framed glasses or if he just wore them to look more serious.

"Hi, Kathleen," he said. "I just wanted to check in with you to make sure we're still on track to do one last check of the alarm system tonight." He glanced over at Susan and gave her a quick smile.

She beamed back at him.

I nodded. "We're closing at six. After that the building is all yours."

"Good." He looked around. "Is Larry here? He had a couple of questions for me about the wiring for the alarm system."

"He's down in the basement," Susan said.

"Will you be in your office when I'm done?" Gavin gave me an inquiring look.

"I will," I said.

"Okay, I'll talk to you in a bit." He headed for the back of the building.

Susan handed the plastic cooler over the counter to me. "Go have lunch," she instructed. "I told Marcus I would nag you to eat, so go do it."

She narrowed her eyes at me, and her topknot bounced. It looked as though she'd secured it with a red-and-white straw. I was never quite sure if it was because of Susan's own absentmindedness that so many odd things ended up stuck in her hair or if it was the twins' handiwork. "I can get spinach into the boys," she continued. "Don't make me show you how I do it!"

Susan's boys were preschool twins with genius-level IQs and seemingly no fear of, well, anything.

"I'm going," I said, picking up the cooler and heading toward the stairs.

"Warm up the two square containers," she called after me.

The two square containers held lasagna and rhubarb crisp. There was also a mason jar of salad, utensils, and the note Susan had mentioned lying on top of a cloth napkin. I poured a cup of coffee and unfolded the piece of paper.

Sorry I couldn't join you. I miss you.

M

There were no X's and O's. That wasn't Marcus's style, but that was okay with me. I found the carefully packed lunch romantic enough.

I'd finished eating and was coming out of the lunchroom with another cup of coffee when Gavin Solomon came up the stairs. "Hi," he said. "Do you have some time for one last run-through of how everything works?"

"I do," I said, gesturing at my office door. "Come in."

It took close to an hour for Gavin to walk me, step-by-step, through the complexities of the security measures he'd put in place. We were the only ones, along with Margo, who would have the system's code, which meant for the ten days of the exhibit I'd have to open up the building and lock up again at night.

"Are you going to be here tonight while we're testing the system?" Gavin asked. He was leaning forward, using the edge of my desk as a writing surface, his left arm curled around as he wrote.

Both Gavin and Margo expected me to be available pretty much twenty-four hours a day. I'd tried turning off my cell phone a couple of times, but they'd both—at separate times—ended up on my doorstep. I wanted the exhibit to be a success. It could be good for Mayville Heights and it could also be very good for Maggie, Ruby and the other artists from the co-op. Still, the merits of one brand of light bulb over another were hardly an emergency. So I was trying to put my foot down when it came to letting the exhibit eat up all my personal time. But I had given Everett my word that I'd do everything I could to make sure things went well, so sometimes it went down a little firmer than others.

"Do you need me?"

Gavin shrugged. "I'll call you if we do. I don't expect any problems, but that doesn't mean there won't be a few glitches. I'd rather have everything worked out before the artwork arrives." He closed the leather folder he'd been writing in and stood up. "I suppose this all seems a bit like overkill to you."

I got to my feet and walked around the desk. "No," I said. "I understand that some of the artwork is very old and very valuable."

He grabbed his jacket from the back of the chair where he'd been sitting. "The Weston drawing in particular probably shouldn't even be out of the museum right now."

I walked Gavin downstairs and then did a quick look around. Mia was working with Margo, Susan was at the desk, and Abigail was shelving books.

It was busy for a Tuesday and the afternoon passed in a blur. It seemed like every time I sat down at my desk Margo had another question, and I talked to Lita so many times I was glad she was on speed dial. Everyone who had been invited to the opening of the exhibit had RSVP'd with a yes, and both *USA Today* and *National Geographic Traveler* were sending writers.

"The reporter from *USA Today* wants to talk to you as well as Margo," Lita said.

"Me? Why?" I asked.

"He wants to do a little background piece on the refurbishment of the library."

"That's easy. I like talking about the library," I said. I turned in my chair so I could look out the window at the gazebo at the back of the building.

"And if you can work in what a nice place Mayville Heights is to visit, that would be wonderful," Lita said. I could hear the smile in her voice.

"That'll be easy, too," I promised. I hung up the phone and looked up to see Susan leaning around my office door.

"Knock, knock," she said.

I motioned at her with one hand. "C'mon in."

She was holding a small cardboard box. She came over to the desk and handed it to me. "This came in the mail for you."

The box was heavy. I checked the return address. It was from Lise, my best friend in Boston.

"I have to get back downstairs," Susan said, pushing her glasses up her nose, "but if that's food, remember who your favorite staff member is."

I smiled sweetly at her. "Don't worry," I said. "I would never forget about Abigail."

She wrinkled her nose at me and stuck out her tongue before disappearing into the hall.

I slit the tape on the top of the box and opened the flaps. Inside was something wrapped in bubble wrap and padded with crumpled newspaper. I used my scissors to cut the tape on the bubble wrap and then unwrapped what was inside. It was a small brass cat statue.

Found this in a little shop in Maine and thought of you.

Love, Lise

I felt an unexpected prickle of tears. I swallowed a couple of times and set the little cat next to the photo of my family. Lise had taken that when I'd been home on a visit. I was so lucky that distance hadn't ended our friendship.

By the end of the day I was happy to be heading home. I was hungry and I had a headache from smiling and nodding so much. I was just shutting off my computer when Marshall Holmes tapped on my open office door. I sighed inwardly and silently and immediately felt guilty for it.

Margo was out continuing her search for the "perfect" light bulbs. I came around my desk and met Marshall in the middle of my office.

"Hello, Marshall," I said. "If you're looking for Margo, I'm sorry. She isn't here."

He glanced at his watch. "Are you expecting her back soon?" He was wearing a dark sport coat with a pale yellow shirt and black pants, everything casually expensive.

"Not before we close," I said.

He made a small sound of dissatisfaction. "She had an update on the security system for me."

"I have her cell number, if that will help," I offered.

"Thank you. I have it," he said. He looked down at his watch again, and when he looked back up at me his expression cleared. "You must be tired of us all invading your library."

I gave him my best professional librarian smile. "I'm happy to have the exhibit in my library. Any inconvenience is worth it."

He smiled. "That's very nice of you to say. Will you tell Margo I was here, please?"

"I will," I said.

He turned to leave and then stopped. "Would you by any chance have a phone book? I mean a real, paper one." He pulled his cell phone out of his pocket. It was an older flip-phone model. "I'm a little bit of a dinosaur."

"Yes, I do," I said. I moved over to the bookshelves and pulled down the Mayville Heights phone book. "We have the books for the entire state, but no one ever used them so we moved them up here." I brushed a dust bunny off the top of the directory and gave him a sheepish grin. "As you can see, they don't get used much up here, either."

Marshall smiled. "I know I should get a smartphone

with all the features and apps. I'm just not sure I *want* to be available all the time."

He took the phone book from me and flipped through the pages, fishing a pen from his pocket. I reached over and grabbed a pad of sticky notes from my desk, handing them to him so he could write down his number. He stuck the square of paper to his phone and dropped it in his pocket. Then he handed everything else back to me.

"I'll tell Margo you were in," I repeated.

"I appreciate it," Marshall said. We shook hands and he left.

There were no decapitated yellow chickens in the kitchen when I stepped in the back door. Owen and Hercules seemed to have called a truce.

"I'm home," I called.

After a moment there was a distant answering murp from Owen. The basement door was open a crack. I had no idea why he liked to prowl around down there, but I suspected what he was doing was napping in the laundry basket. Maybe there was some way to teach him how to push the buttons with a paw and at least start the washing machine.

The fact that for a fleeting moment I'd actually considered the possibility proved how tired I really was. Still, I couldn't help laughing at the mental image of the little gray tabby dragging towels over to the washer in his teeth.

Hercules peeked around the living room doorway.

"Hi," I said, kicking off my red boots.

Hercules came over to me and I reached down and

picked him up. "How was your day?" I asked. "Did you have coffee with Everett again?"

His whiskers twitched. I knew that was a yes.

I yawned and he turned his head to one side and studied my face. "Long day," I said.

He gave a soft murp of sympathy. I stroked his fur and padded into the living room. There were two banker's boxes of files sitting beside my coffee table. It was all paperwork pertaining to the exhibit. Margo and I had spent an hour and a half organizing it all a few days before. Strangely, the cats seemed to like her. They were less enthusiastic about Gavin Solomon.

"I should take those boxes down to the library."

Herc looked at the two cartons and then back at me. "Merow?" he asked. Or maybe I was imagining the question in the sound.

"Okay, I guess I don't have to take them tonight," I said.

He nudged my hand with his head and I began to scratch the space just above his eyes where the white fur on his nose met the black fur on the top of his head.

Hercules sat by the bedroom closet and I told him about my day as I changed into my tai chi clothes and brushed my hair back into a ponytail. He trailed me into the bathroom when I went to wash my face, making occasional murping comments as I talked. When we came back out into the hallway, Owen was waiting. They exchanged looks and soft meows that made me think of people making polite conversation in some awkward social situation.

I crouched down and gave Owen a scratch behind

one ear. His eyes narrowed to slits and he began to purr. "I don't suppose you threw in a load of towels while you were in the basement?" I asked. One golden eye fixed on me for a moment as though he were saying, "Don't be ridiculous."

"How about some meatball soup for me and some sardine crackers for you two?" I asked, straightening up.

Hercules had been cleaning his tail, but he lifted his head when I said, "sardine crackers."

Owen opened both eyes and gave an enthusiastic meow.

They followed me downstairs, where I put a bowl of soup in the microwave for myself and set a tiny stack of my homemade crackers in each of their dishes. Hercules immediately ate the top cracker off his pile without knocking it over. Owen, as he always did, picked up one little square, set it on the floor, and sniffed it cautiously before he took a bite.

Roma and I had speculated about why he always did that. She thought that he'd probably eaten something he shouldn't have and gotten sick from it in the time before I found him and Hercules as kittens out at Wisteria Hill. She was probably right, but sometimes I thought it was just Owen's skeptical personality that made him check his food like some paranoid despot.

My cell phone buzzed in my jacket pocket and the coat shook on its hook. Two furry faces immediately looked at me.

"I'm not answering that," I said, getting my soup from the microwave. "I'm having my supper. It's either Margo or Gavin, and whatever they need can wait."

A pair of green eyes and a pair of golden ones continued to regard me unblinkingly.

I didn't retrieve my phone until my bowl was empty. There were two missed calls from Margo and three texts from Gavin. I called Margo first, but all I got was her voice mail. I sent a quick text to Gavin and waited a couple of minutes to see if there would be a response.

Nothing.

"See?" I said to the boys. "Gavin and Margo both tend to act like everything is life or death, but it never is."

In retrospect I probably shouldn't have said that.

4

By the time the library building closed at one on Thursday for the final preparations before the exhibit opening, I'd had probably two dozen texts from Gavin. Margo, on the other hand, was surprisingly laid-back about everything.

The artwork arrived a little ahead of schedule, just before we closed, but for once Margo took the disruption in stride. She even called me into the workroom so I could see the Weston drawing I'd heard so much about. It wasn't any bigger than a piece of plain paper. The sketch was beautifully detailed and I understood much better now why Margo worried about something happening to it.

I'd expected that they'd want me to stay around as they set up, but I was hustled out of my office and the building. Diana Holmes was just coming across the parking lot as I came down the steps. She wore red leather pants and a cropped black jacket, her wavy dark hair in a short shag that I knew from my own experience with short hair took a lot of styling to look so casually tousled.

"Hello, Kathleen. Is Margo here?" she asked.

"She's inside," I said. "She and Gavin are just taking care of a few last-minute details."

"Perfect," she said. "That means they'll have time to bring me up-to-date on the changes to the security system."

I didn't think that was what it meant at all, but Diana had already started up the main stairs. I stood in the middle of the parking lot and sent a text to Maggie to see if she wanted to have lunch at her studio.

Please and thank you, she texted back.

The sky was cloudy but neither the morning's weather forecast nor my left wrist was predicting rain, so I decided to leave my truck in the library lot and walk. Susan was sitting at the counter with a bowl of soup, heat spiraling up and steaming up her glasses, when I walked in to Eric's.

I bumped her with my shoulder. "Hey, what is that?" I asked. "It smells wonderful." My stomach gurgled as if to emphasize my enthusiasm.

Susan took off her glasses and cleaned them on the edge of her sweater. "Italian sausage soup with oregano cheese croutons." She put her glasses back on and smiled at me. "Want to join me? I have an in with the owner."

"Thanks, but I'm taking lunch to Maggie," I said.

Claire was working, as she did pretty much every weekday lunch rush. She set the coffeepot she was carrying back in its place and turned to me. "Did I just hear you say you wanted takeout?" she asked.

"Please," I said. I looked over at Susan, thinking that the soup really did smell delicious.

"How about a couple of containers of soup and a couple of multigrain rolls?" Claire asked.

I nodded. "Sounds good."

It took Claire only a few minutes to get my order ready. "I put in two real spoons," she whispered. "Just drop them off next time you're in."

I thanked her and paid for lunch, adding a generous tip.

Susan waved her spoon at me. "I'll see you Saturday morning. Call me if you need anything before that."

"I will. Thanks," I said.

Ruby was just coming out of the building when I got to Riverarts, so she held the door for me. As I came out of the stairwell on the top floor I caught sight of Maggie in the hallway. She was wearing her favorite red hooded sweatshirt and she was deep in conversation with a woman in a jean jacket and black leggings. It was Rena Adler, I realized.

"I appreciate this," Rena said.

Maggie nodded. "I'll e-mail you everything later this afternoon." She turned to look at me. "Hi," she said. "Did Ruby let you in?"

I nodded. "She did." I smiled at Rena. "Hi."

"Hi, Kathleen," she said, pushing her backpack a little higher on her shoulder. She was wearing her dark hair loose, just brushing her shoulders. Her fingers on the strap of her leather bag were long and slender, like Maggie's, the nails clipped short, buffed but not polished. And like Maggie often did, Rena had a smudge of paint on one finger, a bit of cerulean blue on her index finger. "Is the library closed now for the day?" she asked.

I nodded. "The artwork from the museum arrived"—
I checked my watch—"about an hour ago." I knew
there was enough soup in the two containers to feed
three of us. "Can you join us for lunch?" I asked.

"Yes. Can you?" Maggie echoed.

"I'd like to; thanks," Rena said, "but Ruby and I
have a class in about"—she checked her watch—"half
an hour. I'm just going to grab some tea."

"Next time," Maggie said.

"Absolutely," Rena said. "I'll watch for your e-mail."
She smiled at me. "And I'll see you Saturday, Kathleen." She headed toward the stairs, pulling her phone
out of her pocket as she moved.

"So how was your morning?" Maggie asked as we
moved into her studio. I handed her the brown paper
take-out bag and took off my jacket, dropping it on one
of the stools pulled up to the center workspace.

"Margo decided we had to change all the light bulbs.
Again. She didn't like the color of the light from the LEDs.
She thought they gave everything a faint blue cast."

Mags gave an almost imperceptible nod.

"Wait a minute," I said. "You agree with her."

She opened the bag and took out the two containers
of soup. She'd already made tea. "Yes, I agree with
Margo about the light. I know she can be a little obsessive, but it's all those small details that add up to a successful show."

I swallowed down a grin. Maggie could be a "little
obsessive" about things herself.

"So what happened with the lights?" she asked.

"Larry managed to find enough incandescent bulbs
for all the fixtures."

"Burtis," Maggie immediately said.

"Burtis has a stash of old-style light bulbs?"

"Burtis has a stash of all sorts of things."

"And you would know this because?" I teased with a sly smile.

Her cheeks grew pink. "I know things," she said, just a little too defensively.

Maggie and Brady Chapman had been casually seeing each other for the past few months. The relationship may not have been serious, but I'd noticed that neither one of them was spending time with anyone else.

Brady was Burtis Chapman's oldest son. Burtis was a self-made businessman. Some of his enterprises were legal, some, not so much.

Maggie handed me a mug of tea and I pulled out a stool and sat down. She took a seat opposite me.

I told her about the possible magazine article and the reporter from *USA Today* as we ate.

"How did all this happen?" she asked.

"Lita," I said around a mouthful of little meatballs.

"I should have guessed."

"I think she has more connections than Burtis has light bulbs," I said.

Maggie laughed.

One of Lita's connections was Burtis himself. They'd been dating for close to a year and their relationship had become a lot more serious—and public—in the last few months.

Maggie walked me down to the back door after lunch. She pulled a tiny brown paper bag from the Grainery out of her pocket.

"Ah, Mags, you didn't buy Owen another funky chicken, did you?" I asked, frowning at her.

"He likes them," she said. "And you've been so busy at the library for the last month he deserves a little treat. Hercules, too. There are some of those little crackers he likes in there." She studied my face. "You're not going to give me the 'They're cats, not people' speech?" she asked.

I shook my head. "Uh-uh. But I am going to call you the next time your furry little friend spreads chicken parts all over my kitchen." I took the bag from her.

She hugged me. "I'll see you at class tonight," she said, and then she headed back up the stairs to her studio and I walked back to the library to get my truck, stopping in at Eric's long enough to return the spoons—and get a cinnamon roll.

Hercules was sitting on the bottom step by the back door when I got home. I reached down and picked him up and he nuzzled my face.

"Have you and Everett been solving all the town's problems?" I asked as I juggled the cat, my purse and my briefcase and tried to fish my keys from my pocket.

The cat wrinkled his nose. I was pretty sure that meant no.

I managed to get the key in the lock and the door open without dropping anything. "So if you haven't been eating bacon, why are you in such a good mood?"

It seemed bizarre to say it—especially since generally it was Owen who was scheming—but I knew Hercules had done something. I just didn't know what. The moment I opened the kitchen door I had my answer.

I could hear "Bandstand Boogie"—Barry Manilow—

coming from the living room. Had some Barry Manilow–loving burglar broken in? Or was it a furry Barry Manilow fan?

Hercules was wiggling in my arms. I set him down and dropped the rest of my things on the floor beside him. Then I went into the living room. My iPod was in the dock. The song changed to "Ready to Take a Chance Again."

Hercules had followed me and his head was bobbing like he was grooving to the music, which he was, because the little black-and-white cat loved Barry Manilow just about as much as I did. His brother, on the other hand, didn't get the attraction of the man who makes the whole world sing. In fact, Owen loathed every Barry Manilow song ever recorded.

"Where's your brother?" I asked.

Herc gave me a blank look.

"I know you did this," I said, pointing a finger at him.

I had no idea how Hercules had managed to turn on the music. It certainly seemed to be a skill beyond the average cat's capabilities, but then again neither cat was exactly average.

I turned the music off and went looking for Owen. I finally found him hiding in the back of my closet, his head stuffed in one of the fuzzy Bigfoot slippers my brother, Ethan, had given me at Christmas.

I crouched down on the floor next to him, pushing my shoes aside. "It's okay," I said. "I turned it off."

He lifted his head, the big fluffy bootie still stuck in place. I pulled it off and he shook himself. His gray fur was sticking up on one side and matted down on the other. He put his two front paws on my knee and meowed loudly.

"I know," I said, reaching over to smooth his fur.

He kept up a steady stream of meows and murps. I had no idea how long Barry Manilow had been playing, but for Owen any amount of time was too long.

I picked him up and got to my feet, dodging clothes and hangers as I backed out of the closet. "I'm sorry," I said, continuing to stroke his fur. "What Hercules did was wrong."

"Merow!" Owen said with as much indignation as he could muster.

"But you haven't exactly been a paragon of cat virtue the last week or so."

He grumbled under his breath.

I had no idea what was going on between the two of them. It felt a bit like being caught in a squabble between a couple of middle schoolers. Maybe Roma would have some insight.

I kissed the top of his furry head and set him down on the floor. "Stay away from your brother," I said firmly.

His gaze slid off my face and he suddenly became engrossed in a spot on the bedroom floor.

I changed for tai chi, retrieved the iPod from the dock in the living room and then went into the kitchen to get some supper before class. Hercules was sitting under the coat hooks. Owen had followed me downstairs, and he stopped by the table and glared at his brother, his tail twitching.

I stepped into the space between them. "I don't know what's going on between the two of you, but I want you both to cut it out," I said, feeling a little foolish that I was having this conversation with two cats. I needed a little incentive, I decided, to force détente, even temporarily. I went over to the counter and grabbed the container of sardine cat crackers I'd made on the weekend.

"See this?" I said.

That got their attention. "If you two don't cut it out, I'm taking all the crackers to Marcus's house and leaving them for Micah."

Owen immediately started grumbling. Hercules came over to me and wound around my ankles. I leaned down and gave the top of his head a scratch. "Sucking up is *not* going to work," I said. I set the container of crackers on the table and reached over to give Owen a little scratch on the side of his face. "Neither is complaining."

I picked up the container of crackers and put it in my canvas tote on top of my towel. "Behave yourselves or I'll be swinging by Marcus's house on the way home," I warned.

Maybe they understood the words. Maybe they didn't, but they definitely understood the tone and the actions. This clearly was a much better warning than my previous threat to feed their treats to Harry Senior's German shepherd, Boris.

When I left for class, Owen had disappeared down into the basement and Hercules was upstairs in my bedroom. When I pulled on my jacket I found the Grainery bag Maggie had given me. It didn't seem like a good time to give her gifts to Owen and Hercules. I didn't want to reward bad behavior.

I was the first person to arrive at tai chi. I found Maggie sipping a cup of mint tea and looking out the window.

"You're early," she said. She held up her cup. "Would you like a cup of tea?"

"Yes," I said.

She frowned at me. "Seriously?"

I linked my hands behind my neck and tipped my head up to the ceiling. "I'd like something hot and I've had way too much caffeine today."

Maggie patted my arm and headed toward the table where she always set up the tea supplies before class. "Margo?" she asked.

I shook out my arms and followed her. "And Gavin," I said. "She called me four times while I was eating supper—she doesn't text, which I probably should be grateful for. But Gavin sent me two texts."

"Do you want to put your phone in my office during class?" she asked.

"Could I?" I asked. I reached into my pocket. The phone wasn't there. I remembered setting it on the table while I went to get my hoodie from the living room closet. I didn't remember picking it up because I hadn't. I closed my eyes for a second and sighed. "It's sitting on the kitchen table."

"Good," she said. "There isn't anything that Margo or Gavin is going to need that can't wait. You can take an hour for yourself."

"I'll probably have a dozen messages by the time I get back."

"The world can turn without you for a little while."

Maggie made the tea and added a little honey to the cup before she gave it to me.

I took a tentative sip. It was hot and just a little sweet and the aroma of mint swirled around me.

She cocked an eyebrow.

"It's not coffee, but it's not bad," I said, taking another drink.

Maggie worked us hard in class. I was happy to spend time trying to perfect my Cloud Hands instead of worrying about the exhibit at the library. By the time we finished the complete form at the end of class, the back of my neck was damp with sweat.

Mags came over to me as I was changing my shoes. "Nice work," she said. She held out a small box.

It was the peppermint tea bags.

"What's this for?" I asked.

"Take these with you," she said. "I know you're going over to the library to see if Margo or Gavin needs anything. Maybe you can make them a cup of tea. If not, you can have a cup when you get home."

I wrapped her in a hug. "Thank you," I said. "I'll see you Saturday. You're coming early, aren't you?"

She nodded. "Margo told us to come at noon for a preview. You're opening the doors at twelve thirty?"

"And Everett will cut the ribbon at one."

"I'm excited," Maggie said, her green eyes sparkling.

"You should be," I said as I reached for my jacket. "Your collages are fantastic. This time Saturday everyone is going to be telling you how talented you are."

Her expression turned serious. "Thanks for everything you've done to make this happen."

"I haven't done that much," I said. "But you're welcome." I reached for my bag. "I'd better get over to the library and see what's going on."

She hugged me. "Take deep breaths."

The library was in darkness, except for the security lights, as I pulled level with the building. It looked as though both Margo and Gavin had finished for the night and gone back to the St. James Hotel. Everything must have gone well. Maybe there wouldn't be a dozen messages and texts on my phone when I got home.

I turned around in the parking lot, ready to head back up the hill, when I noticed one light on in the library. In my office.

I gripped the steering wheel tightly with both hands, took a deep breath and exhaled. It didn't help. I couldn't remember if I'd locked my door or not, but either way my office was supposed to be off-limits.

I parked the truck, grabbed my bag and headed for the main doors of the building. Not only did I want to turn the light off in my office. I wanted to see if anything had been disturbed by Margo or Gavin or whoever had been in there. As I unlocked the front doors it occurred to me that I couldn't have locked my office before I'd left for the day. How would someone have gotten inside without a key?

The first thing I noticed was that neither of the alarms had been set. Some prehistoric sense made the hairs come up on the back of my neck. I remembered the little sports car out in the lot. It didn't seem like the kind of car Margo would drive, but I didn't actually know what she was driving. She'd flown to Minneapolis from Chicago and then rented a car to drive to Mayville Heights. I knew the car didn't belong to Gavin; he was driving a silver Mercedes SUV.

Maybe Margo was still working inside. No, that

didn't make sense. If she was working, why weren't the main floor lights on? Was she sick? Had she climbed a ladder in those high heels and fallen? If I'd had my cell phone I would have called Marcus. But my phone was sitting on the table in my kitchen. The closest phone was inside the library. I felt a bit like the heroine in one of those old movies, heading into the spooky house during a storm, carrying nothing but a candle. And I didn't even have a candle.

Margo wasn't on the main floor of the building. I called her name several times and did a quick survey of the space, but there was no sign of her. I thought about calling 911 but there was no emergency.

I could see that my office door was open before I got to the top of the stairs. I called Margo's name again, and again I got no answer. As soon as I stepped into the doorway I saw why. Margo Walsh was lying on the floor. My brass cat was on its side beside her. Someone had used it to smash in the back of her head.

She was dead.

5

I called 911 from the phone at the circulation desk. Then I called Marcus. My hands wouldn't seem to stop shaking.

"I'm on my way," he said. "Go wait in the truck, please."

"I'm going," I said. I didn't want to stay in the building. I could still see Margo lying on my office floor. How could she be dead?

I locked the door again and sat in the truck until the black-and-white patrol car stopped at the curb. I'd met Officer Derek Craig at more than one of Marcus's crime scenes, because more than once I'd ended up involved in the cases—something that had been a big bone of contention between us for a long time. The young police officer had moved to Chicago to start at the John Marshall Law School in January. So it was Officer Stephen Keller who got out of the car. The military vet always seemed to have a serious expression on his face, and I was suddenly glad of his calm, competent presence.

I explained where Margo's body was, stumbling over the words a little, and handed over my keys. I had no desire to go back inside.

Hope Lind's vehicle pulled up to the curb while Officer Keller was still inside. I crossed the sidewalk to meet her.

"Hey, Kathleen," she said as she came around the front bumper of the little blue car carrying a stainless steel coffee mug and a cardboard take-out cup. She was wearing skinny jeans, laced ankle boots and a dark fleece jacket. She handed the take-out cup to me. "I was at Eric's," she said by way of explanation.

"Thank you," I said, taking the cardboard container from her and wrapping my hands around it. I didn't know Hope that well, but what I did know about her I liked. Marcus said she was a good detective—high praise coming from him.

She looked over at the library. "What's going on?"

I explained about forgetting my phone, driving by, spotting the light on in my office and subsequently finding Margo's body.

Hope watched me over the top of her cup, sipping her coffee as I talked. She didn't ask any questions or write anything down. Her expression didn't change, even when I described the wound I'd noticed on the back of Margo Walsh's head.

"You know how this works," she said with a small smile when I finished speaking.

I nodded, bending my head to take a sip from the coffee she'd brought me. I was shivering a little, although I wasn't sure whether it was from the night air or from finding Margo's body.

"Marcus is on his way?" she asked.

I shifted from one foot to the other. "He should be here in a few minutes. He was already home."

Officer Keller came out of the library then. Hope held up a hand in acknowledgment and then looked at me again. "Are you okay out here by yourself for a few minutes?"

"I'm fine," I said. "I'll just sit in the truck until Marcus gets here."

"Okay," she said. She drained her coffee and set the metal mug on the roof of her car. Then she pulled a pair of plastic gloves from her pocket and started for the library steps.

I changed my mind about going back to the truck. Instead I stayed there on the sidewalk with my coffee and watched for Marcus's SUV to come along the street—which happened in just a few minutes. Okay, he hadn't driven the speed limit all the way from his house. On the other hand, he was a detective on his way to a crime scene. He pulled in behind Hope's car and got out. I was already starting up the sidewalk to him.

He brushed a strand of hair away from my face. "Are you all right?" he asked.

I nodded.

This wasn't my first body. Marcus and I had met when I'd discovered composer Gregor Easton's body at the Stratton Theatre.

"I can't believe Margo is dead. I just saw her a few hours ago. How could this have happened?"

"We'll figure it out," Marcus said. He put his hands on my shoulders. "You're shaking."

"I'm okay," I said. I held up the take-out cup. "Hope brought me a cup of coffee."

"How did she get here so fast?" he asked. He was already shifting into what I thought of as "police officer mode," patting his pocket for gloves and scanning the area around the library.

"She was at Eric's," I said. We started walking toward the building and I had a flash of memory of the first time I'd made coffee for Marcus. We'd sat at the table in the staff room and he'd questioned me about my connection to Gregor Easton, thinking that maybe I'd been involved in some kind of torrid relationship with the pompous musician.

Marcus caught my smile in the darkness. "What?" he asked.

"I was just remembering the first time we shared a cup of coffee."

"Best day of my life," he said quietly.

It wasn't what I'd expected him to say. For a moment I didn't have any words, so I just reached over and squeezed his arm.

He put a hand over mine. "Your hands are cold," he said.

"My mom always says, 'Cold hands, warm heart.'"

"Funny, I don't remember her ever saying that. At least to me." A smile pulled at the corners of his mouth. "I remember she did tell me what would happen if I ever hurt you, but she didn't say anything about hands and hearts, just locations where there's no sunshine."

My mother was a larger-than-life person who was more likely to be doing Shakespeare in the dining room than making cookies in the kitchen. But I had never doubted her love for my brother, Ethan, my sister, Sara, or me. She was as protective as a mama grizzly would be with her cubs.

Marcus's lips brushed the top of my head. "I'll just check in with Hope and you can probably go," he said.

This time I did go back to the truck, nursing my coffee until Marcus came back. In the end it was more like half an hour before he and Hope said it was okay for me to leave.

"What's going in the case in the very middle of where the artwork is displayed?" Marcus asked. We were standing at the bottom of the library steps.

"A drawing of a native encampment by Sam Weston," I said, stuffing my hands in the pockets of my hoodie. "It's the focal point of the exhibit." Then his choice of words sank in. I caught a look passing between him and Hope. "Marcus, what do you mean, 'What's going in the case?' The drawing should be in that case now."

"It's not," Hope said, turning to look at the building.

Marcus ran a hand back through his dark wavy hair, a sure sign that he was troubled by the fact that the Weston drawing wasn't where it should be. Margo Walsh was dead on my office floor. It wasn't hard to make a connection between the two.

"Everett should know what's going on," I said. Another look passed between Marcus and Hope. It was as if they had some form of silent communication. I'd seen Owen and Hercules do the same thing.

"I'll call him," Marcus said.

"All right," I said.

He took a few steps away from us and pulled out his phone.

Hope gave me a smile that was mostly politeness. "You can go home now, Kathleen."

I pulled my keys out of my pocket and detached the ones for the building. "This one is for the main doors," I said, pointing to the largest silver key. "This one is the master for all the inside doors."

She took the keys and put them in her pocket.

"You'll need the alarm codes," I said.

"Tell me what they are," she said. "I can remember them."

I recited the sequences for both alarm systems and noticed that Hope was silently repeating them after me. "If you need anything or you have any questions, I'm going right home. You can call me."

The smile she gave me this time was a little more genuine. "Thanks," she said. She tipped her head toward the building. "I'm sorry about this."

I sighed softly. "Me too. Margo didn't deserve this."

Hope went back into the building. I turned just as Marcus put his phone back into his pocket. I knew that part of his mind was already turning over the details of the case, and I didn't want to keep him from his job any longer.

"I'm going to go," I said.

"Okay." He raked his hand back through his hair again. "I don't know how late this is going to go, but I'll call you in the morning."

"Tell Everett I'll be up if he needs to talk to me."

Hercules was waiting for me on the porch, sitting on the bench by the window, when I got home. I sat down beside him, leaned my head back against the window frame and closed my eyes for a moment. When I opened them again Hercules was standing on his back legs, front paws on my chest, looking at me with his head tipped to one side.

"Margo Walsh is dead," I said. I swallowed down the lump in my throat.

"Merow?" he said.

I thought I heard an inquiry in the sound.

"Do you remember the woman who was here a couple of nights ago?" I asked. "She told you how handsome you looked, like you were wearing a tuxedo."

Hercules ducked his head. "Mrrr," he said softly. He'd liked Margo.

It had turned out she was a cat person. She'd been intrigued by my story of how I'd found Owen and Hercules out at Wisteria Hill when they were just kittens, or, to be more exact, how they had found me. She'd spent several minutes talking to each of them and they'd both stayed around once Margo and I had gotten down to work.

I slipped my bag up onto my shoulder again, picked up Hercules and stood up. He leaned in and licked my chin, his way of being sympathetic.

There was no sign of Owen in the kitchen. I set Hercules down and put my things away. I wasn't exactly sure what to do next. I turned around to see the cat staring at the toaster sitting on the counter.

"That's a good idea," I said. I put bread in the toaster and got the milk from the refrigerator. By the time I sat down at the table with a mug of hot chocolate and a plate of peanut butter toast, Owen had appeared, peering around the basement door, whiskers twitching. He walked all the way around the table to get to my left side since Hercules was already sitting on my right.

I pulled a tiny piece for each of them from the toast. I knew Roma would lecture me about feeding them people food, but I rationalized it as being just a bite.

I told the boys what had happened at the library and they both seemed to listen intently. For all I knew it could have been the cat version of listening politely while they were daydreaming about grackles or catnip chickens.

"It has to have something to do with the Weston drawing," I said.

Owen seemed to frown, as though he disagreed. Then he bent his head and licked a tiny dab of peanut butter from one paw.

Okay, so I didn't have his full attention. I looked at Hercules. "If the drawing isn't in the case, where is it?" I asked. "It was the only thing missing. Neither one of the alarms was set. Margo is dead and the drawing is gone. Do you think that's a coincidence?"

"Merow," he said.

"I know," I said. "Me neither."

Everett called at about nine thirty. He was on his way home and asked if we could get together to decide how to handle things.

"Of course," I said.

"I appreciate this, Kathleen," he said. "Rebecca said to tell you she has some of the Jam Lady's marshmallows."

I laughed grimly. "Rebecca knows me well."

I changed out of my tai chi clothes into jeans and a white shirt. I gave the boys fresh water and left the light on over the stove.

"I have no idea how long this will take," I said. Owen meowed and disappeared down the basement stairs. I made a mental note to figure out why he was spending so much time down there.

Hercules wound around my legs as I pulled on my favorite low leather boots. I reached down to pet the top of his head. "I know it's asking a lot," I said in a low voice, "but please try to get along with your brother while I'm gone."

He suddenly found the edge of the mat where I put my shoes incredibly fascinating.

Rebecca had turned on the light at her back door. I cut across my backyard and then hers. She was watching for me and she opened the back door before I could tap on it.

"Hello, dear," she said. "Everett told me what happened. Are you all right?"

Rebecca was one of the kindest and gentlest people I'd ever met. She was tiny, with silver hair and blue eyes and a smile that lit up her entire face. She also had a will of iron. "I'm all right," I said, shrugging off my jacket.

As promised, she made hot chocolate and topped each pottery mug with two fat marshmallows that smelled of vanilla before she set one cup in front of me. "Would you like a rhubarb muffin?" she asked.

"This is good for now. Thank you," I said.

Rebecca sat opposite me with her own cup. "The way Everett spoke . . ." She hesitated. "What happened to Margo Walsh wasn't an accident, was it?"

"I uh . . . I don't think so," I said slowly. I hated that Margo was probably dead because of a drawing.

"That's very sad," she said.

"It is. Very," I agreed.

"Everett said the Weston drawing is missing?"

I looped my finger through the handle of the cup. "It looks that way, unless Margo put it somewhere for safekeeping, and I don't know where that would be, or even why she would."

Rebecca gave a soft sigh. "I've seen the drawing, you know. It's quite lovely and surprisingly detailed, but it's not worth killing another human being over, no matter how much money it's worth."

There was a knock on the back door then. Rebecca got up to answer it, reaching out to pat my arm for a moment as she moved past me.

It was Gavin Solomon. I wasn't surprised to see him. I'd figured that Everett would have called him as well. He was wearing jeans and a black T-shirt and his hair was mussed as if, like Marcus, he'd run his hands through it several times.

"Hello, Kathleen," he said. He didn't seem surprised to see me, either.

"Kathleen and I were just having hot chocolate," Rebecca said to Gavin. "Would you like to join us? Or I could easily make a pot of coffee."

Gavin pulled a hand across his neck. He seemed much more subdued than usual. "I think I've had more than my share of coffee today. A cup of hot chocolate sounds great." He looked at me. "I can't believe Margo is dead. I was just with her a couple of hours ago."

He joined me at the table and by the time Rebecca had the hot chocolate ready Everett was walking through the back door.

We spent the next couple of hours deciding how we would handle the inevitable press inquiries and whether or not the library should be closed. It was after eleven thirty when Everett pushed back the lined yellow pad on the table in front of him and said, "I think we've done all we can do."

Gavin nodded, shifting sideways in his seat and propping one forearm on the chair back. "You're right," he said. "Everything else is going to have to wait until morning." He closed the leather portfolio in front of him on the table. "I'm meeting Detective Lind at nine o'clock to go over the security system with her, but I'll contact everyone else I need to before that." He shook his head. "I was going to say I needed to call Margo."

Hope had called Gavin about half an hour after he'd gotten to the house, looking for more information about the temporary security system. He'd arranged to meet her at the library in the morning and walk her through it. Listening to his end of the conversation made it clear that the system should have been on.

"I appreciate you taking time to walk Detective Lind through the alarm system, Gavin," Everett said. He looked tired. There were deep frown lines between his eyes and bracketing his mouth. Rebecca came to stand next to his chair. She put her hand on his shoulder and I could see him relax a little at her touch. Everett looked at me then. "Kathleen, I'm sorry about all the disruption this is going to cause for you," he said. "But the only thing that matters is that the police catch whoever killed Margo."

I nodded my agreement.

"If you need extra staff hours once the police release

the building, go ahead and schedule them," he continued. "I'll clear that with the board."

"Thank you," I said, getting to my feet. I smiled at Rebecca. "And thank you for the hot chocolate."

"You're welcome, dear," she said.

Gavin got to his feet as well. "Kathleen, can I give you a ride?" he asked.

I tipped my head in the direction of the backyard as I pulled on my hoodie. "Thanks, but I'm just across the back and I left the porch light on. The only thing I might run into is a raccoon."

"If you're sure," he said, looking a little skeptical.

"I am," I said.

"I shouldn't be more than an hour with the detective in the morning, probably less," Gavin said. "Could we get together after that? By then I know I'm going to have a list of things I'll need input on from you."

I ran through the mental checklist of things I needed to get done first thing in the morning. I had more phone calls to make and a quick check-in with Lita. It seemed callous to be thinking about all those mundane details with Margo dead, but they had to be taken care of. Margo would have been one of the first to point that out. "How about quarter after ten at Eric's Place?"

"That should work," he said.

Rebecca walked me to the door and stepped out onto the back stairs. "I don't see any sign of Oswald," she said.

"Oswald?" I asked. I had no idea whom she was talking about.

"The raccoon," she said. "I saw it crossing the Justasons' yard last week and I said to Everett that it reminded me of Uncle Oswald. He had big black-framed glasses and those bushy sideburns called muttonchops. And a rather unfortunate raccoon coat."

She was trying to distract me for a few moments, I realized, from thinking about what had happened. I leaned against the railing and looked out across Rebecca's yard and mine. "I don't see anything with or without a raccoon coat."

I gave her a quick hug. "Thank you for the hot chocolate," I said as I started down the stairs. I cut across the back lawn and all but sprinted through the patch of darkness in between the reach of Rebecca's porch light and my own. I had no desire to meet anything in a raccoon coat, no matter whose family member it might look like. I'd seen enough of what the bogeyman could do for one night.

6

Gavin walked into Eric's Place at about five minutes after ten the next morning. I had called Harrison first thing and postponed our visit, promising we'd get together in a few days. Claire picked up the coffeepot and started toward the table as soon as she caught sight of Gavin. She had a cup poured before he had a chance to sit down.

"Thanks, Claire," he said, reaching for the sugar. "You read my mind."

She put two fingers to her right temple and narrowed her gaze at him. "Now you're thinking about a sausage-and-apple breakfast sandwich," she said, a hint of a smile playing across her face.

Gavin laughed. "I actually am." He looked across the table at me, raising an eyebrow. "And one of those cinnamon roll things?"

"Please," I said. I slid my mug toward Claire and she refilled it for me.

"It'll just be a few minutes," she said. She headed for the kitchen with our order.

Gavin leaned back in his chair and crossed his legs. "Did you get in touch with everyone who was planning on being here for the opening of the exhibit?" he asked, gesturing at my phone, which was on the table next to my cup.

I nodded. "Most people were very understanding, although there was an art historian from Chicago who seemed more concerned about not being able to see the Weston drawing than about Margo being dead."

Gavin rolled his eyes as he took a drink from his coffee. "There's always someone whose priorities are all wrong." He set the cup down. "I take it word's getting out that the drawing is missing."

"How, I don't know," I said with a sigh. "But I think so. I hedged as much as I could."

"Don't worry about it," he said. "That's not something we're going to be able to keep quiet for very long. As I told your detective this morning, the questions are just going to get more pointed."

"How did things go at the library?" I asked.

He gave an offhand shrug. "The Weston drawing is the only piece that's missing. It's pretty obvious that's what the thief was after. And I think it's too much of a coincidence to think Margo's death isn't connected." He pressed his lips together for a moment and picked up his cup again. "I kept expecting her to walk in, you know."

I nodded. "Do you have any idea who turned off the security system?" From the corner of my eye I saw Claire approaching with our food. Gavin waited until she'd topped up our cups before he answered my question.

"It was an inside job," he said.

I frowned at him. "Inside how? Are you trying to say it was someone who works at the library?"

His mouth was full of Eric's latest breakfast sandwich creation, so he held up a hand. I waited.

"I mean inside as in someone shut down both systems from inside the building."

I had to let the words sink in for a moment. "You mean Margo turned off the alarm? She let her killer get into the building?" I broke a piece off the fat cinnamon roll on the plate in front of me but didn't eat it. "C'mon, Gavin. That doesn't make any sense. Margo didn't think the Weston drawing should have been out of a museum setting. Why on earth would she turn off the security system that was protecting it?"

He shook his head. "I don't know. When I left, Margo said she was going to be about another twenty minutes. She locked the main library doors behind me and I can guarantee that the rest of the building was locked up tight because I checked everything personally."

"So she let the thief in?"

"It looks that way." He looked around for Claire, pointing at his mug and smiling when she looked his way. Gavin drank more coffee than I did.

I shook my head. "That doesn't make any sense. Margo wouldn't let anyone into the building. Not with the exhibit set up." I didn't say that I'd half been expecting her to sleep in the building once the artwork arrived.

"I know it doesn't make any sense," Gavin agreed. "And it's completely out of character for Margo from what I know of her, but I can't find any other way that the thief could have gotten into the building. Nothing was tampered with at the keypads."

He paused, looked around the restaurant and then leaned across the table toward me. "Kathleen, I don't imagine your detective would want this getting out, but it's not just that it looks like Margo let someone into the building." He cleared his throat. "You know I set up a perimeter alarm just around the area where the exhibit was?"

"I know," I said.

The day the alarm had been installed, Mary had managed to set it off twice, both times by backing up with a cart of books for reshelving. We'd ended up moving a low unit of bookshelves and borrowing a set of brass posts and a black velvet rope from the Stratton Theatre to keep patrons from straying across the invisible security barrier.

"It had been disabled, too."

The only way to turn off that perimeter alarm was from the circulation desk, with a sixteen-character code that only Gavin, Margo and I knew.

He swiped a hand over his mouth. "I didn't do it and I'm guessing you didn't, either, so that just leaves Margo."

He looked past me, out the front window toward the river. I could see a mix of emotions play across his face. There was sadness over Margo's death. They hadn't been friends, but they had worked extremely well together, and as the poet John Donne had written, "Each man's death diminishes me." But I could also see tight lines of frustration, or maybe it was anger, around his mouth.

I sighed. "If Margo let the thief into the building . . ." I let the end of the sentence trail away. I didn't want to finish the thought.

Gavin grimaced. "Yeah. Was she in on the theft?"

"Do you seriously believe that?" I asked. "You knew her better than I did, but nothing I knew about Margo would make me think she'd do something like that."

"I know, I know," Gavin said, shaking his head. "Maybe there's something we're missing."

"I hope so," I said, reaching for the spiral-bound notebook to my left. "There are a couple of things I need to go over with you."

"Sure," he said, reaching for his tablet. He seemed to be happy to stop talking about Margo.

Gavin and I spent about half an hour coming up with a plan to deal with security at the library until the police at least released the artwork back to the museum. At this point the entire schedule for the exhibit had been put on hold and I suspected in the end the tour would be canceled.

I went home and had lunch with the boys, taking my bowl of rice, topped with some steamed vegetables and leftover chicken, out into the sunshine of the backyard. I sat in the blue Adirondack chair with Hercules beside me while Owen prowled around the lawn like a predatory jungle cat.

As I ate I told Herc what I'd learned from Gavin. Talking about it out loud seemed to help me make sense of everything, and talking to the cats didn't feel as weird as just talking to myself did.

"Why would Margo let the thief into the building?" I asked Hercules.

He looked at me blankly. He clearly had no more idea than I did.

"She had to know she'd be setting herself up as a suspect once the theft was discovered. Why would she do something that careless?"

The cat didn't have an answer to that question, either.

I spent the rest of the day working from home, dealing with paperwork and making numerous phone calls to Lita.

Late in the afternoon Lita called me. "Kathleen, Everett has asked if you'd be willing to go ahead with the two interviews that had been scheduled for tomorrow. He would have called and asked you himself, but he's in a meeting."

"Of course I will," I said. "You know they're going to ask about Margo's death."

"I know," she said. "Everett thinks it would be better if we got out ahead of the speculation as much as we can. To this point the police haven't released a cause of death and it's not common knowledge that the Weston drawing is missing."

I leaned back in my chair and stretched. Owen was sitting on my lap, seemingly engrossed in the revised staff schedule on the screen of my laptop. "I think Everett is right. We need to salvage what we can from this." As soon as the words were out of my mouth I realized how they sounded. "I'm sorry, Lita," I said. "That was disrespectful. Margo is dead. Finding out what happened to her is what matters."

"You weren't being disrespectful," Lita said. "It doesn't serve anyone to have her death sensationalized along with the town. These interviews are a chance to make sure people know how hard she worked on this exhibit and how enthusiastic she was about supporting and promoting the local art community."

Owen turned his head to look inquiringly at me and I smiled at him since I couldn't smile at Lita.

"And that's what I'm going to do," I said. "As usual, you're right. Are you ever wrong?"

"Oh yes," she said gravely. "Last October. I was convinced that I was mistaken about something, but it turned out I was incorrect."

I laughed and she promised she'd send me the details for both interviews once she'd confirmed them with the reporters.

Marcus wasn't available to have supper, so I called Roma. "Are you free for supper?" I asked. "I have pea soup with ham."

"Oh, that sounds good," she said. "Are you free to help strip wallpaper from the little bedroom?"

"Absolutely," I said.

I had some of Rebecca's rolls in the freezer. I got them out to take along with the soup. "I'm going out to Roma's for supper," I said to Owen, who had watched me get the food ready with great interest.

"Mrrr," he said, wrinkling his nose in annoyance. Roma was not one of Owen's favorite people. She was the one who poked him with needles and tried to look in his mouth. I felt the same way about the dentist.

The library was closed on Saturday and stayed closed Monday. I did both of the interviews and tried to keep the conversation on the exhibit and the town and away from speculation about Margo's death.

"Can you at least give me an idea about when we'll be able to reopen?" I asked Marcus as we sat on the swing on his deck after supper Monday night. I leaned over and left a string of tiny kisses down his jawline, ending with a longer, warmer one on his mouth.

"Ummm," he growled. "Are you trying to influence a police officer, Kathleen?"

"No," I said. I straightened up and folded my hands primly in my lap. "I'll stop."

He pulled me against him. "I didn't say I wanted you to stop."

I laughed and laid my head against his chest. Micah padded across the deck and launched herself into Marcus's lap. I reached over to stroke her fur and in a moment she started to purr.

"I think she likes living here with you," I said. The little ginger tabby gently kneaded Marcus's lap with her paw and then stretched out on his leg.

"Ahh, you guys are so cute," a voice said. Hope Lind was standing by the deck stairs.

I straightened up and tugged at my shirt, suddenly feeling self-conscious, which was a little silly since everyone in town knew Marcus and I were a couple. In fact, it seemed, at times, like half of the town had been invested in us *becoming* a couple.

"Is everything okay?" Marcus asked.

"Everything's fine," Hope said, waving away his concern with one hand. She dropped down onto the built-in bench seating that ran around the deck railing.

Micah immediately jumped down from Marcus's lap, crossed the deck, and leapt up next to Hope. "Hey, puss," Hope said with a smile, reaching out to scratch behind the little tabby's ear. She extended the smile to me. "I actually came to see Kathleen." She gave an apologetic half shrug. "I'm sorry to interrupt. I did try your cell."

My phone was sitting on the counter inside. I straightened up the rest of the way and tucked my hair behind one ear. "It's okay," I said. "Did you by any chance come to tell me I can open the library tomorrow?"

She looked a little sheepish. "No, it's actually pretty much the opposite."

I groaned, tipped my head back to study the sky overhead for a moment and then looked at her. "How long?" I asked.

"The rest of this week and maybe next," Hope said, her free hand playing with the zipper pull on her jacket. "I'm really sorry."

I glanced at Marcus, who frowned, his blue eyes narrowing. He clearly didn't know why the library was going to have to stay closed.

"It's not your fault," I said. "Can I at least ask you why the investigation is taking so long?"

"It's not the investigation," she said.

"I don't understand," I said.

"Neither do I," Marcus said. "What's going on?"

Hope blew out a breath. "Part of the reason the museum agreed to this and three or four other exhibits going on the road was to get things out of their building so they could renovate the oldest section."

"I know," I said, curling one foot up underneath me. "Margo and Gavin both mentioned it."

"Contractor was doing something up in the ceiling yesterday and someone set off the sprinkler system."

Marcus pulled a hand over his neck. "Damn. How much damage?"

"A lot," Hope said, one hand still stroking Micah's fur.

"They can't take the pieces back," I said.

Hope shook her head, pressing the back of her free hand to her mouth to stifle a yawn. "They're scrambling to clear up the water damage and find storage for what's there now. You really should talk to Gavin Solomon. All I can tell you is that the insurance company is balking at having the library open as long as the exhibit is still in place."

I exhaled loudly in frustration. We had programs that depended on the library for space.

Marcus got to his feet, which set the swing gently swaying back and forth. He gestured to the mug on the deck boards by my feet. "Do you want a refill?" he asked.

I shook my head.

He looked at Hope. "How about a cup of coffee?"

"I don't want to interrupt anything," she said.

"You're not," I said.

Hope turned to Marcus. "Okay, I could use one."

His fingers brushed my hair and then he went into the kitchen.

"So what is going to happen to all the artwork at the library?" I asked.

"The plan is to leave it where it is for now. Mr. Solomon has a backup security system up and running, plus a security guard."

I thought of Margo's reluctance to have the pieces out of the museum. I was beginning to think she'd been right.

"Wouldn't it make more sense to repack everything? Or better yet, send it all on to the next stop on the tour." *And give me back my building,* I added silently.

"There is no more tour," Hope said. "The insurance company refuses to take on the additional risk with the Weston piece missing. As for packing up everything, apparently there are some extra security measures in the display cases that are supposed to make them safer than just putting everything back in their crates." She stretched one arm along the railing. "That security system is probably the most complicated one I've ever come across. That's why Solomon has come onto the case as a consultant."

"What?" Marcus said. He had just come out from the kitchen with the coffee.

"Oh yeah," Hope said, taking the steaming cup he held out to her. "The word came down from on high."

I knew by the set of Marcus's jaw that he wasn't happy about Gavin being involved in their case.

"You don't want to work with Gavin," I said, framing the sentence as a statement and not a question.

A look passed between them.

Hope took a sip of her coffee and gave an offhand shrug. "It's not that," she said. "It's just that anytime someone else gets tied up in an investigation, things always get more complicated."

It was more than that, I knew, but I also knew it wasn't the right time to ask more questions.

Marcus sat down next to me again. He didn't say anything.

"Okay, if we can't reopen, can I at least get into the building to get a couple of things from my office and clear the book drop?" I asked. "It has to be overflowing by now."

Hope nodded. "I don't see why not. If you call Mr. Solomon I'm sure he'll clear you with the security guard. Why don't you come by about nine thirty or so?"

She was trying just a bit too hard to keep things light, but I just smiled and thanked her.

Hope finished her coffee and we talked about the water levels and how lucky the town was that there hadn't been any real flooding this spring. She gave Micah one last scratch behind the ear and stood up, yawning again as she tipped her head toward one shoulder.

"Sorry," she said. "It's not the company. It's just been a long day." She handed her cup to Marcus. "Thanks for the coffee." Then she looked at me. "I'll see you in the morning?"

"Yes," I said.

"I'll walk you," Marcus said, getting to his feet again. He glanced at me. "Be right back." He and Hope disappeared around the side of the house. I could hear their voices, too low to make out the words.

Micah studied me from her seat on the bench. Then she jumped down, came across the deck and launched herself onto the swing, timing her jump to match its slight sway. "Mrrr," she said softly, tipping her head to one side inquiringly.

If it had been Owen or Hercules sitting beside me, I would have convinced myself the cat was asking if everything was all right.

Micah put a paw on my lap and continued to give me that look.

Feeling a little silly, I leaned toward the cat. "Marcus doesn't like Gavin," I said, keeping my voice low, because after all, I was talking to a cat. "Why?"

"Mrrr," she said again, pawing the leg of my jeans. I had no idea what she meant.

"You and Hope are awfully friendly," I said.

The little tabby turned and looked at the back door before resting her chin on my leg next to her paw. I "spoke enough cat" to know that meant "scratch behind my ears." So I did.

"Hope has been to the house a lot."

Micah opened her eyes, looked at me and then dropped her head back onto my lap.

"I sound jealous, don't I?" I said. Did I actually think I was having a conversation with her?

I had conversations with Owen and Hercules all the time, which I told myself was just a way of thinking out loud. But the truth was, deep inside I did think they understood what I was saying. Was it really that farfetched to think a cat who could walk though walls or disappear at will would also be able to follow a conversation?

"It makes sense that Hope would be out here," I said to the little cat. "She works with Marcus. It's just that . . ." I shifted in my seat, trying not to disturb her. She opened one eye, looked at me as if to gently chastise me and then closed it again. "Why didn't he ever say so?"

Marcus was very private person. So much so that it had been a big stumbling block to our relationship getting off the ground.

"And what's taking him so long?" I whispered.

Micah meowed softly without opening her eyes, and Marcus came around the side of the house. He sat down beside me. The cat sat up, stretched, shot me a look and jumped down to the deck. Then she disappeared down the steps and into the backyard.

Marcus put his arm around me. "Sorry that took so long," he said. "There were just a couple of things we needed to talk about that had to do with the case."

"That's okay," I said. "Micah kept me company."

"She likes you," he said.

I leaned my head against his shoulder. "The cat or Hope?"

"Well, both, but I was talking about Micah." I felt his lips brush my hair. "I think Maggie is right. I think maybe you are the Cat Whisperer."

Maggie had given me the nickname for my ability to get so close to Lucy and the other cats in the feral cat colony that called the old carriage house out at Wisteria Hill, where Roma now lived, home. And she had jokingly dubbed Marcus my sidekick, the Cat Detective.

"Well, I am pretty much a cat person," I said lightly. "But I do like Hope as well. And so does Micah, it seems."

The moment the words were out I was sorry I'd said them. There was a sour taste at the back of my throat. I was fishing, and I didn't want to be *that* kind of girlfriend.

"She's been out here a few times," Marcus said, "you know, when we've been working on a case."

"That's what I thought." I leaned forward and picked up my cup. "I should get going," I said, standing up. "Who knows what Hercules and Owen could have gotten into, and I need to call Everett and see how he wants to handle the building being closed."

Marcus reached out and caught my hand. "The cats are fine, and couldn't you call Everett from here?" The space between his eyebrows was furrowed into two frown lines.

I turned to face him, setting my mug on the deck railing and rolling my arm in his grasp so I could link my fingers through his. "You and Hope work together a lot. You're close," I said.

"Yeah, I guess we are," he said. There was just a hint of color on those gorgeous cheekbones.

"Close as in colleagues who work together a lot or close as in this?" I held up our clasped hands.

"I should have told you sooner," he said. "We went out a few times. Before us. Before I even knew you." To his credit, he didn't look away.

"So why didn't you?" I asked.

He swiped a hand across the stubble on his chin. "I don't know. I didn't want things to be awkward. The longer I waited, the harder it got. I'm not good at sharing personal stuff. You know that." He did look away then and swallowed hard. "I am sorry."

I leaned over and plinked the middle of his forehead with my thumb and index finger.

"Ow!" he exclaimed.

I dropped back down beside him on the swing. "What did you think I'd do when you told me? Jump on Hope's back, pull her hair and yell, 'Keep your hands off my man!'"

"No," he said, looking a little embarrassed. "Probably not."

I leaned back and started the swing swaying slowly back and forth. "My mother, on the other hand, would be perfectly capable of doing something like that, but she's not here." I nudged him with my shoulder, smiling at him because I felt better.

"I know," Marcus said with a wry smile. "She made it very clear what would happen if I made you unhappy."

I kissed his cheek. "Lucky for you that you make me very happy."

"Lucky for me, period," he said, turning his head so my second kiss landed on his mouth.

I could have stayed there for another half an hour just kissing him, because oh my, could he kiss, but I made myself pull away and stand up. "I really have to call Everett," I said. "I'm sorry. And talk to Gavin, and I need my computer and my date book so I can keep everything straight."

Marcus got to his feet as well. "Why do you need to talk to Solomon?"

"You heard what Hope said." I started for the back door, looking around to see if Micah was close by and wanted to come in. I didn't see her. "The insurance company wants to keep the rest of the exhibit in my library until the museum cleans up after that sprinkler malfunction. I don't want to stay closed for another two weeks. Maybe he can satisfy them and we can find a way to open."

My phone was lying on the kitchen table. I picked it up and sent a text to Gavin asking if we could meet for breakfast to talk about things at the library. He texted right back suggesting Eric's first thing in the morning.

"I could join you," Marcus said, leaning against the counter as I pulled on my sweater.

"Thanks, but we're going to spend the whole time talking about the exhibit and the security system," I said, tucking my cell in my pocket. "I know you have better things to do with your time than listen to that."

"I don't mind," Marcus said with an offhand shrug. "I'll pick you up."

I laid a hand on his cheek for a moment. "It's a business meeting and I need the truck because Hope is going to let me into the library and there are some things I need to take home." I smiled at him. "How about lunch?"

He hesitated just a moment too long.

"You're jealous," I said slowly.

"I just want to spend some time with you," he said, reaching out with one hand to pull me closer. "You've been so busy getting ready for the exhibit, and now Hope and I have this case."

I held up one finger. "True I've been busy." I held up a second finger. "True that you're going to be tied up investigating Margo's murder." I added a third finger to the first two. "Also true that you, Marcus Gordon, brilliant detective, are jealous."

I felt his breath against my hair as he exhaled slowly. "I'm not jealous," he finally said. "I just don't like the way Solomon looks at you."

I pulled back so I could see his face. "And how does he look at me?"

His cheeks reddened. "It doesn't matter," he said. "I'm sorry."

I felt my shoulders tighten, and this time I was the

one who took a deep breath and then exhaled slowly, once, twice. "How does Gavin look at me?" I asked again, my dark eyes locked on Marcus's blue ones.

His mouth twisted and he broke the gaze, looking over my shoulder. "He looks at you like you're a hamburger and he hasn't eaten for a week."

"Gavin's a flirt," I said. "He flirts with me; he flirts with Lita; he flirts with the senior women in the book club."

"If Burtis catches him flirting with Lita, we'll have another case to investigate," Marcus said, with, it seemed to me, just a touch of petulance in his voice.

"You're missing the point," I said, struggling to keep the frustration I was feeling out of my voice. "It doesn't matter if Gavin puts on a G-string and dances around to Beyoncé at the next meeting we have with him. Neither Lita nor I am interested." I was pretty sure I could speak for Lita, given how serious the relationship seemed to be with Burtis.

"I trust you," he said, his gaze coming back to my face. Trust had been an issue in the past between the two of us, with Marcus feeling I didn't trust him enough to share an instinct I had about one of his cases and me feeling shut out because he hadn't shared any details about his family. I didn't really think this was about trust. I was pretty sure it was a guy thing.

"You just want to mark your territory."

"I'm not a dog, Kathleen," he said, reaching out to run a hand down my arm. "I'm not trying to lift my leg and—"

I held up one hand. "I get the picture," I said. "And I think you're more like Owen."

Marcus frowned. "I'm sorry. I don't understand."

"Before he figured out that Hercules had no interest in catnip in general and yellow chickens full of catnip in particular, whenever he got a Fred the Funky Chicken, the first thing he'd do is lick it from one end to the other. It was his way of saying, 'Mine.'" I folded my arms over my chest. "You're trying to do the same thing by joining us for breakfast. And you're not invited." I caught his hand and gave it a squeeze. "I'll talk to you tomorrow."

"You're mad," he said, frowning in surprise.

I held up my thumb and index finger about an inch apart. "Little bit," I said.

Micah was sitting on the top of the deck railing by the stairs, next to my empty cup. I stopped to give the top of her head a scratch. "Sometimes he makes me crazy," I whispered to her.

She gave a soft "mrrr" and nuzzled my hand in what I decided was solidarity.

7

The détente between Owen and Hercules seemed to still be holding. They ate breakfast while I got supper started in the slow cooker the next morning, and then Owen decided to go outside while Hercules came upstairs to watch me brush my teeth and do my hair.

When we got back downstairs I went to the back door to call Owen. He was already coming across the grass. And he was limping. I cut across the lawn to him, bending down to pick him up. He held out his left front paw, somewhat sheepishly, it seemed to me. A large sliver of wood protruded between his first and second claw.

I sucked in a breath. "What happened?" I asked. That had to hurt.

Owen looked in the direction of Rebecca's house.

"The woodpile," I said.

"Merow," he said sadly. He liked to sit on the top of the wood Rebecca had split for her fireplace and survey both our yards like a ruler on his throne.

I started back to the house, keeping a firm grip on

the cat, because I knew once he figured out what my next move was going to be he was going to disappear.

Literally.

As soon as I was in the kitchen, I reached for the cat carrier bag hanging by the door, swept Owen inside and zippered the top shut with one smooth motion. His howl of outrage brought Hercules from the living room.

"I'm sorry," I said to Owen. "This is something Roma has to do."

His golden eyes glared at me through the mesh panel in the top of the bag. As I picked up my phone, Hercules approached the bag and meowed softly in inquiry at his brother. Owen held up his injured paw and gave a pitiful meow. Hercules looked over his shoulder at me.

"No," I said as I pulled up Roma's number on my phone. "I'm not doing this. He needs a doctor." I shook my head. Why was I explaining myself to them?

Roma agreed to meet us at the clinic. Once we got into an examination room she gave me a towel to wrap around Owen and pulled on her Kevlar glove. I tried to stroke his fur, but he twisted his head away and glared at me.

"I know it hurts," I said. I took hold of his paw with my right hand, keeping his body against my body with my arm. At the same time I held a catnip chicken in front of his face with the other hand. He turned his head, his eyes narrowed in suspicion. Owen knew a bribe when he was presented with one, and he wanted to ignore the yellow chicken, but there's principle and then there's funky chickens.

He grabbed the toy in his mouth and at the same

moment Roma yanked the sliver of wood from his paw with a large pair of tweezers. Owen gave a yowl of surprise and Fred the Funky Chicken fell into my outstretched hand. He tried to shake his paw but I was still holding on to it.

"Let Roma make sure she got it all," I said.

He shot me a baleful glance and took the catnip chicken in his teeth, biting down through the yellow fabric into the tightly packed catnip with a crunching sound.

Roma straightened up. "I don't see any other slivers of wood, and the skin is barely broken. I'm going to rinse the area, but that's about all. Given that Owen is . . . well . . . Owen, I'm not going to put on a bandage, but if you see any sign at all of infection, bring him back."

She leaned sideways to get in the little tabby's line of sight. He stared, resolutely, at the floor. "Good job, Owen," she said.

He made ungracious grumbling sounds in his throat.

By the time we were back in the truck it was almost time to meet Gavin. I decided Owen would be okay for about half an hour in the truck. I gave him a pile of sardine crackers.

"I'll bring you something from Eric's," I promised.

He licked his whiskers but refused to look at me.

I left him spreading his crackers all over the seat.

Gavin smiled when he saw me walk in. I didn't see anything in his expression that suggested he saw himself as a starving man and me as a hamburger.

"I'm sorry I'm late," I said. "I had a small cat emergency."

"Is everything all right?"

I nodded. "Owen got a sliver of wood stuck in his paw, but it's out and he's okay. In fact, he'll probably be milking it for the rest of the week."

"Can't fault him for that," Gavin said, grinning at me.

Claire was at the table with coffee for me before I'd pulled off my jacket. Gavin gave her his toothpaste-commercial smile. "Thanks, Claire," he said. "You know you're going to have me ruined for anywhere else to eat when I go back to Chicago."

She smiled back at him. "It's all part of my master plan for world domination." She looked at me. "We got some tomatoes from the hydroponic place. They're pretty good." One eyebrow went up. "Are you interested in a breakfast sandwich?"

"Very," I said. "Thank you."

Once Claire had started back for the kitchen, Gavin leaned forward, his forearms on the small table, and smiled at me. "I think I may have found a way to satisfy the museum's requirements for keeping the artwork safe."

"Seriously?" I said.

He nodded and reached for his tablet. "There's a line in our contract with the insurance company about using 'all reasonable measures' to protect the artwork during the times it's not on exhibit."

I added cream and sugar to my coffee. "Which means?"

"Keeping the library closed is not a reasonable measure." He turned the tablet so I could see the paragraph he was talking about in the contract. "I talked to Lita to get her thoughts. She agreed with me. She even ran it by a lawyer she knows."

That had to be Brady.

Gavin took the tablet back and set it on the table again. "He agrees."

"Yes!" I said.

He held up one hand, and even though it felt a little silly I high-fived him because being able to open the library once the police were finished had just made my life so much easier.

I leaned back in my seat and folded my hands around my mug. "Thank you," I said. "I appreciate you going through the contract."

He reached for his own coffee. "Hey, it was the least I could do after all the disruption having the exhibit here has caused for you." His expression changed. "Have you heard anything more about the investigation into Margo's death? Or should I not ask you that?"

"No, it's okay," I said. "I haven't heard anything."

Claire came out of the kitchen with a tray and started toward us.

"There's a memorial being planned for Margo in Minneapolis the first of next week," Gavin said. "I'm going to try to be there. Her, uh . . . service will be in Chicago."

"I'm glad you're going," I said.

Over breakfast we went over the plans to keep the artwork secure until it could be moved and how that might affect day-to-day operations at the library. With a few adjustments I felt confident we could make things work.

When Claire came back to the table, she handed the bill to Gavin, something I realized he must have arranged in advance. "No," I said, shaking my head. "I asked you to meet me for breakfast."

"And I'd been about to make the same request when I got your text," he countered. "This was business. My company's business. You can get it next time." He turned to Claire. "Would you add a chicken salad sandwich to that, please?" he held out the bill and his credit card.

"Of course," she said. "How would you like the sandwich?"

"Hold the bread, mayo, celery and green onions."

Claire frowned but at the same time a hint of a smile played around her mouth. "So what you really want is the chicken."

"Yeah," Gavin said. "I'm trying to take a more minimalist approach to lunch."

"Okay," Claire said, giving up and letting the smile out. "I'll be right back."

He pulled on his leather jacket and grabbed his messenger bag. I told him I'd call Lita and get back to him once I'd talked to her and checked out the library.

Claire came back with his receipt and a small takeout container that I was guessing held the chicken. Gavin thanked her and passed the cardboard container over to me. "For Owen," he said. "Guys have to stick together."

I laughed. "Thank you. You'll have a friend for life now."

"You can't have too many of those," he said. His phone buzzed.

"I'll talk to you later," I said.

If Owen had been a person, I would have said his eyes lit up when his nose detected the aroma coming from the take-out container. His whiskers twitched and he momentarily forgot about his injured paw as he walked across the front seat of the truck to sniff the box.

"Are you feeling better?" I asked.

He immediately sat down, held up his paw and meowed, giving me his sad-kitty face.

"I'm sorry to hear that," I said. I leaned over and carefully lifted him onto my lap. "You were very brave," I told him, "and you didn't try to bite Roma even once."

He ducked his head and then looked up at me with his exotic golden eyes. It was Owen's way of trying to seem modest.

"I have to go to the library," I said. "You can stay in the truck or you can come inside if"—I narrowed my gaze at him—"if you stay in the bag."

He seemed to consider my words. Then he reached out and put his uninjured paw on the take-out box.

"You can have a couple of pieces now and the rest after we're done."

That seemed to be okay with him. He climbed down off my lap and looked expectantly at me.

I fished two slices of grilled chicken out of the container and held them out to Owen. He took each piece from my hand and set it on the seat so he could go through the little ritual of sniffing and checking that he always followed before he ate anything. If there was anything to reincarnation, Owen had probably been some autocratic ruler poisoned by a cadre of disgruntled noblemen, with enough trace memory lingering that he wasn't going to let it happen again even though in this life he was a small tabby cat.

"Gavin sent that, by the way," I said as I pulled away from the curb.

Owen lifted his head, looked around and gave a loud meow. Sending a thank-you out into the universe perhaps?

Owen climbed into the cat carrier without objection when we got to the library. For a moment I debated leaving him in the truck, but I knew if he got pissed off he'd just render himself invisible and follow me anyway. An Owen I could see and hopefully corral to some degree was preferable to an unseen cat roaming around the building, poking his furry nose into whatever struck his fancy.

Hope was waiting for me.

"I have Owen," I said, putting one hand on the side of the carrier bag. "I had to take him to Roma and I didn't have time to take him home after that."

"Is he all right?" she asked, eyeing the carrier.

An indignant "merow" came from inside before I could answer.

"He got a big splinter between two claws on his paw," I said. "Roma came to the rescue."

Hope made a face. "Sounds painful."

Owen gave another loud meow.

Hope laughed. "I swear that cat knows what you say to him." She leaned toward the bag. "I'm sorry about your paw," she said. "I hope you're feeling better soon."

He gave a little murp of acknowledgment and shifted

against my hip. It occurred to me that maybe I was worrying way too much about people finding out how much I talked to the cats.

The book drop was more than overflowing, if that was possible. Two sets of shelves to one side of the circulation desk had been turned sideways and there were bits of dirt and dried grass on the floors. By my standards things were a mess. Still, I felt a huge sense of relief now that I was inside again and could start dealing with it all.

The exhibit space looked pretty much the same as it had when I'd last been in the building on Thursday night, except that Gavin had created a half wall, maybe four feet high, of Plexiglas panels in metal frames, attached to temporary supports bolted to the walls at each end. I knew Harry Junior had put in the panels, which were actually part of a railing system, and Oren had already assured me he could fix the walls where the supports had been screwed in.

A middle-aged man in a dark blue uniform was sitting in front of the half wall. He got to his feet. "Good morning, Ms. Paulson, Detective," he said.

"Good morning, Curtis," Hope said, smiling across the room at him.

I raised a hand in acknowledgment. Curtis Holt was one of Gavin's security guards. Gavin had e-mailed him my photo so he'd recognize me. The man sat back down and went back to whatever he was reading on his tablet.

"Did you manage to work anything out as far as reopening?" Hope asked, looking around the space.

I pushed a stray piece of hair out of my face and set

Owen in his carrier on the circulation desk. "I think so," I said. "Gavin and Lita may have found an out in the contract with the insurance company that will let us get the building open again."

"I like him," Hope said. "He's a bit of a flirt, but he knows his stuff." She gave me an appraising look. "He kind of has a bit of a guy thing going with Marcus."

"A guy thing?" I said. "You mean a 'Who's going to win the cup', 'Let's grab a cold one' thing?"

She laughed and put a hand on her pocket for a second as if she were checking for her phone. "No. More like 'Let's bang our heads together like a couple of big-horned rams on one of those nature shows on PBS.'"

I'd pretty much known that based on how Marcus had reacted to my breakfast meeting with Gavin. I shook my head slowly.

"It's not a big deal," Hope said. "They mostly stand around puffing out their chests like a pair of lowland gorillas while they try to outdo each other with obscure bits of technical stuff about electronics." She laughed. "Can you tell I've been on a nature documentary binge?"

"Maybe just a little." I grinned back at her. "Although I can picture the two of them grunting and pounding on their chests."

Because I'd been talking to Hope and imagining Marcus and Gavin acting like a couple of posturing apes, I hadn't noticed that Owen had managed to work the zipper on the carrier bag from inside, sliding it open so he could work out a shoulder and then his whole body. He climbed out, shook his head and jumped down to the floor.

"Crap on toast!" I exclaimed. "Owen, get back here. What did I say about staying in the bag?" It was a total waste of words. He listened only if it suited him or he was trying to placate me in some way.

Owen was making his way purposefully across the mosaic tile floor. He didn't seem to be having any problem with his paw. He stopped at a spot in the middle of the space, under the domed ceiling with its curved skylight, bent his head and sniffed at something on the floor. He scraped at whatever he'd found and then sat and looked over his shoulder at me.

"Really bad thing to do if you want the rest of that chicken," I said, glaring at the small cat. I reached down to pick him up. He twisted away, put his paw on the same spot on the floor he'd been pawing at and meowed at me.

"Do you happen to have a cat-size set of handcuffs?" I asked Hope.

"Sorry," she said. "I left them in my other jacket." She frowned at Owen. "What's he scratching at?"

"I don't know." I crouched down beside the little tabby. He looked at the floor and then he looked at me. I knew that expression. It was his "So do you see it?" look.

There was something stuck to the tiny square tiles. I scraped the edge with a fingernail. It was a dried pine needle sticky with sap. I held out my finger to show Hope. I was certain Owen had a reason for pointing out this particular bit of dirt, but I couldn't exactly tell that to Hope. No, that wouldn't seem at all peculiar, would it?

"That's pine sap," she said. She turned and squinted toward the front entrance.

I waited. I could tell from her expression that she was making connections in her head. I didn't need to tell her Owen thought the sticky pine needle was important; clearly she thought it was as well.

Hope sat back on her haunches. "Kathleen, there aren't any pine trees out front, are there?"

I shook my head. "No. There's one by the loading dock."

She pressed her lips together. Owen was watching her intently. "I don't suppose you know when this floor was last cleaned?" she asked.

Suddenly I understood why both she and Owen were so interested in the pinesap. "I do," I said, slowly. "This entire level was steam mopped late last Thursday afternoon." I picked up Owen, who made no move to wiggle away from me now, although he kept all of his focus on Hope. "Do you think the thief might have gotten into the building through the loading dock?" I asked. Hope got to her feet and so did I.

"We went over the entire building, but I'm thinking it might be worth a second look," she said. "My guys wore booties when they were in here, and if the floor was cleaned not too long before the break-in . . ." She held out both hands.

"Maybe this was tracked in by the person who took the Weston drawing and killed Margo," I finished.

Hope looked at me. "Maybe," she said. She got her camera and took some photos of the spot on the floor as well as of my finger. Then she scraped the sticky pine needle off my finger into an evidence envelope.

"I should call Marcus," she said. She peeled off the latex gloves she'd pulled on to collect the sap from my finger, pulled out her phone and called Marcus. The call went to voice mail.

"Damn!" she muttered almost under her breath. "He's in a meeting with the prosecuting attorney."

While she'd been making the call I'd put Owen back in the cat carrier. He'd climbed in without objection—something he didn't often do. He seemed to have forgotten about his injured paw.

Hope dropped her phone back in her pocket. She looked at me and one eyebrow went up. "Do you want to go take a look back there? Off the record?" She blew out a breath. "Way, way off the record."

Before I could say anything, Owen answered for me. "Merow!" he said loudly.

"We're in," I said.

She turned to the security guard. "Curtis, we're just going to check something outside."

He nodded.

I swung the bag over my shoulder and followed Hope out, stopping to lock up and set both alarms. Owen and I stood on the grass and watched while she examined the loading-dock area and the heavy metal door.

After a few minutes she pushed her hair back from her face and sighed. "I don't see any sign that someone broke in through this door," she said. She looked at the cat carrier. I could see a pair of eyes watching her. "You got any more clues, Owen?" she asked.

"Murp," he said.

Hope came to stand beside us. "I guess I was just grasping at straws," she said, scanning the area.

Harry Junior had just started working on the library

grounds, collecting small branches that had blown down over the winter and uncovering the shrubs that had been protected from the cold and snowy Minnesota weather.

Hope was focused on a spot to the side of the loading dock, where the bronze rain chain hung down the side of the building. It looked like a sequence of tiny pots.

"What's that?" she asked.

"It's a rain chain," I said. "It guides the water down to the ground from the gutter."

"Why don't you have a downspout?" she asked without taking her eyes off the side of the building.

"That was Harry's idea," I said. "Kids kept using the downspout to climb up onto the roof over the loading dock."

Hope's eyes met mine then. "Stay right here," she said. She took a couple of steps forward, her gaze fixed to the ground. Then suddenly she stopped and back-tracked.

"What size would you say Harry's feet are, Kathleen?" she asked. "Fourteen maybe?"

I thought about the big black rubber boots he had been wearing when he'd last been working on the library grounds. "At least," I said.

Hope looked at me. "I think I know how the killer got into the building," she said, pulling out her phone.

8

"The thief came in through the roof?" Ruby said. "C'mon, Kathleen, tell me Bridget got that wrong."

We were in the tai chi studio. Maggie and Ruby were holding mugs of some kind of tea that smelled of orange and spices, and I was wishing I'd stopped for coffee at Eric's. The current edition of the *Mayville Heights Chronicle* was on the table.

I shook my head. "She didn't." The latest developments at the library were front-page news. Once again, Mary's daughter, Bridget, had all the details.

What Hope had seen on the ground by the loading dock to make her back up so quickly was part of a footprint. A footprint that was smaller than anything Harry would have left in his rubber boots. Not that he would have stepped in a flower bed that was still too wet to work in in the first place.

It appeared that Margo's killer had some kind of gymnastic or climbing skills, as far-fetched as that seemed. There was no other way to have gotten up onto the roof without leaving evidence behind. Hope had called in her crime scene team, Marcus had arrived, and any hope I had of reopening the library had evaporated. I'd taken Owen home and then spent the rest of the day at Henderson Holdings with Lita, doing damage control.

"It sounds like something out of a Tom Cruise movie," Maggie said, stretching one arm over her head.

"I didn't know that skylight even opened," Ruby said. She'd changed her hair color back to grape-jelly purple.

I made a face. "I knew it could be opened—in theory. What I didn't know was that Will Redfern and his crew had left it unsecured."

Will Redfern was the contractor who had been in charge of the library renovations that had brought me to Mayville Heights in the first place. Will had been having an affair with the librarian before me, Ingrid, and as far as he was concerned, if I gave up and went back to Boston things would work out just right for him.

The renovations had been plagued with problems, and in the end the only way we'd managed to have the building ready on time for its anniversary celebrations was to replace Will and his crew with Oren Kenyon.

Lita had shaken her head when I'd told her about the skylight. "No good deed goes unpunished," she'd said.

The work on the library had been Everett Henderson's gift to the town for the Carnegie building's centennial. He'd agreed to hire Will for the job because he'd had a good reputation up to that point and because Everett had gone to school with Will's father. Lita had very strongly advised him not to do it. It was one of the rare times, I was guessing, that Everett had let sentiment and nostalgia influence a decision.

"How did the thief get up onto the roof in the first place?" Ruby asked. She drained the last of her tea and set the cup on the table. "You can't exactly walk around Mayville Heights carrying a ladder. It's something people would notice."

"They think he climbed up from the loading-dock roof," I said. I wasn't telling them anything that Bridget wouldn't be printing in the next issue of the *Mayville Heights Chronicle* in the morning. She'd had a reporter on the scene while Hope was still securing the library grounds. I was beginning to suspect Bridget had some kind of contact at the police department.

"Do you think Margo surprised this burglar and he killed her?" Maggie asked.

I shrugged. "It looks that way."

She linked her fingers around her mug of tea. "It's hard to believe someone would risk that much bad karma over that little drawing."

"I don't think whoever took that drawing was thinking about their karma," Ruby said. "They were probably thinking about money."

Taylor King appeared in the doorway then. She looked in our direction.

"Excuse me," Ruby said. "I have something for Taylor." She headed across the studio.

Taylor King collected vintage purses and bags. The teenager, who was part of our tai chi class, was becoming quite an expert on them. Ruby had found a small

embroidered clutch at a flea market she and Maggie
and I had gone to in Red Wing and paid a dollar for it.
She was planning on giving it to Taylor as a thank-you
for the work Taylor had been putting in, helping get
everything ready for a yard sale at the Riverarts building, where most of the town's artists had studios.

· "Mags, is that Weston drawing really worth that
much money?" I asked, linking my hands behind my
back and squeezing my shoulders together to loosen
the knots that seemed to have settled in at the base of
my neck.

"In the end, a piece of art is worth whatever someone is willing to pay for it." She took a sip of her tea.
"You saw it, right?"

I nodded.

"I've seen the drawing a couple of times. The detail
is exquisite." She put her mug on the table next to Ruby's. "It was the only thing stolen? You're certain of
that?"

I nodded. "Gavin and someone from the museum
did an inventory."

Maggie glanced at her watch. It was time to start
class. "Whoever stole that drawing went to a lot of
trouble to get into the library. Doesn't it seem like they
would have at least made sure the building was
empty?"

"You think the thief planned to kill Margo?" I said
slowly.

"You don't?" she said. She gave me a look and then
moved toward the center of the room, clapping her
hands and calling, "Circle, everyone."

Maggie had given voice to the niggling little thought

that had been way in the back of my mind since the moment I'd walked into my office and discovered Margo Walsh's body. If the thief hadn't planned on murdering Margo, then why had he or she gone up to my office? Why stay in the building any longer than was necessary? Everything of value was on the main floor. But if the thief had planned to kill her, why hadn't that person brought along a weapon?

Since the library was closed at least until the end of the week, I decided not to set my alarm clock, and sleep in a little in the morning. Owen had other ideas. He put both paws on the edge of the bed, licked my chin, and then breathed on me. Let's just say his breath wasn't exactly minty fresh.

I opened one eye. All I could see was his golden ones staring back at me, slightly out of focus because he was so close to my face.

"Fifteen more minutes," I said.

His response was to lick my chin again.

I groaned and threw an arm over my face. "Ten minutes, then. You can wait for your breakfast for ten minutes."

A paw began to bat a strand of my hair. I knew if I didn't get up in a minute or two, Owen would be standing on my chest despite my edict that furry people did not belong in my bed. I thought about trying to negotiate for five more minutes under the covers, and then I remembered I was dealing with a cat.

The phone rang while I was eating breakfast. "Stay away from my oatmeal," I told Owen as I headed for the living room to answer the phone. He glared darkly at me. Oatmeal was pretty much the only thing he didn't try to mooch from me.

"Hi," Marcus said when I picked up. "I called to see what your day's like."

I dropped onto the footstool. I couldn't help grinning like an idiot at the sound of his voice. Sometimes—a lot of times—Marcus had me acting like a teenager.

"I have to check in with Lita, and I'm having dinner with Maggie and Roma, but otherwise I'll be here," I said.

"Hope and I have a couple of interviews this morning. How about lunch at Eric's?"

"Umm, that sounds good," I said.

Owen was peeking around the living room doorway. "Merow," he said loudly.

"Was that Owen?" Marcus asked.

I laughed. "Uh-huh. That's his not very subtle way of telling me he's ready to go outside and check the yard for interlopers."

"Oh well, I wouldn't want to mess up his schedule." I could hear the smile in his voice.

We agreed on a time and said good-bye.

Owen was sitting by the back door, his tail moving restlessly on the floor. I knew that meant he was in a bad mood. I held the door open without comment and he went outside without making a sound.

"What's with your brother?" I asked Hercules when I went back into the kitchen.

He was washing his face. He looked blankly at me, one paw paused in midair. Owen was usually the one giving me the faux innocent look. I had to admit Hercules was a lot better at it than his brother.

"You're not fooling me," I said, narrowing my gaze at him.

He gave an offhand murp and went back to his grooming routine.

Marcus was sitting at a table by the window when I walked into Eric's just before twelve thirty. He was talking to Hope, who was standing by the table, and he got to his feet, smiling when he caught sight of me.

I walked across to them. "Hi," I said.

Hope turned halfway around. "Hi, Kathleen," she said. "I'm sorry. I didn't mean to horn in on your lunch. I seem to always be interrupting."

"You're not," I said, unzipping my jacket and hanging it over the back of a chair. "Can you join us?"

She shook her head. "Thank you, but I have a pile of paperwork back at the station." She inclined her head in the direction of the counter at the back of the small restaurant. "I'm just waiting for takeout." She looked at Marcus. "I'll meet you at Riverarts in an hour," she said. "Have a good lunch," she said to me. She headed to the counter as Nic came out of the kitchen carrying a brown paper take-out bag.

"How was your morning?" Marcus asked as I sat down.

"All right," I said. "Everett talked to the insurance company. And the CEO of the museum. They're making space in another part of the museum. We should be able to get the artwork back to them early next week."

Hope was on her way out the door. She raised a hand at us as Nic approached the table. "Hello, Kathleen," he said. He refilled Marcus's cup and poured coffee for me. "The lunch special is macaroni and cheese with ham and chopped tomatoes." He turned to me. "Eric said to tell you he also has a roasted vegetable sandwich on sourdough."

"That sounds good," I said, imagining two thick slices of Eric's sourdough bread soaked with juicy roasted tomatoes, mushrooms and peppers.

Marcus ordered the macaroni and cheese.

"It'll just be a few minutes," Nic said.

I reached for the cream for my coffee. "You're going to talk to Maggie and Ruby," I said.

He nodded. "We're putting together a timeline for last Thursday."

"Let me know if you need anything else from me."

We spent the next several minutes talking about my family back in Boston. I was telling Marcus about my mother's latest efforts directing my dad when Nic slid an oval-shaped stoneware dish in front of him. I could smell the aroma of cheese and ham. He put a heavy plate at my place and my mouth began to water as the scent of warm grilled bread, tomatoes and spices reached my nose.

I'd just reached over and snagged a forkful of macaroni and cheese from Marcus's bowl when Gavin Solomon stepped into the restaurant. He looked around and came in our direction once he caught sight of us.

"I'm glad I found you, Kathleen," he said to me. "I just spoke to Detective Lind. I think I know who took the Weston drawing."

"You know who broke in to the library?" Marcus said with just an edge of skepticism in his voice.

"Possibly," Gavin said. If he'd heard Marcus's disbelief, he was ignoring it. He grabbed a chair from a nearby table, pulled it over and sat down. "A criminal named Devin Rossi."

"And he is?" Marcus asked.

"She," Gavin corrected. He leaned sideways, managed to catch Nic's attention and mimicked drinking. Nic nodded and reached under the counter for a coffee cup. "Devin," he repeated. "With an 'i' and an 'n.' As soon as Detective Lind told me how the break-in was done, I thought of her."

"So you're saying this person is some kind of professional cat burglar?" I said.

Gavin laughed. "Yeah, I know how ridiculous that sounds—a cat burglar, here." He held up both hands for a moment in a "what can you do?" gesture. "But this isn't an old Cary Grant movie. And Mayville Heights is the perfect place for a thief like Rossi to be operating. It makes more sense than trying to rob a high-security art museum in Paris."

I thought he had a point, but I could tell from the set of Marcus's jaw that he didn't agree.

Nic arrived then with a cup of coffee for Gavin. "Could I get you anything else?" he asked.

Gavin gestured at his cup. "Let me finish this first, and then I'll decide."

Nic nodded. "No problem."

Gavin added cream to his coffee, then reached across the table for my spoon to stir it, smiling at me as he did so. He took a long drink and leaned back in his chair.

"Devin Rossi stole artwork on demand for specific customers. She'd been operating mostly in North America and Great Britain for the past few years."

"Stole?" I asked. "Past tense?"

"It looks that way. She dropped out of sight about two years ago. It was like she just disappeared."

"Why haven't I heard of this person?" Marcus asked.

"She'd been eluding law enforcement for pretty much the entire time." Gavin shrugged. "No one is really sure what she even looks like. There was some speculation that she'd given up stealing for a living and was living on a beach somewhere in Costa Rica."

Marcus speared a forkful of macaroni and ham but didn't actually eat it.

"You think she's the one who broke in to the library?" I said. "Why?"

"Because she was a gymnast as a kid who segued into rock climbing as a teenager. Can you think of someone better equipped to get onto the roof of the library and climb down from a skylight?"

"You're saying she deliberately chose the most difficult way she could think of to break in to the building—assuming she even did this?" Marcus asked. He set his fork down on the table and gave up on pretending to eat.

"In a way, yes. Devin was always very careful *not* to be seen, *not* to be caught, but it was as if she liked the rush from doing things the hard way." He held up one finger. "Excuse me a minute." He pulled his cell out of his pocket, looked at the screen and put it away again. He turned to Marcus. "I have a contact at the Chicago Police Department. He's sending you everything he has on Devin Rossi."

Marcus's jaw tightened, but all he said was, "Thank you."

Gavin turned his smile on both of us. "And I've interrupted your lunch enough." He looked at me and the smile widened just a bit. "Kathleen. I'll call you later and we'll coordinate getting the exhibit packed and out of your library as soon as the police are certain they're finished." His gaze moved to Marcus and the smile faded. "Detective, let me know if you have any questions."

He stood up and put the chair back in one smooth movement, raised a hand and made his way over to the counter.

Marcus's mouth moved but he didn't say anything. I took a bite of the last bit of my sandwich and waited.

"A cat burglar," he said finally.

I nodded. "Uh-huh."

His eyes flicked over to the counter where Gavin was talking to Nic. "Okay, even I have to admit this whole thing is starting to seem a little . . . out there. A cat burglar for hire, female no less, ends up here, in Mayville Heights. She climbs up onto the roof of the building, gets inside via a skylight no one knew was working, and makes it down to the floor like some kind of ninja."

I reached across the table, took another forkful of macaroni and ate it before I answered. "Number one. Women can be cat burglars. What we lack in upper-body strength we make up for with persistence." Marcus opened his mouth and I waggled a finger at him. "I wasn't finished."

"I'm sorry. I should have known that," he said.

I held up another finger. "Two. It certainly looks like someone did get into the building via that skylight that Will Redfern left unsecured. Whoever it was probably didn't somersault down onto the stairs like a ninja, but they did get inside. And that at least partly explains how they managed to circumvent the alarms on the windows."

I picked up my fork again, speared the last chunks of ham and tomato in Marcus's dish and ate them.

He leaned back in his chair and folded his arms over his chest. "There's no number three?" he said.

I held up three fingers. "And number three: Again, you're jealous."

His blue eyes narrowed. "I'm jealous? Of Gavin Solomon?"

I reached for my cup and when I realized it was empty leaned sideways and caught Eric's eye at the counter.

I turned my attention back to Marcus. "You get a little caveman when he's around."

"I don't get a little caveman," he protested, "and what does that mean?"

"It means you want to throw me over your shoulder, beat on your chest and then carry me back to your cave."

"I'm not jealous and I'm not going to beat on my chest," he said. Then he raised an eyebrow. "Although throwing you over my shoulder and carrying you back to my cave does have a certain appeal."

I was saved from having to answer by Eric with fresh coffee. "Any idea when the library is going to open?" he asked as he filled my cup.

"I don't know for sure," I said. "A couple of days at least, if everything goes well."

Eric reached for Marcus's mug. "Susan and the boys

made Gak yesterday. Do you know what Gak is?" he asked.

"It's like Silly Putty, isn't it?" Marcus said. He looked around as though he couldn't quite figure out what Gak had to do with when the library was going to re-open.

"Yes, it is. It's slimy and stretchy and it will stick to the ceiling if you throw it high enough, where it will then remain until there is a lemon meringue pie cooling on the counter." Eric looked from Marcus to me. "Susan needs to come back to work. She *really* needs to come back to work."

"Oh, Eric, I'm sorry," I said. I couldn't quite swallow a grin.

"Go ahead and laugh, Kathleen," he said darkly. "Maybe I'll send all three of them up to visit you." He moved to another table with the coffeepot.

Marcus smiled at me across the table. "Poor guy."

"He loves every minute of it," I said. Eric had had some tough times growing up, and I knew that having a family meant the world to him. It wasn't an exaggeration to say they were his life.

Marcus looked at his watch.

"Are you heading over to the library?" I asked.

He nodded. "You and Maggie are going out to Wisteria Hill to have supper with Roma, aren't you?"

I stood up and reached for my jacket. "We are. Which reminds me, I should stop in at the co-op store and let her know the local artists aren't going to be able to pick up their artwork for a few more days." I glanced in the direction of the counter, where Nic was handing a take-out order to Ella King.

Marcus put a hand on my arm. "I've got this."

"You got the last one," I said.

"And I have this one, too."

He gave me a look that made my knees turn to pudding, and I held on to the back of my chair for a moment. "Um . . . thank you," I said after the silence had lasted just a little bit too long.

"Are you staying downtown for a while?" he asked as he pulled on his own jacket.

"I am." I fished my keys out of my purse. "Is there any chance I could get a few things from my office with an official police escort? I kind of got sidetracked when I was there with Hope yesterday."

He nodded. "I don't see why not. Call me when you're ready." His hand trailed down my arm.

"Okay, I'll talk to you later," I said. I was so busy looking at him, I walked right into a table. I gave him an embarrassed smile and managed to get out of the restaurant without running into anything else.

9

When I stepped inside the artists' co-op building, Maggie was just maneuvering her way down the stairs from the second-floor studio space, clutching two large cardboard cartons by their flaps in one hand and three in the other.

"Hey, Kath," she said and at the same time lost her grip on one of the boxes. It careened down the steps and landed at my feet. I picked it up and reached up for one of the others before she dropped it, too.

"Maggie, what are you doing with all these boxes?" I said.

She came the rest of the way down the steps and headed into the co-op store, and I followed her. She set the three cartons she was still holding on to down by the counter, where Ruby was on the phone. Ruby waggled her fingers at me. I put the other two boxes down next to Maggie's three.

"Thank you," she said, smiling at me. She swiped a hand over her neck. "We're starting to pack up things so Oren can start working." The artists' co-op was adding a small space for demonstrations and workshops to the store. Oren was going to be moving a wall, among other things. Maggie's plan was to keep the store open for as much of the time as she could during the renovations.

"But I thought Oren wasn't starting until next month," I said.

"That was when we thought—hoped—that we'd get more traffic in here from the exhibit. Since it's not happening anymore, there didn't seem to be any reason not to get started. Oren has the time in his schedule."

"I'm sorry that all of you lost the chance to be part of the exhibit," I said with a sigh.

"Hey, it's not your fault," Maggie said. "Oren has the time, and now the work will be done before the peak tourist season." She smiled at me again. "In the grand scheme of the universe I think it balances out."

That was Maggie. She had a deep belief in the ultimate balance and fairness of the universe.

"Would you like some help getting things packed?" I offered.

Her blue eyes narrowed. "Don't you have things to do at the library?" she asked.

I shook my head. "Not right now. I'm going to meet Marcus there later. "

"Good dog!" Ruby said behind me. "What's taking so long?"

"The police are still collecting evidence," I said.

"Whoever broke in to the library? What did they do? Rappel down from the roof? Use giant suction cups and walk down the wall like Spider-Man?"

I shrugged. "I'm not sure," I said. "But if I had to

guess, I'd say whoever it was used rope, not giant suction cups."

Ruby gave me a smirk. "Yeah, people always make the conventional choice," she said.

I turned back to Maggie. "That's why I stopped by. You'll need to let everyone know they won't be able to pick up their artwork for a few more days. Or if you want to give me phone numbers, I can do it."

Ruby leaned sideways so she was in Maggie's direct line of sight. "Want me to take care of that?" she asked.

"Please," Maggie said. She gave me a hug. "I'm sorry you can't get back into the building."

I tucked a stray strand of hair behind my ear. "The worst part is that there are so many programs that don't have anywhere else to meet: the seniors, story time, Reading Buddies. We've just got the new group of kids paired up and started in Reading Buddies."

Reading Buddies was a program that paired kindergarteners and first graders with older kids who helped the little ones with their reading skills. The little ones benefited from the one-on-one attention and the older ones from the responsibility. Right after Thanksgiving we'd had a fundraiser that had managed—after some major roadblocks—to leave us with enough money to expand the program and add more kids. Now every younger child had a match and the older ones had finished their training with Abigail. The kids had had only one session together. I hated that they were losing momentum.

"They meet after school, don't they?" Maggie asked. I knew that gleam in her green eyes. She had a plan.

I studied her face. I swear I could see her mind

working, or as Mary would say, the little hamsters running in their wheels. "Yes," I said. "The little ones come right after school lets out and the older ones get their last period off. We usually get started about two thirty."

"They can come here," she said. "I mean upstairs in the studio. You don't have to have chairs and tables, do you?"

"No," I said slowly. "But they're not exactly quiet. I know they're reading, but—" I held out both hands. "They're kids. They don't always do it quietly."

Maggie pulled a hand through her blond curls. "First of all, we're not exactly packed with customers at two thirty in the afternoon in April. And second, anyone who has a problem with children learning to read can—"

"—bite me," Ruby said behind us.

Mags laughed. "Anyone who has a problem can take it up with Ruby."

I laughed too. "All right. Yes."

This time I hugged Maggie. "Okay, put me to work," I said, taking off my jacket. Ruby put it and my purse behind the counter.

"We need to get those shelves apart," Maggie said, pointing to a wide, ceiling-high shelving unit against the end wall. Her neon orange toolbox was sitting on the floor.

I studied the unit for a moment. "I think we need to detach the shelves first," I said. I took a look at the underside of one of the long barn-board planks and then opened the toolbox to find the right screwdriver.

Maggie had the neatest toolbox I'd ever seen. Everything was organized by size and function and there wasn't a speck of dirt or rust on anything. She picked up the cordless drill that had been lying on the bottom shelf of the unit. "Do you want this?" she asked.

"No, the screwdriver is fine," I said. I knelt down and started on the lowest shelf while Maggie, who was taller, used the drill to work over my head.

"Do Marcus and Hope have any suspects?" she asked. She smelled like lavender oil.

"Not exactly," I said. I was twisted so my head and one shoulder were under the shelf and my voice was muffled.

"So what do they have, exactly?"

I gave the screwdriver one more twist and the screw in the back corner of the shelf came loose. I pulled my head out from under the length of barn board and sat back on my heels. "Have you ever heard of a woman named Devin Rossi?" I asked.

"Yes," she said. "Is that who they think took the Weston drawing and killed Margo Walsh?"

"It's what Gavin thinks," I said.

Maggie frowned. "He could be right."

I looked up at her. "Seriously?"

She adjusted the drill bit, tightening the chuck. "You could say she 'works on commission.' She never hits the big galleries or museums. And I heard she used to be a gymnast, so getting in through the roof would be something she could do." She turned the drill over in her hands. "But no one's ever been hurt as far as I know. In fact Devin Rossi has a bit of a Robin Hood reputation."

"I think Robin Hood's thing was take from the rich, give to the poor. Not take from the rich, give to the rich."

She smiled. "Okay, it's not a perfect analogy."

I pushed my hair back off my face and leaned under the shelf again. "What you're saying is she has her fans."

"In the art world, to some people, she's kind of a folk hero, yes," Maggie said. "Not everyone is a fan of big museums and galleries."

I twisted onto my left shoulder so I could reach the screw in the other back corner of the shelf. "That doesn't mean it's okay to take things that don't belong to you."

"I know," Maggie agreed. "Some people just seem to lose sight of that. Robin Hood was probably nothing like Sean Connery or Kevin Costner in tights."

I grunted as I tried to get some torque on the screw. "No, he wasn't. Some historians think Robin Hood was a real person. Others think he was a character based on the exploits of people like William Wallace. Still others say he's totally a creation of folklore—the outlaw hero of ballads."

Maggie laughed. "How did I know you'd know that?"

I slid my head out from under the shelf. "Was I being obnoxious?" I asked.

She nudged me with her foot. "No," she said. "It just fascinates me how you know so many things."

"I spent a lot of time in the library when I was a kid," I said, just a little self-consciously.

"And I spent a lot of time taking pictures with my mother's Polaroid instant camera and then coloring in the image with magic markers," she said. She looked over at Ruby. "Hey, Ruby, what did you like to do for fun when you were about ten or twelve years old?"

"Shoplift Kool-Aid and use it to dye my hair," she said immediately. Ruby had been on the road to being a juvenile delinquent as a kid before her school principal, Agatha Shepherd, had taken an interest in Ruby's flair for art. When Agatha died, Ruby had used the money the older woman had left her to fund an art program for children as well as an art school scholarship.

I looked up at Maggie and smiled. "It seems our destinies were set before we even hit puberty."

She smiled back at me. "No doubt the universe is unfolding as it should."

I spent about an hour and a half helping Maggie; then I walked up to Henderson Holdings to see Lita. I called Marcus before I left. "Any chance I could stop by the library and get some files from my office now?" I asked.

"You can," he said, "but I'll have to take a look at whatever you take out. Will that be a problem?"

Even though I knew it was impossible, it seemed as though I could feel the warmth of his voice against my ear. "It's just some files on books I want to buy and a draft report on the library's new damage-control strategy. You're welcome to look at all of it."

"I'd rather look at you," he said.

I felt my cheeks flood with color. Marcus wasn't a wildly romantic hearts-and-flowers kind of man, but every once in a while he'd say something that would make me either blush or forget how to breathe.

"I'll be there in about . . ." I glanced down at my watch. How long did it take to walk over to the library? Why couldn't I remember that? "A few minutes . . . I mean ten minutes," I said, stumbling over my words.

"I'll see you soon, then," Marcus said, and I could picture the smile I knew was on his face.

I ended the call and took a deep breath, exhaling slowly.

I liked to think of myself as being pretty unflappable, growing up with my eccentric actor parents and a younger brother and sister who could both be pretty out there sometimes. Someone had had to be the sensible, practical person who remembered to buy milk and carry the health insurance cards. Marcus had the ability to turn me into a blushing, giggly teenager. I'd never really been that and, truth be told, I liked it.

Lita was watching me, a knowing smile on her face. "You two are so adorable," she said.

"And you and Burtis are?" I teased.

"A mature love ripened by time," she countered. "Like a bottle of fine wine or an aged wheel of Brie."

It sounded like an answer she'd given before. I laughed as I picked up my bag. "I'm sure Burtis would like the comparison to a wheel of stinky cheese," I said.

Lita threw back her head and laughed. "He certainly eats enough of it for it to be an apt comparison."

I thanked her for her help and headed out. I couldn't get the image of barrel-chested Burtis, whose hands were big enough that one of them would cover my head, holding a tiny water cracker with a smear of soft cheese, his pinkie raised in the air. The image made me smile all the way to library.

Marcus was waiting for me on the steps to the building. He smiled when he caught sight of me.

"Hi," I said, reaching out to touch his arm.

"What were you thinking about?" he asked. "You

were smiling all the way up the sidewalk." He pulled a set of keys out of his pocket and unlocked the doors.

I told him what Lita had said about Burtis's love of old cheese. "I just always thought of Burtis as a beer-and-brats kind of guy," I said.

Marcus punched in the codes for both security systems and we stepped into the library proper. "Burtis is a complex man," he said. "There's a lot more to him than just what you see on the surface."

Marcus was very much a law-and-order, the-rules-apply-to-everyone kind of person, while some—or maybe all, for all I knew—of Burtis Chapman's business enterprises danced on the edge of illegality and sometimes fell in. But Burtis was intensely loyal to the town and to people he called his friends. I was lucky to be one of them. And Marcus was the same way, so the two of them had always had a grudging respect for each other. But last winter Owen and I had been trapped in a burning building and Burtis and Marcus had worked together to get me out. It had changed the relationship between the two men in ways I couldn't exactly figure out.

Curtis Holt was in his chair next to the Plexiglas half wall that still separated the exhibit area from the rest of the library.

"Good morning, Curtis," Marcus called.

"Morning, Detective," the guard replied. "Detective Lind is upstairs." He smiled at me. "Good morning, Ms. Paulson."

I smiled back. "Good morning, Curtis."

Hope Lind was at the top of the stairs on the second floor with, I guessed, a couple of crime scene technicians.

"Thank you for letting me get some things from my office," I said. Hope was the lead detective on the case and I knew it was because of her that I had been allowed in the building, not because of my relationship with Marcus.

"No problem, Kathleen," she said. Her eyes flicked to Marcus for a second and I found myself wondering about those dates the two of them had had.

I stepped into my office and glanced around the room, trying not to look at the spot on the floor where Margo's body had been lying. I tried instead to think about what I wanted—needed—to accomplish in the next few days. I pointed out the files I wanted on my desk and Marcus retrieved them, looking carefully through each manila folder before he handed them to me. "Sorry," he said with shrug. "I have to follow procedure."

"It's okay." I smiled at him.

"Is there anything else you need?" he asked. "I still have no idea when you'll be able to reopen."

I stuffed the file folders in my bag. "That's all right. I can work around the building being closed. Maggie's offered to move Reading Buddies to the tai chi studio. And Lita is going to offer the boardroom at Henderson Holdings to the seniors' reading group."

"They couldn't get any more raucous than some of the board meetings we've had in there," she'd said, looking at me over the top of her glasses.

"I'm glad to hear that," Marcus said. "Everyone— but especially you—worked hard to raise the money to expand Reading Buddies. That's really nice of Maggie to let you use the studio. But, uh, does she have any idea how loud that could get?"

Marcus had helped out with the kids at the library a few times. Because of his own dyslexia he was very good with reluctant readers.

"I warned her."

"Maybe you should drop off some earplugs, just in case," he said with a grin.

"By the way, she thinks Gavin might be right about Devin Rossi." I glanced toward the hall again.

His smile faded. "You told her what he said."

I studied his face as it closed into what I thought of as police officer mode. "I didn't think it was a secret and I wanted to know if she thought Gavin's idea had any credence."

His eyebrows went up slightly. "Did she?"

I shifted a bit uncomfortably from one foot to the other. I could feel the skepticism coming off him. He'd made it clear he thought the idea of a cat burglar dropping into the library from the roof to steal a drawing that wasn't any bigger than a piece of copier paper was outlandish.

"She confirmed everything Gavin told us." I paused. When he didn't say anything, I added, "She's at the shop all afternoon if you'd like to talk to her."

"Okay," he said. He leaned against the edge of my desk. "By the way, I talked to Solomon's police contact from Chicago." He gave me a small smile. "You didn't think I would, did you?"

"No, I didn't," I admitted, feeling my cheeks get warm.

"The only thing they have on Devin Rossi is a fingerprint from a robbery they *think* she committed at a private gallery about three years ago."

"Did you find any fingerprints on the skylight?" I asked.

Marcus nodded. "Yes."

"So did they match?"

He shook his head. "The only prints we had belong to Will Redfern, and I don't think it was him who stole that drawing."

I sighed. "And you don't think it was Devin Rossi, either."

He straightened up. "Sorry. I just don't think some cat burglar broke in here, stole that drawing and killed Margo Walsh."

I nodded. It was just so far-fetched, but I couldn't help wishing things really were that simple.

10

Owen went to sit by the back door about five minutes before Maggie was due to drive out to Roma's with me. "She'll be here soon," I said. He shot a backward glance in my direction as if to say, "I know that."

And he did. I had no idea how he knew when Maggie was going to show up or when Rebecca was about to knock on the back door with treats or even when Marcus was going to stop by unexpectedly. He just did. It was just one of the many things about the cats that I'd stopped trying to find an explanation for.

"Hey, Fuzz Face," Maggie said when she caught sight of Owen.

He looked up at her, adoration written all over his furry gray-and-white face. I pulled on my hoodie while the two of them "talked."

Finally, Maggie looked at me. "Hi, Kath, where's the bench?" she said. We were taking a long, low bench that I'd painted and Mags had made a pillow for out to Roma as surprise. Maggie had surreptitiously measured the space and we were fairly confident that it would fit under the window at the end of the upstairs hallway. Roma had found a similar bench in an antiques store in Red Wing but had balked at the price. Maggie and I had found this one at a flea market a few weeks ago, painted a bilious pea soup green. Marcus had tightened one wobbly leg and Hercules had "helped" as I sanded away the old paint—from a distance, of course.

"It's in the basement," I said. "It's kind of awkward for one person to bring up the stairs alone and I forgot to ask Marcus to help me when he was here."

She lifted her right arm and made a muscle. "We can do it," she said. "We don't need any boys."

Owen gave a sharp meow.

Maggie smiled down at him. "I didn't mean you," she said.

He went over to the basement door and pushed it open with a paw, then looked expectantly at Maggie.

"Thank you, Owen," she said.

With Owen supervising, we got the bench up the basement stairs. Hercules came to watch as we carefully wrapped it in an old blanket, sniffing and poking the padding with a paw. Once the bench was set in the bed of the truck and Maggie had given both cats a couple of sardine crackers to thank them for their assistance, we headed out to Wisteria Hill.

I backed the truck up to the side steps of the house. Roma had come out onto the verandah when she'd heard the truck. "What is this?" she asked as Maggie and I got out.

"We brought you a little housewarming gift," I said.

Roma looked from Maggie to me. "I should say you shouldn't have, but I'm really curious about what it is." She cocked her head to one side and studied the blanket-wrapped shape. "It looks a little small to be another Eddie."

Eddie Sweeney, aka Crazy Eddie Sweeney, was a star player for the NHL's Minnesota Wild and was Roma's significant other. Mags had made a life-size Eddie for a Winterfest display a couple of years ago. Faux Eddie had led to a lot of rumors swirling around town about Roma and the real Eddie, and eventually to the two of them meeting. Real Eddie had bought Faux Eddie as a gift for Roma.

I climbed into the truck bed and Maggie and I got the bench off it and up onto the verandah. I unfastened the bungee cords that were holding the blanket in place and Maggie pulled it away.

"Oh my word," Roma said softly, putting one hand to her chest. "Did . . . did you two do this?"

I nodded. I suddenly felt the unexpected prickle of tears. I was so incredibly lucky to have friends like Roma and Maggie. I caught Maggie's eye. She swallowed and blinked a couple of times. I had a feeling she'd felt the same rush of gratitude I had.

Roma leaned over and trailed a hand across the cushion fabric and down over the wood. "It's beautiful," she said, her voice raspy with emotion. "It's more beautiful than the one in Red Wing."

She threw her arms around Maggie and reached out to pull me into the hug.

As we carried the bench up to the second floor of the old farmhouse, I crossed my fingers—metaphorically, since I couldn't do it literally—that it would fit in the space under the tall multipaned window at the end of the hall.

It did.

Roma beamed at us. "How did you know it would fit?" she asked.

"Maggie measured the space," I said.

Roma looked up at Mags. "When did you do that?" she asked.

Maggie had been studying the bench, head tipped to one side. She shifted it about a half an inch to the left and moved it back even less than that, then nodded with satisfaction. She looked at Roma and then shook her head. "Sorry," she said. "When did I measure for the bench? Remember when the three of us were stripping the wallpaper in the closets?"

Roma nodded.

There had been so many layers of paper on the old walls I'd been half-afraid they'd fall down when we got it all off.

"You lost the drawstring in your hoodie," Maggie said to me.

I made a face. "Right. The vacuum ate it."

Her eyes darted from side to side. "I took it. That's what I used to measure the space because I didn't have a tape measure and I couldn't exactly ask Roma if I could borrow one."

"I didn't know that," I said. Roma was running her hand over the cushion again. I nudged her with my elbow. "It's okay to sit on it."

She laughed, her cheeks turning pink. "It's so beautiful, I don't want to mess it up."

Maggie put her arm around Roma's shoulder and gave her a squeeze. "You can't 'mess it up,'" she said.

Roma sat down in the middle of the bench. She grinned up at us.

"Your drawstring is hanging on the bulletin board in my studio, by the way," Maggie said to me.

"Don't worry about it. Owen turned that hoodie into the cat version of a futon."

"See?" she said. "I told you he was smart. He's creative, too."

I laughed, wrapping my arms around her shoulders in a side hug, and thought that she didn't know the half of it.

Roma had made chicken corn chowder for supper. We sat around the kitchen table talking about her plans for the yard and the outside of the old house. "Oren's going to start painting as soon as it gets just a little bit warmer," she said, glancing out the window to her right.

"What did you finally decide on for colors?" Maggie asked. Her spoon was paused midway between her bowl and her mouth. She had made several "mood boards" for Roma, highlighting the different color combinations she'd been trying to choose between for the old farmhouse.

Roma nodded. "Buttercream yellow, vintage white and winter-lake blue. And thank you for putting those boards together for me. I never would have been able to decide with just those little swatches."

"You're welcome," Maggie said. "You picked my favorite colors, by the way."

"Eddie's, too," Roma said.

Something in her voice, or maybe something in the way she said Eddie's name, told me something was off.

"How is Eddie?" I asked, pushing my empty bowl to one side.

"Eddie's good." Roma couldn't help smiling whenever she said his name, so I knew whatever was wrong between them was fixable. "Nobody expected them to make the playoffs this year and now it seems as though everyone wants to interview him." She glanced out the window again.

I shot Maggie a sidelong warning glance to stay quiet and waited, letting the silence settle at the table with us. Roma looked from me to Maggie and back again. "Can you two keep a secret?"

It wasn't really a serious question. I trusted Maggie and Roma as much as I trusted anyone, and I felt certain they felt the same way about me as well. Still, I nodded.

"Of course," Maggie said softly.

Roma glanced down at her hands for a moment, then looked up at us. "Eddie won't be going public with this until the playoffs are over, but . . ." She hesitated. Took a deep breath. "He's decided to retire."

I wasn't really surprised. The last time Eddie had been in town he'd been full of plans and ideas for Wisteria Hill. In the back of my mind I'd wondered if he was thinking about making a permanent move to Mayville Heights.

"That's good, isn't it?" Maggie asked, picking up her spoon again.

Roma leaned both forearms on the table, reached up

and began idly tracing the shoulder seam of her shirt with one finger. "It is and it isn't."

"I'm guessing the good part is that Eddie's retiring while he's still healthy," I said.

"That's *why* he's decided to retire now," Roma said. "Kathleen, do you two know who Ben Crossley is?"

"Only the best center to ever play the game," I immediately said.

Maggie's eyebrows went up. "Excuse me," she said. "Sidney Crosby?"

I gave her a Cheshire cat smile. "I don't think so, Mags. Check the numbers." Then I turned to Roma. "Crossley was Eddie's mentor, wasn't he?"

She nodded. "They met at a hockey camp when Eddie was just eleven. Ben has been part coach, part mentor, part father figure." She swallowed. "And he's showing signs of early dementia. He suffered more than one concussion in his day."

"Oh, Roma, I'm sorry." Maggie reached across the table to give Roma's arm a squeeze.

"So that's why Eddie's decided to retire," I said.

Roma nodded. "Yes. He had a serious concussion himself, three years ago. He's been thinking about retiring for a while now. If this hadn't happened I think he might have played for another year, but that probably would have been it."

She was still playing with her shirt. I would have expected her to be happier about Eddie's news. There had to be something she hadn't told us yet.

"So what does he want to do?" Maggie asked. "I mean aside from stripping all the trim upstairs." She glanced at the ceiling over our heads.

Roma got an odd look on her face. It was a mix of panic and . . . happiness?

She looked down at the table for a moment, then lifted her head and met our eyes. "He says he wants to marry me."

11

Maggie and I both gave squeals of excitement.

"Roma, that's wonderful," I exclaimed, grinning at her. I knew she loved Eddie, and you only had to spend a few minutes with the two of them to know he was crazy about her, too.

"He's a lucky man," Maggie said, green eyes shining. Then her smile faded.

Because Roma wasn't smiling at all.

"What's wrong?" I asked.

"How can I marry him?" She pressed her lips together and stared down at the flowered tablecloth.

"It's easy," Maggie said. "Kathleen and I take you shopping for a pretty dress. We put lights and flowers in the living room the way we did when Everett and Rebecca got married, and then you say 'I do.'"

Roma shook her head. "I can't."

Maggie shot me a sidelong glance.

"Why not?" I asked.

"I'm older than Eddie. A lot older."

I reached over and put my hand on her shoulder for

a moment. "It doesn't matter. You know he doesn't care."

Roma had been married young, widowed when her daughter, Olivia, was very small, and she had put herself through college. She was in her late forties now, but most people were surprised when they found that out. She was older than both Maggie and me and it had never mattered to our friendship.

"It does matter," Roma insisted. She reached up and raked her fingers through her hair, tipping her head toward me. "Look. I found a gray hair yesterday."

I couldn't see a single white strand among her glossy dark brown hair.

"So what if you have a couple of gray hairs?" Maggie said. "So what if they're all gray? Eddie loves what's on the inside." She laid a hand flat against her chest. "Sure, he appreciates your colorful candy shell."

I knew she was referring to Roma's propensity for carrying a bag of M&M's along with a roll of duct tape so she was covered for pretty much any emergency that might happen.

"But it's your sweet inside that Eddie fell in love with."

The whole analogy was so silly even Roma had to laugh. But then her expression turned serious again. "Eddie loves kids. I'm too old to have a baby. I'm not going to let him give up something I know he wants just for a life with me. So I can't marry him." She held up a hand. "And I don't want to argue about it."

I struggled to find the right words. "Roma, Maggie and I are with you, no matter what you decide to do," I said. Out of the corner of my eye I saw Maggie nod in agreement. "Just . . . before you make a final decision, try living with the idea a little while." It was something my father had said to me more than once, and it was the best thing I could think of to say.

We went back to talking about Roma's plans for the yard, but Eddie's proposal was the proverbial elephant in the room. When it was time to leave I wrapped Roma in a hug. "Call me anytime you want to talk," I said. "Or not talk."

"I will," she promised. She waved from the steps as we started down the long driveway.

We were out on the road back to town before Maggie spoke. "Roma isn't too old for Eddie. And there are other ways to make a family besides having a baby."

I nodded without taking my eyes off the road. "I know that, but I don't think she does."

Gavin called me early the next morning. I was standing in the kitchen, wild haired, trying to decide between oatmeal with fruit and a scrambled egg. Owen and Hercules had already started on their breakfasts.

"Hey, Kathleen," he said. "Could I buy you breakfast, or have you already eaten?"

I pushed my hair back off my face. "Is this about the library or are you just looking for company?" One night we had worked late on plans for the exhibit and Gavin had admitted that he didn't like eating alone, even with a good book for company.

"I like conversation," he'd said, a bit sheepishly.

"You need a cat," I'd told him. "Owen and Hercules are great at making mealtime conversation, as long as you consider meows, murps and grumbling conversation."

He'd laughed. "Where do they stand on the Wild's playoff chances?"

"Stanley Cup in six," I'd said, straight-faced.

Gavin laughed now. "I always enjoy your company, Kathleen, but this is about the library, specifically about the Weston piece. I have an idea I want to run by you and it's a bit too complicated to get into on the phone."

"And you don't like eating alone," I finished.

"You're right, I don't. So come join me. I'm at Eric's Place. The coffee is hot, and I have an idea that might help us figure out who took that drawing." He paused for a moment and when he spoke again the laughter had gone out of his voice. "And who killed Margo."

I looked at the clock over the refrigerator. "I'll be there in twenty minutes."

I went back upstairs, wrestled my hair into a low twist with the help of lots of bobby pins and hairspray, and brushed my teeth. Back downstairs again I pulled on my favorite ankle boots while Hercules watched with curiosity and Owen moved the rest of his breakfast from his dish to the floor so he had more room to sniff each bite.

I leaned down and stroked the top of Hercules's head. "I'm going to have breakfast with Gavin," I said. "Have a good day."

Owen's gray tabby head shot up and the brothers exchanged a look; then two sets of cat eyes focused on me.

Neither Owen nor Hercules had taken to Gavin, probably because by his own admission he was a dog person. Their eyes stayed locked on me as I checked that I had everything I needed in my bag and reached for my coat, pretending to ignore them the whole time.

Still, it was disconcerting to be stared at. I should have been used to it, given how many times they'd used the technique on me when they were dissatisfied with something I'd done.

I turned and stared back at them, arms folded over my chest. "First of all, dog people are not the Evil Empire."

That got no reaction, not even a blink.

"You like Harrison," I continued, "and Harry Junior, and they're dog people."

The Taylors—Harry Junior and Senior—had a big German shepherd named Boris. Owen and Boris had had one "unfortunate" encounter that as far as Owen was concerned made them mortal enemies for life. The truth was that Boris was an intelligent and gentle dog. I'd made the mistake of calling him a pussycat once. Owen had been understandably offended.

The cats exchanged another look. Owen wrinkled his nose at me and meowed loudly.

I smiled at him, wrinkling my own nose back at him. "No, that's not different," I said firmly.

He dropped his head over his food again. Clearly, as far as he was concerned the discussion was over.

Gavin was sitting at a table by the end wall of the small café when I got to Eric's. Claire was just refilling his coffee cup. Gavin raised a hand in greeting and when Claire caught sight of me she reached for the other stoneware mug on the table.

"Oh, thank you," I said to her, dropping my bag on the chair opposite Gavin.

"You're welcome," she said. "Do you need a menu or do you know what you'd like?" She gave me a knowing smile. "Eric's sourdough breakfast sandwich, maybe?"

"Definitely," I said. Clearly I was getting to be predictable.

Claire headed for the kitchen and I slipped off my jacket, put my bag on the floor and sat down. "Okay, I'm here, so tell me your idea. You really think you might have a way to figure out who took the Weston drawing?" I reached for the small pitcher of cream in the middle of the table.

"Maybe." Gavin ran the fingernails of one hand over his bearded chin. "I have a . . . connection in Minneapolis."

I took a drink of my coffee. It was strong and very hot, just the way I liked it. Not that I would necessarily turn down coffee that was cold and weak.

"A connection could be anyone from someone you worked with to someone you dated to the kid you ate erasers with in kindergarten," I said.

"I didn't eat erasers in kindergarten," Gavin said. "But remind me sometime to tell you the story of what happened when I tried that paste stuff they use for papier-mâché."

I laughed. "You didn't."

"Oh, I did." He grinned across the small table at me. "I didn't have the discriminating palate that I have now."

I laughed. Even though I knew that Gavin was trying to charm me, I still enjoyed his company.

He held up a hand and the grin faded. "Seriously, my connection to Big Jule is professional."

"Big Jule?" I said, not even trying to keep the skepticism out of my voice. "Like the character from *Guys and Dolls*?"

Gavin nodded. "I know what you're thinking. Big Jule—whose real name is Julian McCrea—is a huge musical theater fan. He's played the role of Big Jule nineteen times in amateur productions." He shrugged. "He's a little . . . eccentric, but if a piece of artwork is"—he paused for a moment, searching for the right word—"generating interest, Big Jule knows who's interested."

I took another sip of my coffee. "So he's what? A thief? A fence?"

Gavin leaned back in his chair. "He's more of a relocation specialist."

"A fence, then," I said. "So does he say 'youse guys' and shoot craps in a back alley?"

He laughed again. "You're not going to break out in a chorus of 'Luck Be a Lady,' are you, Kathleen?" he asked.

A mental image of my dad in a snap-brim fedora and a black pinstripe suit when he'd played Sky Masterson in *Guys and Dolls* flashed into my head.

I raised one eyebrow. "You joke, but I can do the choreography."

Gavin folded his arms over his chest and grinned across the table at me. "I'd like to see that," he teased.

Claire was on her way from the kitchen with our breakfast. "Maybe some other time," I said.

"Saved by a breakfast sandwich," he countered with a laugh.

Gavin told me a little more about "Big Jule" while we ate. Julian McCrea had had an art gallery for many years. He'd represented several up-and-coming artists.

With a degree in art history, he'd even been called as an expert witness in a number of cases in which the provenance of a piece of artwork was in question. Now McCrea specialized in helping a select group of clients add to their private collections. And it was clear that, like the character in *Guys and Dolls*, this Big Jule's deals weren't always aboveboard.

Gavin put down his fork and looked around for Claire. "Come with me, Kathleen," he said. "I'm going to see Big Jule tomorrow and, well, you do know the choreography for 'Luck Be a Lady.'"

I laughed. "I think you'll do just fine without me."

He leaned toward me across the small table. "Come with me," he repeated. "I'll do even better with you. You can talk about musicals with the guy and he'll be a lot more susceptible to your charms than he is to mine."

"I have work to do," I said, using the last bite of sourdough bread to soak up a bit of tomato on my plate.

"It won't take that long," Gavin countered. "And I'm serious. Big Jule is more likely to talk to you than he is to me."

Claire came to the table then and poured each of us more coffee. Marcus walked into the café as she was topping up my mug. The smile that flashed across his face when he saw me was tempered when he saw Gavin. I raised a hand in hello, and Marcus came over to us, crossing the space between the door and the table in about three strides of his long legs.

"Hi," I said, smiling up at him.

Gavin got to his feet and offered his hand. "Good morning, Detective," he said with an easy smile.

"Good morning," Marcus replied, shaking Gavin's

hand and then, once he'd let it go, resting his other hand on my shoulder. "I didn't know you two had a meeting this morning," he said. His eyes flicked briefly to me, and while I knew the words were directed to me, he kept his gaze on Gavin.

"It was a last-minute thing," I said. "Gavin may know someone who can help us figure out who might have wanted the Weston drawing."

"I'm sure Detective Lind will be happy to have that information," Marcus said.

"Actually, Kathleen and I were planning on going to talk to my contact tomorrow. No offense to Detective Lind, but I think we'd have better luck." Gavin's tone was offhand, but there was nothing offhand in the way he returned Marcus's gaze.

"This is a police investigation," Marcus said. His eyes shifted to me for a moment. "You know how this works, Kathleen."

His hand was still possessively on my shoulder. I suddenly felt like a fire hydrant between two dogs.

I looked up at Marcus. "I do," I said. "But Gavin has contacts the police don't." I couldn't quite picture a man whose business clearly wasn't completely legal and who liked to be called Big Jule—even if the name did come from a fifties musical—wanting to share a lot of information with the police, but I wasn't going to say that to Marcus with Gavin standing right there.

The muscles were tight along his jawline, but he turned to Gavin and forced a cool smile. "I'm sure your contacts are more likely to talk to you than to us," he said as though he'd read my mind. "But please let Detective Lind know if you find out anything."

"Of course," Gavin said.

"I need to get my order and get back to the station," Marcus said, motioning toward the counter.

"I'll walk you over," I said, getting to my feet. His hand fell away from my shoulder. "I'll be right back," I said to Gavin. I followed Marcus to the back of the small restaurant.

"Hi, Detective," Claire said. "Eric's just putting your order together in the kitchen. I'll be right back."

I waited until she'd passed through the swinging door and then I turned my head to study Marcus. "So you're really not jealous?"

He glanced over at the table. Gavin's back was to us and he was talking to someone on his cell phone. Marcus's blue eyes narrowed. "Of him? No. I just don't want him interfering in the case."

"He's acting as a consultant," I said gently. "That's not exactly interfering."

"I know that," he said. He sighed softly. "Kathleen, I don't trust him. There's something he's not being honest about."

"You don't think he had something to do with the robbery and Margo's death, do you?" I asked.

Marcus shook his head and his gaze darted across the restaurant again for just a moment. "He has an alibi. He was in the bar at the hotel. At least a dozen people saw him, so, no, I don't think he had anything to do with what happened at the library. Not directly."

An unspoken "but" hung in the air between us.

I studied his face. "How about indirectly?" I asked. "Is there something about Gavin you haven't told me?"

He swiped a hand over the back of his neck. "No. I just . . . I just get a bad feeling from the guy."

It took effort to keep from smiling. "A feeling?" I said. "You?" Marcus was very much a "just the facts, ma'am" kind of person. I was the one who relied much more on feelings, nuance and body language. It was one of the reasons we'd butted heads so much in the past. It had taken a case that involved his sister, Hannah, for both of us to be able to see the other person's point of view.

The corners of Marcus's mouth twitched. I realized that meant he could see the irony of his words, too. "I guess that's what happens from spending so much time with you," he said, the tight lines around his eyes softening.

"I guess it does," I agreed, wiggling my eyebrows at him.

Just then Claire came out of the kitchen carrying a large brown paper bag. She set it on the counter in front of Marcus.

He smiled at her. "Thanks, Claire. Could I get two large coffees to go, please?"

"Of course." Claire smiled back at him. "Black with two sugars for you and one sugar no cream for Detective Lind."

He nodded and looked at me again. "The coffee-maker at the station died. Again. And we did an extra run this morning." He fished his wallet out of his pocket.

Hope was training for a triathlon and Marcus was running with her a couple of mornings a week. Brady

Chapman was helping her with the cycling portion and I knew that Mary had been working with Hope on a strength program for her legs using kickboxing moves. It was one of the things that had made me fall in love with Mayville Heights, the way people were willing to help one another.

Claire came back with the coffee. Marcus handed her a couple of bills. "The rest is for you," he said.

She smiled again. "Thanks. Have a good day, Detective." She moved down the counter to the cash register.

"I can drop you at the library," Marcus said, reaching for the paper bag of take-out food. "It looks like rain."

I turned and looked out the front window of the restaurant. It was cloudy but it didn't look like rain to me. And more important, my left wrist, which was a pretty good indicator of wet or snowy weather, felt fine.

I realized that maybe Gavin's invitation to breakfast had been motivated, a tiny bit, by wanting to spend time with me. The two of us eating at Eric's was getting to be a habit. On the other hand, I also believed that he wanted to catch whoever took the Weston drawing and killed Margo as much as I did. If I went with him to talk to Big Jule, maybe I could find out if there was anything more to Marcus's "feeling" about Gavin than just a smidgen of jealousy that he didn't want to admit to.

"Thank you," I said, brushing his hand with my fingers. "But there are a couple of other things I want to talk to Gavin about."

Marcus picked up the bag of take-out food with one hand and the pressed-paper tray holding the coffee with the other. "You're going to go with him, aren't you? To talk to his *contact*." Something in his voice when he said the word "contact" made me suspect that he didn't really believe there was one.

I nodded. "Yes. And just so you know, I keep that little can of industrial-strength hair spray that Mary gave me in my bag. It's more lethal than pepper spray." I held up my first three fingers. "I'll be careful. I'll call you when we get there and as soon as we get back. Librarian's honor."

"There's no such thing as librarian's honor," he said.

"Don't make me shush you," I countered, narrowing my gaze at him in a mock glare.

He smiled and gave my fingers a quick squeeze. "I'll call you later," he said.

I nodded and watched him go, thinking for what had to be the millionth time by now that he looked good no matter in what direction he was headed.

I walked back to the table.

"Everything okay with you and your detective?" Gavin asked.

I nodded and sat down again. "You wanted to get a rise out of him. That's why you told him that 'we' were going to talk to Big Jule."

I thought he'd deny it, but he just gave me that easy grin. "Guilty as charged," he said, leaning back and propping one arm on the chair back. The smiled dimmed. "I'm sorry, Kathleen. I shouldn't have done that. It was juvenile."

He seemed sincere, so I decided to accept his apology.

"When do you want to go talk to Julian McCrea?" I asked.

The smile came back. "You're coming with me?"

I reached for my coffee. The cup was empty, but Claire, with her seemingly sixth sense about when I needed a refill, was already headed our way with a full pot. "Yes, I'm coming with you," I said. "I hope it's not a waste of time."

"I'll pick you up at nine."

I nodded. "That's fine."

"I'll call Big Jule in a little while and if anything changes I'll let you know," he said. He made a gesture at the table. "Breakfast is on me."

"Thank you," I said, getting to my feet and sliding the strap of my bag over my shoulder. "I'll see you in the morning."

I stopped at the counter for a cup of coffee to go even though I was probably already overcaffeinated. It gave me the opportunity to quietly pay for both my and Gavin's breakfasts, my subtle way of letting him know that all the charm in the world wasn't going to work on me.

12

Gavin pulled into my driveway exactly at nine the next morning, something I was pretty certain he'd timed for effect since I'd once seen him check his watch and linger for a moment at the library when he'd had a meeting with Margo.

"I'm leaving," I said to the boys, reaching for my jacket.

Owen looked up from the stack of stinky crackers that he was arranging on the floor like a bingo player spreading out cards before the numbers were called. It could have been my imagination, but his expression looked sour, as though he'd just gotten a whiff of something rotten. Hercules didn't even acknowledge that I'd spoken. "I'll see you later," I said.

Gavin was just coming around the side of the house as I stepped outside. "Good morning," he said. After a pause he added, "You look nice."

"Thank you," I said. I'd waffled on whether it was manipulative to wear a skirt and heels for the meeting with Julian McCrea, standing, undecided, in front of the closet. Hercules, who had been sitting just inside, seemingly eyeing everything I pulled out and rejecting it like a feline Tim Gunn, had finally reached out and set a paw on my black boots and blinked his green eyes at me.

Ruby would have said that was a sign from the universe. It was more likely a sign that Hercules wanted his breakfast, but I decided I was overthinking things. I'd chosen a black skirt with a lavender shirt and the boots.

"We're meeting Big Jule for brunch at the Rose and Gray," Gavin said as I settled into the passenger seat of his Mercedes and fastened my seat belt.

I'd never been to the restaurant that specialized in cuisine made exclusively with ingredients from within a hundred-mile radius of Minneapolis, but I knew Roma and Eddie had had dinner there a few times and it was only his position as a local celebrity that had gotten them a reservation on short notice. Either Julian McCrea or Gavin had some clout.

We talked about Gavin's work for much of the drive, and that led, eventually, to a conversation about Margo.

"She had talent in her own right, you know," Gavin said, his eyes flicking away from the road for a moment to look at me. "One night we were working in the bar at the hotel and she showed me photos of her artwork. I can't even draw a stick man, but Margo had done some paintings of these old buildings, and I know it sounds crazy, but she could actually make you feel something when you looked at them."

I thought of Ruby's oversize pop-art acrylic renderings of Owen and Hercules. I couldn't explain it, but she'd managed to capture Owen's mischievous streak and Herc's sensitive side with her vivid colors. "It doesn't sound crazy to me," I said.

"She painted this barn—it was half falling down—and I kid you not, when she showed it to me I got a little choked up just looking at it. But she had another one she'd done of this old farmhouse, and be damned, but the feeling I got was that I wanted to live in the thing." He shook his head.

"Had she ever exhibited her work?"

"Somehow I don't think so. Margo was her own worst critic."

I exhaled slowly. "I know she could be"—I hesitated, looking for the right word—"challenging. But she was very encouraging to the local artists who had pieces in the show."

I remembered the smile on Nic Sutton's face after he'd come out of his meeting with Margo, and how Ruby had been literally bouncing with enthusiasm after hers.

"Lita said Margo didn't have any family. Is she right?" I felt a twinge of guilt that it had taken me until now to ask the question.

"She is," he said, moving into the passing lane and accelerating to pass a high-sided furniture delivery truck. "She told me once that her parents had died when she was a child and she'd been raised by her grandmother." His gaze flicked over to me for a moment. "I think that's why she was so exacting. Her grandmother was a doctor in an era when there weren't that many women doctors. I got the impression the woman had very high standards for Margo."

He looked at me again as the sleek silver Mercedes hugged a wide turn of the highway. "Margo has"—he paused for a moment—"had a degree in molecular biology. I think studying art history was a huge act of rebellion for her."

"I didn't know that," I said.

Gavin smiled. "I know. 'Rebellious' isn't really the first word you'd think of to describe her."

I couldn't help smiling myself. "No, it isn't," I agreed. Knowing a bit of Margo's history helped me understand her a little more. I found myself wishing I'd known all of this before she'd died.

"What about you, Kathleen?" Gavin asked, his eyes fixed straight ahead as he moved into the left lane to pass a slow-moving minivan and then back to the right to get by a tractor-trailer. He drove the way he did everything else: with a confidence that teetered on the edge of arrogance. I felt safe—he wasn't taking stupid chances, and he was a good driver. It reminded me of driving with Marcus, a comparison neither man would probably have liked.

"What do you mean?" I said.

"Do you have a rebellious streak?"

I couldn't help laughing.

"What's so funny?" Gavin asked, his eyes gleaming with curiosity.

I put one hand flat on my chest and took a moment to get my breath. "I'm sorry," I said. "It's just that 're-bellious' is pretty much the last word anyone would ever use to describe me, either." I cocked an eyebrow at him. "What about you?"

"Rebellious is my middle name," he teased.

"So, what or who were you rebelling against?" I asked, shifting sideways a little under my seat belt so I could watch his face.

"Three generations of Solomon men who always worked in the paper mill, married girls from the neighborhood and turned out a yard full of babies, and a high school that said people from my side of the river didn't go to college." He shrugged, and the bad-boy smile seemed a little forced. "You might say that bringing you along to meet Big Jule was an act of rebellion." He shot me a quick glance. "I saw Lita yesterday and I told her what we were doing today." The smile got wider and more genuine, it seemed to me. "She said I was poking the bear with a stick."

Clearly Marcus was the bear.

Lita wasn't the kind of person to judge other people's choices; she was involved with Burtis Chapman after all, and he had a reputation. But when she did share her opinion, she wasn't shy about it. I was guessing she'd done more than just compare Marcus to an angry bear. Whatever she'd said, it was none of my business.

"That's because Lita is immune to your charm," I said lightly.

"I'm like a bottle of fine wine," Gavin said, moving the car into the right lane so we could take the exit that would take us downtown. "You may not be captivated at the first taste, but after a little time the nuances will win you over."

I waited for a moment and then looked pointedly at my feet. "Good thing I wore boots," I said.

Gavin frowned. "Why?" he asked.

"Because my shoes would have been ruined by that load of fertilizer you're spreading around."

He gave a snort of laughter. "Busted," he said with a grin. "And I worked hard on that line."

Gavin had a brief meeting scheduled at the Walker Art Center, so I looked around the pop-art exhibition while I waited for him, thinking Ruby's portraits of Owen and Hercules would have fit right in with the artwork. My thoughts kept wandering to our lunch with Julian McCrea.

I hadn't been able to find anything more than what Gavin had told me about the man through my usual online sources, so I'd ended up calling Lise, in Boston. Her expertise was music, but I knew she had contacts in the art world. Unfortunately, she didn't know anything about McCrea.

"Do I want to know why you're asking about this Julian McCrea person?" she'd asked.

I'd stretched my feet out on the footstool, and Hercules, who was sprawled on my lap, had moved his head so it was resting against my arm and closed his green eyes. "Remember that exhibit I told you was coming to the library?" I'd said.

"The centerpiece was an early Sam Weston drawing," she immediately said.

I'd exhaled softly. "It was stolen."

"What?"

"It looks as though the thief came in through a skylight in the roof I didn't even know would open."

"You're not serious."

I pictured her, elbows propped on her kitchen table, making a face at my words. "I wish I wasn't."

"I'm beginning to think that Mayville Heights is the crime capital of the Midwest," she'd said. "You're okay, right?"

"I'm fine," I had said, shifting my arm a little, which got me a one-eyed glare from Hercules. It evaporated once I began to stroke his ebony fur. I'd decided not to tell Lise about Margo or how the brass statue she'd sent me had been used to kill her.

"That Weston drawing could be worth quite a lot of money," Lise had said. "Though actually, some experts believe it's not Weston's work."

Hercules had been purring, a low rumble coming from his chest. "If it's not Weston's work, then how can it be worth a lot of money?" I asked.

"Because some experts think the drawing was done by Weston's first wife. She was Native American."

"Do you know anyone I could talk to who could tell me more?"

"I can tell you more."

"I didn't know you were interested in nineteenth-century American art."

"I'm interested in lots of things," she'd said, and I had felt her smile through the phone. "Did I ever introduce you to Edward Mato?"

Hercules had lifted his head and looked at me. My hand had stopped moving. "I don't think so."

"Back about 1990 the federal government passed the Native American Graves Protection and Repatriation Act—as a way of hopefully returning remains and artifacts buried with them to the Native American tribes they belonged to. Ed's ancestry is Sioux and he's an expert on native burial rituals."

"What does that have to do with the Weston drawing?" I'd asked.

"He's also interested in native art," Lise had said. "He's very knowledgeable. About a month ago we bumped into each other at a cocktail party and I was telling him about the exhibit coming to your library. He's the one who told me there's some controversy about who the real creator of that drawing is. I think he actually might have appraised it at some point."

After I'd talked to Lise I'd pulled out my computer to see what I could find out about Sam Weston and his art. It was a fascinating story.

Sam Weston had been a graduate of West Point and a mapmaker and artist for the United States Army. He'd spent three years at Fort Snelling, which was located near where Minneapolis is today. Weston had learned the language of the Sioux people and created detailed sketches and paintings of their lives. And he had married fifteen-year-old Wakaninajiinwin, or Stands Sacred, leaving her and their daughter behind when he was reassigned two years later.

Weston kept very detailed sketchbooks during his time at Fort Snelling, I learned, but there was also a portfolio of individual sketches and watercolors from that time. That's where the controversy began. There was a school of thought that believed some of the drawings in that portfolio, including the village scene missing from the exhibit, weren't done by Weston, but by Stands Sacred, his teenage first wife.

"If there was any kind of proof that those disputed drawings weren't done by Sam Weston, they could be worth a fortune to collectors of Native American art, not to mention the historical value to the Dakota Sioux people," I'd said to Hercules, who'd been "helping" me with my research. "Which could explain why someone wanted to steal the drawing."

The cat had murped his agreement.

If Stands Sacred was the real artist, the drawing would be one of the few intact pieces of native art from that period. And it could call into question the provenance of every other Weston drawing from that time.

I'd told Marcus what I'd learned about the drawing. Now I wondered if Margo had known how potentially valuable the drawing was. Was that why she had had reservations about the exhibit?

Gavin touched my shoulder and I jumped. "Sorry," he said. "I called your name but you didn't hear me. Where were you?"

"I got a little distracted," I said. "Are you ready to leave?"

He nodded. "Big Jule is meeting us at the restaurant." He glanced at his watch. "And we should get going."

The Rose and Gray restaurant was on the bottom floor of a restored brick building close to the river in downtown Minneapolis. Inside there was wide plank flooring and high windows overlooking the waterfront. We were shown to a round table in the middle of the room. The ponytailed waiter dressed all in black held out my chair for me. "Would you like coffee?" he asked.

"Please," I said.

Gavin nodded his agreement and sat down as the waiter headed to the far side of the room. "Big Jule should be here in a couple of minutes," he said. "He likes to make an entrance."

The waiter returned with our coffee and I was just taking my first sip when Julian McCrea entered the restaurant.

He was a large man, tall and round in a double-breasted pinstripe suit with a white shirt and a white tie with navy polka dots. His black wingtips gleamed and he was carrying a charcoal fedora. He did make me think of the character from *Guys and Dolls*, but he could just as easily have been a fashion-forward businessman.

Gavin got to his feet as McCrea approached the table, and I did the same.

"Gavin, it's been too long," the big man said, shaking the hand offered. I saw a glint of gold cuff links at the cuffs of the crisp white shirt.

"It's good to see you," Gavin replied with what sounded to me like a touch of deference in his voice. "This is my friend Kathleen Paulson." He gestured to me. "Kathleen, I'd like you to meet Julian McCrea."

McCrea smiled and took the hand I held out in both of his. "It's truly a pleasure to meet you, Miss Paulson," he said. I caught a hint of an accent in his cultured voice—not British or Australian; maybe South African.

"Thank you for making time to talk to us," I said.

"Gavin told me what happened at your library," he said. "I don't know if I can be of any help, but I'm happy to answer your questions."

We took our seats again. McCrea set his fedora on the empty chair between him and Gavin and turned his attention to me. "Tell me a little more about the exhibit. I didn't get a lot of details."

I gave him a brief background on how the library had come to be one of the stops on the exhibit of mid-nineteenth-century artwork and explained how Margo had convinced the museum to include a contemporary local segment of artwork at each stop on the tour. Gavin sat silently, nodding on occasion but letting me do all the talking.

"I met Margo several times, socially," McCrea said. "The art world—at least here—is a very small world. I was sorry to hear what happened." He reached for his menu, which had appeared at his elbow along with a cup of tea about thirty seconds after he'd sat down. Our waiter had to have been watching and waiting for his cue.

"Do you like fish, Miss Paulson?" he asked.

"Yes, I do," I said.

"Then I suggest the fish cakes with lemon dill sauce."

"They sound delicious." I closed my menu and set it back on the table.

The waiter appeared at McCrea's elbow again, almost as though the big man had given some kind of signal. He took our orders, refilled my and Gavin's cups and headed for the kitchen.

McCrea talked in general terms about the art scene in Minneapolis while we waited for our food. He was well spoken and clearly knowledgeable about his subject. The man was charming but in a different way from Gavin. Gavin's charm was all about pulling you in. Julian McCrea's was all about keeping you at arm's length. I didn't think I was going to get any information from him unless I could find a way to bring that wall down.

The fish cakes were delicious, a mix of catfish and

salmon, with a thin, crispy bread-crumb coating. "These are excellent," I said, raising my fork in acknowledgment to the art dealer. "The last time I had fish cakes this good was in a little roadside diner just outside of Rockport, Maine, when my parents were doing *Noises Off*."

"Your parents were involved in community theater?" McCrea asked.

I shook my head. "Summer stock. They're both actors, although they also teach at a private school and my mother has been doing more directing lately."

His blue eyes focused in on me. "May I ask their names? I'm wondering if I may have seen either of them on stage."

"John and Thea Paulson," I said. "If you're a Shakespeare fan at all and you've seen any theater at all on the East Coast, it's possible you've seen them."

Julian McCrea's eyes widened and a smile stretched across his face. "Thea Paulson is your mother?" he exclaimed.

It wasn't the first time my mom's name had gotten that kind of reaction. She'd just recently wrapped up her third visit to the daytime drama *The Wild and the Wonderful*. My father liked to tease that they couldn't go anywhere without at least one young woman coming up to tell her she rocked.

"And men half my age stare at her," Dad had said, laughing and shaking his head. "And the kind of looks they give her aren't because they're looking at her like she's a mother figure."

"Yes, she is," I said in answer to McCrea's question. His smile grew wider. "I saw her maybe a dozen years ago as Portia in *The Merchant of Venice*, and two years ago as Ella in *Last Love*, in Boston. She's very talented."

"Yes, she is," I said, smiling back at him. "Thank you."

"What about you, Kathleen?" he asked. "Do you act?"

I shook my head. "I'm afraid the talent gene skipped me." I speared a forkful of arugula. "You clearly enjoy the theater. Have you done any acting?"

"I've played the role of Big Jule in *Guys and Dolls*," he said. I noticed that he sat up a little straighter as he said the words.

"It's one of my favorite musicals," I said. That was true. I'd loved watching my dad rehearse his role as Sky Masterson and I really could do the choreography for "Luck Be a Lady."

I gave Julian McCrea a quick once-over. "I can see you as Big Jule," I said.

He patted his midsection. "I do have the 'big' part."

"I was thinking more that you have the presence to play the role. It's very easy for the character to turn into a caricature." That was also true. I'd heard my mother express her dissatisfaction with the way the part had been cast a couple of times because the director had turned Big Jule into comic relief instead of using him to move the story forward.

We spent the rest of the meal talking about musical theater. Gavin didn't say a word. When the waiter arrived with the bill, discreetly presented inside a small black folder, he indicated with a flick of his gaze that it should be given to him.

"Thank you, my friend," McCrea said.

"Thank you for taking the time to talk to us," Gavin replied.

The art dealer turned to me. "I'm sorry I couldn't be of any help to you. I can promise you that no one is shopping that missing drawing around this area. If someone were, I would know. Unfortunately, you're just going to have to take my word for that."

"It's good enough for me," I said.

I hesitated. McCrea must have seen the uncertainty in my face. "Is there something else, Kathleen?" he asked.

"The name Devin Rossi has . . . come up in the investigation," I said, hoping I'd chosen my words wisely.

He turned his head to look at Gavin for a moment before bringing his attention back to me. "Interesting," was all he said.

"She acquires art for her customers."

The big man tented his fingers over his midsection. "You're very diplomatic," he said, an amused expression on his face.

"My mother always says you can catch more flies with honey than with vinegar," I countered. I didn't add that she also said you could get the best result by spreading a little bull around.

"I'll put out a few discreet inquiries," he said. "If I find out anything I'll be in touch."

"Thank you," I said. "I appreciate that."

He pushed back his cuff, glanced at his watch and then got to his feet. Gavin and I did the same. McCrea took my hand in both of his. "It's truly been a pleasure to meet you, Kathleen," he said. "I hope to see you again."

I smiled. "I'd like that."

"It's always good to see you, Gavin," the big man said, reaching for his hat.

They shook hands and McCrea headed for the door.

Gavin flashed a credit card to the waiter, who had been hovering nearby. "He plays his cards very close to the vest, but you made a good impression on him. He may very well ask around."

"Good," I said.

He gave me a sidelong glance. "You played him like a five-string banjo."

I shook my head. "We both like the theater. I meant everything I said. I'm guessing he's very good in the role of Big Jule." I pulled out my cell phone. "You tried to play me, though."

I'd half expected him to deny it, but he didn't. He gave me his "I've been a naughty boy" smile. "I knew Big Jule would be a lot more responsive to your charms than mine. And like you said, you both like the theater."

"You knew if you just came and asked him directly if he knew anything, he wouldn't tell you."

He nodded. "I told you, he doesn't show his hand for any reason."

He pulled his car keys out of his pocket. His expression went from lighthearted to serious then. "Kathleen, I liked Margo. It was my job to keep the exhibit and anyone involved with it safe. Now it's my job to find out what went wrong."

"That's a job for the police," I said, not unaware of the irony that I was the one saying those words.

"From what I've heard you don't always follow your own advice," he said.

"Do you think Julian can help?"

Gavin's mouth twisted to one side. "Truth? I don't know. I do know that he knows the art world in this part of the country better than anyone else."

"I guess we'll just have to keep our fingers crossed," I said. I held up my phone. "I just need to make a quick call."

Gavin nodded. "I'll wait for you at the car."

Marcus answered on the second ring. "How was lunch?" he asked. "Did you learn anything?"

"Just that Julian McCrea is a fan of my mother and as far as he's heard, no one is trying to sell the Weston drawing and no one had been putting out feelers about the piece before it was stolen."

"You're on your way back now."

"Uh-huh." I could see Gavin standing next to the car, talking on his own cell. "We're just about to leave."

"Can you stop at the library when you get here?" he asked.

"I can do that," I said slowly. I couldn't put my finger on what it was in his voice that told me he'd found something, but somehow I knew he had. "What's going on?"

I heard voices in the background. "I'll explain when you get here," he said. "I have to go. See you soon."

He was gone. I put my phone in my bag and headed outside.

I couldn't shake the feeling that once we were back in Mayville Heights, things were going to get a lot more complicated.

13

Gavin asked me more about my family on the drive back. I noticed that when I tried to steer the conversation into his personal life he'd deftly move it back to me, the way he had when I questioned him about being rebellious.

I hadn't told him about my conversation with Marcus. When we turned off the highway he glanced at me. "Where can I drop you?" he asked.

"The library, please," I said. "

Gavin nodded as the car hugged the curve of the exit ramp. "I'll come with you. I did promise your detective I'd report in."

In the parking lot of the library I recognized the car Hope and Marcus used when they worked together. Gavin followed me up the steps to the building. The first set of doors was unlocked and the old-fashioned wrought-iron security gates were also open. I tapped on the inside door and after a moment Hope came to let me in.

"Hi," she said. "Marcus said you were on your way. You made good time."

"And stuck to the speed limit, Detective," Gavin said. "More or less." His eyebrows went up and a small smile played on his face.

Hope rolled her eyes and shook her head. "Why do I think it was less rather than more?"

Marcus was standing by the circulation desk. He smiled as he caught sight of me and I couldn't help smiling back as I walked over to him. Curtis Holt was doing a circuit of the exhibit area, checking the windows—part of his security guard duties, I guessed.

"Before you ask, we didn't find out anything useful," Gavin said.

I turned to look at him over my shoulder. "Yes, we did," I said. I shifted my gaze to Hope and Marcus. "Julian McCrea told us that he hadn't heard anything about anyone being interested in the Weston drawing, not before it was stolen and not since."

"Do you think he was being honest with you?" Hope asked.

"I don't think he had any reason to lie," I said. I looked questioningly at Gavin.

"Big Jule doesn't lie. He might split hairs or shade the truth, but he won't tell an outright lie."

Hope looked skeptical.

"He won't," Gavin repeated. "He went to Catholic school. He told Kathleen no one had approached him about acquiring the drawing. You can take that to the bank, for what it's worth."

"Every little piece is part of the puzzle." Hope made a gesture like she was fitting two pieces of a jigsaw puzzle together. "You never know which small piece will help you figure out the entire picture."

"We found something, too," Marcus said. There was a piece of paper on the checkout desk. He reached over and picked it up.

Gavin shot me a puzzled look. I gave an almost imperceptible shrug.

"Margo Walsh kept a date book," Marcus continued.

I nodded slowly. "She kept everything in it. It was a small book with a maroon leather cover." Like Maggie, Margo had kept a paper schedule instead of using her phone or computer.

"We found it today."

Hope looked at me for a moment before looking back at Marcus. Did that mean anything? I wondered.

"So what does that mean?" Gavin asked, restlessly shifting his weight from one leg to the other. "Did Margo happen to make a note that someone wanted to kill her?"

Marcus opened the folded sheet of white paper, looked at whatever was written on it, then looked at Gavin. "No. But she did make a note about having lunch with you three weeks before you told us you'd met her for the first time."

Gavin exhaled loudly and shrugged. "I should have guessed she'd write it down," he said. "Margo wrote everything down."

"Why did you lie to us?" Hope asked.

"Not because I killed her," he said. "I was in the bar at the hotel. You know that. People saw me." He looked from Hope to Marcus. Neither one of them said a word.

"You told me this was the first time you'd worked with Margo," I said.

"It was," Gavin said. "It just wasn't the first time we'd met. I didn't lie. I just didn't tell you everything."

"So stop playing games and tell us everything now," Hope said.

He exhaled loudly. "Fine. Margo and I had lunch when the schedule for the exhibit was finalized." His mouth moved like he was working on shaping his words before he spoke them. "She had big concerns about the artwork being out of a museum."

"Why did you let everyone think you'd never met before?" Hope asked.

I glanced over at the stairs to the second floor of the building. Margo and I had been standing there when Gavin had walked into the library for the first time. I remembered her holding out her hand and saying, *"Hello. You must be Gavin Solomon. I'm Margo Walsh."*

"Wait a minute," I said. "Why did Margo pretend she didn't know you?" I looked from Hope to Marcus. "I was here with her when Gavin arrived for our first meeting." I turned to Gavin. "She introduced herself as though she'd never seen you before."

"That's because I asked her not to let on we'd already met." He exhaled loudly and looked up at the ceiling. "When we met for lunch it was to go over the security details for the exhibit. The insurance company had certain requirements that had to be met. Margo . . . had some questions." He dropped his head and looked at me. "The thing is, I work for ILG Security as a consultant, which means I can also work for other companies in the same capacity . . . as long as there isn't a conflict of interest."

"Which there was this time," Marcus said.

"Who else were you working for?" I asked.

Gavin shifted restlessly again. "The insurance company."

"You were working for the company that required the security and the one that was providing it." Hope's tone and her body language told me that she and Marcus had already figured out his conflict of interest.

I shook my head. "I don't understand. Why on earth would Margo have gone along with keeping that a secret?"

Gavin swiped a hand across his face in exasperation. "Oh, c'mon, Kathleen. You worked with the woman. You know what she was like. She was dead set against any of the artwork being displayed anywhere other than a museum where she could control everything from the way the lights were angled to the alarm system. We could have had laser beams crisscrossing the room like a James Bond movie and she was still convinced someone was going to steal one of her precious drawings."

"Someone did," I said softly.

"And maybe she helped whoever it was," he retorted. "She wanted to know a lot of the technical details on how the system worked. She *said* it was so she could keep moving things around and not set it off. I didn't have any reason to think she wasn't telling me the truth." He pulled a hand over the back of his neck. "Maybe I was wrong."

"Maybe," Marcus said.

Gavin looked directly at him, his jaw clenched and tight lines around his mouth. "I didn't kill her."

Marcus came to stand next to me. "We should take this down to the station," he said.

"Are you going to arrest me?"

"We just want to ask you a few more questions," Hope said, her tone even and nonconfrontational.

Gavin looked directly at Marcus. "So go ahead and ask them. I don't need a lawyer if that's what you're worried about. I have the right to remain silent and anything I say can be used against me. I get that." His dark eyes flicked to me. "Kathleen, you're my witness." He held up both hands. "Ask your questions."

"This is a bad idea," I said softly. Hope shot Marcus a warning look.

He ignored both of us. "Before you worked for ILG Security, who did you work for?" he asked.

"Myself," Gavin said. "I have a background in art and I've always been pretty good with electronics. People hired me to evaluate their security systems. It was pretty much a word-of-mouth business, but I can give you the contact information for some of my satisfied customers."

A muscle twitched in Marcus's cheek. "What about dissatisfied customers?"

Gavin smiled, although there wasn't a lot of warmth in his expression. "There were none."

"Ever been in any trouble with the police?"

The smile didn't waver. "You wouldn't ask the question unless you knew the answer. Yes. When I was a *kid*." He emphasized the word "kid."

He looked away from Marcus then, over to me. "I was fourteen. I broke in to a teacher's house. I got probation and community service. I wore an orange vest that was two sizes too big for me and picked up garbage along the highway for six weeks including the hottest July on record."

Gavin continued to focus his attention on me. "You're the only one who doesn't know the rest of the story, Kathleen, so here it is. I took a drawing from that teacher's house. I guess that constitutes some kind of pattern." He shrugged.

"Was that the only time you ever took something that didn't belong to you?" Marcus asked. He continued his laser focus on the other man.

"I picked up a quarter from the sidewalk," Gavin said. "Strictly speaking it didn't belong to me. And last week I ate a muffin from the staff room here in the library, although they were on a plate in the middle of the table so you could argue there's a reasonable assumption they were intended for everyone." He looked away from me then, and the look he gave Marcus was a mix of flippant and defiant.

Marcus sighed softly, so softly I was probably the only person who heard him. I knew he didn't like Gavin. He'd admitted something about the man bugged him, but did he really think the security expert had had anything to do with the theft and Margo's death? How could he? More than one person had seen Gavin in the bar at the hotel.

Hope looked at Marcus. Something passed between them.

"Mr. Solomon, do you know a man named Alastair Darby?" Marcus asked.

I'd heard the name somewhere but I couldn't remember where.

"He's a collector," Gavin said. "Fancies himself a patron of the arts."

"You were at a fundraising event hosted by Alastair Darby a couple of years ago."

Gavin nodded. "I was. It was a garden party at his summer home. Mediocre wine, excellent food."

"You and Alastair Darby got into an argument at the party." Marcus squared his shoulders and crossed his arms over his midsection. He tipped his head to one side and studied Gavin as though he was some kind of science experiment.

If Gavin was intimidated, it didn't show. "Actually, I got into an argument with the mountainoid who worked for him. He got a little frisky in a pat down. He wasn't my type." He raised an eyebrow at Hope and gave her a sly smile.

"Darby thought you'd taken something that belonged to him," Marcus said.

"He was mistaken," Gavin said. "Which he learned after his gorilla felt me up."

Hope smiled back at him. "You didn't take a painting that belonged to Mr. Darby?"

Gavin laid a hand over his chest. "I promise you, Detective, I didn't take anything from that party that belonged to Alastair Darby."

"Two people saw you stuff something in your pants."

He laughed. "That was all mine."

"So you're not a thief?" Marcus said.

Gavin held up both hands again in a gesture of surrender. "I'm just a security expert. I'm not a thief. I didn't take anything of Mr. Darby's. And for the record"—his eyes flicked to me again—"I wasn't a thief

at fourteen, either. The teacher? He took a piece of artwork that had been done by a student, that she didn't
give to him and that he lied about having. All I did was
retrieve it." He shrugged. "I have some unique skills. I
use them to prevent things from being lost. A few times,
in the past, I acted as a retrieval agent for people whose
artwork had, let's say, been borrowed without their
permission. I was paid a fee when that artwork was
returned to its rightful owners. I don't think that's
against the law, Detective."

"Mr. Solomon, were you in the bar all evening the
night Margo Walsh was killed?" Hope said. "Because
nobody seems to remember seeing you after about
quarter to eight."

"No, I wasn't."

"So where were you?" I asked. This game of cat and
mouse had been going on too long for me.

"With Mary," he said, gesturing at the checkout desk.

"Mary Lowe?" I said.

He nodded. "Uh-huh. It turns out we have an interest in common."

I should have known. I really should have known at
that point. But instead I frowned and said, "You're interested in kickboxing?"

Gavin threw back his head and laughed. "No. Mary
and I were at The Brick."

I got it then. I felt my cheeks flood with color. Marcus
and Hope hadn't figured out what Gavin was talking
about, and before I could say anything he spoke again.

"It was amateur night. We performed." One eyebrow went up and the sly smile returned to his face.

"To 'Proud Mary,'" he said. "Together."

14

There was no reason for Gavin to stay, so he left. Marcus got on his cell phone and moved a couple of steps away. Hope walked over to me. "Mary Lowe and Gavin Solomon dancing at The Brick." She shook her head. "My mind just won't go there."

"I was there once for amateur night," I said.

Her eyebrows went up.

"Not to perform. It was during the investigation of Agatha Shepherd's murder."

Hope grinned. "Sure it was, Kathleen," she teased.

"Mary's act was very popular." I didn't add that I had only seen a moment of her performance because I was so embarrassed at seeing one of my staff members on The Brick's stage in high heels, fishnets, a corset and pretty much nothing else that I'd grabbed Maggie and literally dragged her to the parking lot.

Hope put her hands over her ears. "I don't want to hear this," she said.

I leaned my head close to hers. "I have one word for you. Feathers."

She made a face and dropped her hands. "Okay. You're going to have to start delivering books to my house because I'm never going to be able to come into the library and look Mary in the eye ever again."

Marcus stuck his phone in his pocket and walked over to us. "I have to go back to the station," he said to Hope.

"Go ahead," she said. "I want to go out back and see how the crime scene techs are doing." She smiled at me. "I'll see you later, Kathleen."

I nodded.

"I'd better get home and see what Owen and Hercules have been up to," I said to Marcus. I reached out for his hand and gave it a squeeze.

He looked around, then leaned down and kissed the top of my head. "You'll find some papers kind of spread around the living room. Don't give Owen a hard time about them, because really, he was the one who found Margo Walsh's date book."

"Owen found Margo's date book?" It occurred to me that if anyone heard us talking they would have thought that Owen was a person. Of course, he seemed to think he was.

Marcus nodded. "Uh-huh."

We started for the door. "I have a feeling this is going to be good," I said. "How exactly did *my* cat find a piece of *your* evidence?"

"I stopped at your house just before lunch to check on the cats. I realized I'd forgotten the drawing I'd made of the cabinet."

Maggie and I had found an old 1960s vintage wooden cabinet at the same flea market where we'd gotten Roma's bench. I'd sanded off the old finish and Marcus was going to add shelves and legs before I painted it.

"It's on the counter by the toaster," I said.

He nodded. "Yeah, I know. I found it. But I checked the living room first."

Marcus locked up the building and set the alarm and we stepped outside into the afternoon sunshine.

"So exactly how did these papers end up spread around my living room?" I asked.

"You had a couple of boxes next to that big chair."

I bent to pick up a candy wrapper on the second step. "Those were my files about the exhibit. "Don't tell me Owen got the top off one of the boxes."

"I think he just wanted to see what was inside."

I stopped at the bottom of the stairs. "What did he do?" I said.

Marcus hesitated.

"What did he do?" I repeated.

"He kind of spread everything around the living room . . . a little," he said somewhat sheepishly.

"That little fur ball isn't going to see a stinky cracker for a very long time," I said, shaking a finger for emphasis. "I just got those files finished and organized so I could bring them down here and put them away. Now I have to start all over again. I can't believe he got that lid off the box."

Marcus smiled. "He's pretty resourceful."

I shook my head. "Oh no."

He looked surprised. "What do you mean, no? I didn't ask you anything."

"You want me to let Owen off the hook. In fact, you

probably want me to give him a treat." I stopped at the edge of the parking lot and squinted up at him.

"I wouldn't have found Margo's date book if Owen hadn't gotten into that box. Do you have any idea how it ended up there, by the way?"

"Margo helped me put all those files in the boxes. It probably got mixed up with one of the piles of paper and got put in by mistake."

"If I hadn't found Margo's date book I wouldn't have known Gavin was lying about when he and Margo met. And I might not have found out that his alibi was a fake."

"Which doesn't do you any good because he has another alibi, which I'd just as soon not know about."

Marcus rolled his eyes. "You and me both. But my point is, Owen helped me find that date book. Once I finish going through it, who knows what other bits of evidence I might get from it."

"You make it sound as though he knew the date book was in the box and opened it so you'd find it." I had an uncomfortable feeling, niggling away at the base of my brain, that that was exactly what had happened, which meant I'd just made Marcus's point.

"Okay, I know that didn't happen, but he did help." Marcus raised his eyebrows and smiled at me. He had a gorgeous smile that still had the ability to make me feel like a love-struck teenager when I wasn't imagining what it was like to kiss his equally gorgeous mouth.

I realized then that he was waiting for me to say something while I was focusing on his mouth instead of the words coming out of it.

I let out a small sigh. "You win," I said, reaching up

to brush back the lock of dark hair that had fallen down onto his forehead.

"Thank you," he said.

"That little fur ball owes you," I said.

Marcus laughed. "A cat in my debt," he said. "Now, that's useful."

Given what Owen was capable of, it really was, but I didn't say that.

Marcus gave me a drive up the hill because my boots weren't really made for walking up Mountain Road.

"Thank you for the ride," I said as I undid my seat belt after he'd pulled into my driveway.

"You're welcome," he said, leaning over to kiss me. "I'll call you later. And by the way, you look beautiful."

I felt my cheeks flood with color as I got out of the car.

Owen was sitting by the table in the kitchen. He meowed the moment he saw me, coming over to wind himself around my legs. I bent down and picked him up and he immediately nuzzled my cheek.

"Never mind trying to get on my good side," I said. He tipped his head to one side and looked at me, the absolute image of adorable kitty.

Hercules appeared in the living room doorway. "Mrrr," he said softly; then he looked back over his shoulder.

I kissed the top of Owen's head and set him down. "I know," I said to Hercules. "Marcus told me." I crossed the kitchen to him and leaned over to stroke his dark fur. "I heard he helped Marcus find some evidence."

I know cats can't shrug, but it almost seemed that he did. Then he took a few steps into the living room,

turned and looked at me. I went to stand beside him.
The contents of one file box were strewn all over the
living room. All over. There were papers on the floor,
under the wing chair and on the footstool. I blew out a
breath and looked at Hercules.

"Was this all Owen?" I asked.

"Merow," he said.

"Some of it was Marcus, wasn't it?"

The floor was suddenly very interesting.

"That's what I thought," I said. "It explains why
Marcus was so quick to spring to Owen's defense."

Hercules kept me company while I piled the papers
in the box again. He even managed to snag an empty
file folder that had somehow ended up underneath the
sofa.

I scooped him up once we were finished. "Thank
you," I said. "What would I do without you?"

He narrowed his green eyes at me as though he were
actually contemplating the question.

I spent the rest of the afternoon making phone calls,
taking a break long enough to make a pan of cinnamon
rolls and call Harrison to see if he would be free after
supper for a visit. I still wanted to hear about the
woman he'd met online. By suppertime I'd managed to
coordinate moving most of the library's programs temporarily over to Maggie's studio, with the seniors heading to Henderson Holdings for their reading group.
And Harrison had called back to say he'd see me at
about seven thirty.

After supper I sat on the living room floor with Hercules beside me and reorganized the box of papers.

And played *Barry Manilow Live* from the iPod dock. There was no sign of Owen.

Young Harry dropped off Harry Senior just before seven thirty. "I'll be back to get him in about an hour," Harry said to me.

"There's no rush," I said.

"We're just fine. Go," the old man said, waving one hand at his son. Harry mouthed a "thank you" at me and left.

Harrison settled himself at the table. "Something smells good," he commented.

"Cinnamon rolls," I said. "Would you like one?"

"Are they good for me?" he asked reaching in his pocket for something. Hercules had wandered in from somewhere and was sitting next to Harrison's chair looking up at him.

"Probably not," I said.

"In that case, yes, I'll have one along with a cup of that coffee I smell." He pulled what looked like a small piece of old shoe leather out of his pocket and held it out to Hercules. The cat sniffed it curiously and then took it from him, holding it in place on the floor with one paw and chewing happily on the other end.

"What are you feeding my cat?" I asked as I set a plate in front of the old man.

"Turkey jerky," he said. Hercules looked up at him and seemed to almost smile just as the basement door opened and Owen appeared. He lifted his head and sniffed the air, then headed toward our guest.

"I didn't forget you," Harrison said. He reached into his pocket and pulled out a small plastic bag. He took out a second piece of the jerky and held it out to Owen, who meowed his thanks and took it.

"Turkey jerky?" I asked as I poured our coffee.

"Burtis and the boys made it," Harrison said. "It's pretty good. Sorry I didn't bring a piece for you."

"That's okay, I'll take your word on it," I said, joining him at the table.

He grinned at me. "It's good stuff." He patted his chest with one large hand. "It'll put hair on your chest."

I smiled back at him. "That's just what I need."

He laughed and leaned back in the chair with his coffee. "So tell me, when's the library going to reopen? I've got about a half a dozen books requested."

"It's going to be sometime next week at least," I said adding cream and sugar to my cup. "But if something you've been waiting for comes in, I'll bring it out to you."

"That's good of you, Kathleen," Harrison said. He took a bite of his cinnamon roll, smiled and licked a dab of icing off the side of his thumb. "That's better than Burtis's jerky."

"That's high praise," I teased.

He reached over and patted my hand. "You're darn right it is." He took a long sip of his coffee and then his gaze focused on my face. "So start with the questions."

I pulled one leg up underneath me. "No questions," I said. "I'd like to hear about this woman you've met."

"My son's time would be better spent finding a date of his own."

I nodded. "Maybe. But we're not talking about Harry; we're talking about you."

"I met a woman. Yes, I know how to use a computer.

I'm old, not dead. We decided it's time we met in person. End of story."

"Harry and Elizabeth are worried about you."

He broke off another section of cinnamon roll, popped it in his mouth and ate it. "Kathleen, you know I love my kids. Harry is a damn fine man." He mock frowned at me. "And if you repeat that to him I'll pretend I had a stroke and was just mumbling nonsense." He reached for his coffee again. "For a while I wasn't even sure I was going to meet Elizabeth, let alone get to be part of her life, and I'm grateful every day that it all worked out. And I'm grateful for your part in that."

I smiled across the table at him. "I did very little, but I'm glad it helped."

"They worry too much, Kathleen," Harrison said. "We're meeting in a public place and I'm going to that meeting with my eyes wide-open. I know my lady friend could be a bald fella in sweatpants, but I don't think she is. All I can tell you is when you're looking at life from my end of things, it looks pretty damn short."

"All right," I said.

"All right?" He looked surprised. "That's it?"

I smiled at him. "You didn't see that coming, did you?"

He gave a snort of laughter. "No, I did not."

"You have good judgment, Harrison," I said. "I don't think you're going to do anything stupid."

"I had a whole argument worked out, you know," he said. His eyes were twinkling.

"And I'm sure it was a good one," I said, taking the last bite of my own cinnamon roll. "I'll listen to it if you'd like."

His shook his head and fingered his white beard. "I should have known I didn't need an argument for you. You're pretty much the most sensible person I know."

I got up to get myself more coffee and squeezed his shoulder as I passed behind his chair. "More like I know what a waste of time it is getting into any argument with you."

He put his hand on mine for a moment and laughed. "Are you trying to say I'm a bit stubborn?"

"A bit?" I countered.

Harrison laughed. "There are damn few perks to being as old as I am, Kathleen," he said. "Having my own way is one of them and I'm not about to let it go."

We spent the rest of our time together talking about what was going on around town. When Young Harry arrived to pick up his father, the old man got to his feet and gave me a hug. "Always good to see you, Kathleen," he said. "Come out to the house sometime for supper. It's been too long."

"I'd like that," I said.

He looked at his son.

"I'll set it up," Harry Junior said.

Harrison headed for the porch door. "I'm going out to the truck so you two can talk about me behind my back."

"Yeah, we appreciate that, Dad," Harry said drily. Once we heard the outside door close he turned back to me. "You didn't have any luck, did you?"

I shook my head. "You know what he's like. He has his mind made up and nothing is going to change that."

Harry swiped a hand over his neck. "That's pretty

much how I figured things would go. Thanks for talking to him."

"I didn't mind. I like spending time with your father," I said.

"I'll call about supper," he said. "The old man will be like a dog with a bone until I do."

I laughed. "The way things are at the library right now, my schedule is pretty open."

"Marcus getting anywhere on that?"

I sighed. "The drawing that was stolen might be worth a lot more than anyone knew."

"Which means there could have been even more people who wanted it," he finished.

"Exactly," I said.

"Larry said she was a nice woman," Harry said as we headed out into the porch.

I knew he was referring to Margo. Larry had worked well with her because he didn't mind her perfectionism. He was a bit of a perfectionist himself.

"But you know, I think his head's been turned by that new artist who's working with Ruby."

"You mean Rena Adler, the painter?" I asked.

Harry pulled off his Twins ball cap and smoothed a hand over his bald pate before putting the hat back on. "That's the one. I pulled up to the library the day before the robbery. Larry was supposed to be making some last-minute changes to a few lights. He's in the parking lot in the van checking his hair in the rearview mirror."

He laughed. "I tapped on the window and almost gave him a heart attack."

"Has he asked her out?"

Hercules had followed us out to the porch. He'd

jumped up onto the bench and seemed to be intently following the conversation, head tipped to one side. I reached over and stroked his fur.

Harry shook his head. "Lord no! He's the opposite of the old man. Larry pretty much moves at a snail's pace when it comes to women. But I'm thinking she might like him. He said they spent a lot of time talking. She even brought a cup of coffee down to the basement to him while he was working."

I thought about all the cups of coffee Marcus and I had shared while we were getting to know each other. "It sounds like she might be interested," I said.

"At least she's real," Harry said, rolling his eyes. "And we know she's a woman."

"Your father's not going to do anything stupid," I said.

"I hope you're right, Kathleen." He smiled again. "I'll call you about dinner."

I nodded.

Hercules watched Harry disappear around the side of the house. Then he looked at me and meowed. I leaned down and picked him up, heading back into the kitchen.

Before I could set him down the phone rang. I went back to the living room to answer it. It was Marcus.

"How was the rest of your afternoon?" he asked.

"Good," I said. "I have every program from the library relocated, and Harrison came for coffee. By the way, did you know Thorsten got a piercing?"

"You're kidding."

The seemingly straitlaced caretaker of the community center didn't seem like the type for a piercing.

I dropped onto the footstool, still holding on to the cat. Hercules kneaded my lap with his paws and stretched out. "No, I'm not."

"I just saw him about an hour ago. I didn't notice an earring."

"That's because it wasn't in an ear," I said, struggling not to laugh.

"Well then, where was— No, don't tell me. I don't want to know."

I did laugh then, picturing him holding up one hand and shaking his head even though I couldn't see either gesture.

"Okay, let's change the subject," I said. Hercules was eyeing me as though he was trying to figure out what was so funny. "How was the rest of your afternoon?"

"I went out to The Brick," Marcus said. "Mary's in Red Wing so I couldn't confirm Solomon's alibi with her. Did you know they record their amateur shows?"

"No," I said slowly.

"Solomon wasn't lying," he said. "Let's just say I've seen way more of him and Mary than I ever wanted to see."

"Oh, I know what you mean," I said. I heard him laugh on the other end of the phone. "So now what?"

He sighed and I pictured him running one hand back through his hair the way he did when he was frustrated. "I don't know. It looks like we're back to square one."

15

I'd planned to sleep in Saturday morning, but Owen had other ideas. He'd swatted my face with a paw and grumbled because I didn't seem to be getting dressed fast enough for him.

"Do you have plans this morning?" I asked as I followed him down to the kitchen.

"Merow!" he said loudly.

Owen had already started his breakfast when Hercules wandered in, yawning. He came over to me, leaned against my leg and eyed his brother curiously.

"He has plans," I said, reaching down to scratch the top of Herc's head.

I put half an English muffin in the toaster and scrambled an egg with onions, pepper and tomatoes. It made a very good breakfast sandwich—not quite what Eric served but delicious just the same.

Owen finished breakfast, washed his face and then headed toward the back door like a cat with a purpose. At the door he looked back over his shoulder and meowed sharply at me.

"I'm coming," I said, padding across the floor to let him out. I paused with my hand on the doorknob. "I didn't hear any 'please.' "

"Murp," he said, much to my amusement.

I opened both doors and let Owen out onto the back step. He headed down the stairs and I wondered if he was going to Rebecca's.

"I'm going to the library if I hear back from Marcus this morning," I said.

That got me another murp, but he didn't even slow down.

I finished my breakfast, threw a load of bedding in the washer and then sat at the table, making a list of things I wanted from the Farmers' Market, with Hercules settled on my lap. "Do you think the Jam Lady will have any marmalade?" I asked.

The cat's whiskers twitched. He liked the occasional dab of marmalade on a sardine cracker, information we didn't share with Roma.

I pulled on my hoodie and got my cloth shopping bags from the hall closet. Hercules followed me out into the porch and watched while I tied my sneakers. He looked a little at loose ends to me.

"You want to come for a ride in the truck?" I asked, canting my head in the direction of the driveway and feeling a little foolish as I said the words. At least half of a cat's life was spent lying around at loose ends, as far as I could see.

He had been washing the white fur on his chest. He lifted his head, shook himself and then went to sit by the outside door. That was a yes.

I stood in the middle of the backyard and called

Owen several times. There was no sign of him. Hercules meowed at me from the steps. "I know," I said. "He's probably over at Rebecca's mooching a treat. Let's go."

I found a parking spot on the street not too far from the market. "I won't be very long," I told the cat, grabbing a bag from the floor on the passenger side of the truck. He stretched out on the seat.

"Maybe we'll go to Tubby's when I'm done," I said, "as long as you promise not to tell Roma—or your brother." I wasn't really sure who would be more annoyed to find out I'd let Hercules have a taste of Tubby's bestselling strawberry frozen yogurt: the cat or the vet.

I'd long since come to the conclusion that not only were the boys not exactly ordinary house cats; they didn't have the digestive systems of regular cats, either. But I didn't want to take any chances on their health, so when Roma had gotten after me about feeding them people food, I'd gotten a lot stricter about what they ate.

Hercules looked at me and at the same time crossed one paw over the other. Was that cat for "cross my heart"? It was good enough for me.

I got some onions, a dozen brown eggs, the marmalade and some spring lettuce and onions from the greenhouse Taylor King's parents kept. I was just about to head back to the truck when I bumped—literally—into Diana Holmes. I was surprised to see the owner—or to be exact, half owner—of the Weston drawing. I hadn't had any contact with her since Margo's death.

"I'm sorry," she said, reaching down to pick up the bag of lettuce she'd knocked from my hand. "I had my eye on a red velvet cupcake and wasn't paying attention to where I was going." She was wearing a long, slim black-and-white-patterned skirt with a white cotton sweater and a short jean jacket. I felt a little under-dressed in jeans and a hooded sweatshirt.

"It's all right," I said. "I've been distracted by Georgia's cupcakes more than once myself." I took my lettuce from her and put it back in my shopping bag. "I didn't realize you were still in town."

Diana smiled with more politeness than genuine warmth. "Marshall has been discussing some business with Everett Henderson. He decided to stay for a few more days. It's such a lovely little town, even with everything that happened, I thought I'd do the same."

"I'm sorry about the Weston drawing being stolen," I said.

She nodded. "So am I. It was my father's favorite piece in his collection."

It seemed to me I could see a glimpse of real sadness in her expression for a moment.

"I'm trying not to lose sight of what's really important," she continued. "The drawing is . . . a thing. And it was insured. I just want the police to find whoever killed Margo Walsh."

"So do I," I said.

"Have you heard anything?" she asked.

I shook my head. "No. But Mayville Heights has an excellent police department. They'll find whoever did this."

"That's good to hear." She gave me the polite smile again. "It was nice to see you, Kathleen," she said. "Enjoy your weekend."

I walked back to the truck, wondering what kind of business Everett was doing with Marshall Holmes.

I put the shopping bags on the floor of the passenger side. Hercules leaned over to sniff each one and then straightened up and looked at me.

"Yes, we're going to Tubby's," I said.

I parked by the waterfront and Hercules and I sat in the truck with the windows rolled partway down and enjoyed a small cup of creamy, icy strawberry frozen yogurt. I got Hercules his own flat-paddle wooden spoon and gave him a couple of tastes. Then he curled up on the seat next to me with a sigh of contentment. He was so relaxed that when my phone buzzed on the seat next to him he started and almost fell onto the floor.

I put one hand on his back and picked up the cell with the other. It was Marcus.

"Where are you?" he asked.

"I'm at Tubby's, sitting in the truck with Hercules eating frozen yogurt."

"Why? Was Owen busy?"

"As a matter of fact, he was," I said. Hercules turned his head to lick a tiny smear of yogurt off the side of my thumb.

Marcus laughed, the sound tickling my ear as it came through the phone. "Do you still want to clear the book drop?" he asked.

"Please," I said.

"I can meet you at the library in about fifteen minutes."

That didn't give me time to take Hercules home. "The only problem is, like I said, I have Hercules with me." The cat looked up at me and narrowed his green eyes as though he didn't like be referred to as a problem.

"That's not a problem," Marcus said. "He can't hurt anything. We've wrapped up everything we want to do in the building. We're releasing it back to you. You could probably reopen on Monday."

I leaned against the back of the seat as relief flooded my body. "I'm going to need to get the cleaners in, and there are stacks of books to reshelve. And I'll have to call Gavin to see if we can get the artwork moved on Monday. Maybe we should wait and reopen Tuesday." I rummaged in my purse, looking for a pen and the notebook I usually carried.

"Kathleen, take a breath," Marcus said.

"What?" I said.

"Take a breath," he repeated. "You don't have to do everything at once."

"You're right," I said. "How about Hercules and I come and meet you and we'll go from there?"

"I'll see you in a few minutes," he said.

Hercules sat up, took a couple of passes at his face with a paw and then looked expectantly at me.

Marcus was waiting by his SUV in the library parking lot. I popped Hercules into the spare shopping bag I'd brought with me and got out of the truck. I knew there was no point in leaving him in the truck when he didn't want to stay there. He'd just climb out through the door—literally—and how would I explain that to Marcus?

"Hi," I said as we walked over to him.

"Hi," he said, leaning down to kiss me. "Hey, Hercules," he said to the little black-and-white cat, who was poking his head out of the top of the bag.

"Merow," the cat said.

Marcus let us into the building, and before I could take more than a few steps toward the checkout desk, Hercules jumped out of the bag, shook himself and looked around. "No, no, no," I said, reaching for him. "You need to stay with me."

Marcus turned to look at me. "It's okay, Kathleen," he said. "We're finished in here. He can't hurt anything."

The cat gave me a look and headed straight for Curtis, who was in his usual spot.

"Is this your cat?" the guard asked.

I started toward them. "Yes. This is Hercules. Please don't try to pet him. He was feral. He doesn't have the best people skills."

Curtis laughed. "Yeah, people say that about me, too." He looked at the cat. "Hello, Hercules," he said.

"Merow," the cat answered. He considered the security guard for a moment and then moved around the circulation desk.

I handed a take-out container of coffee to Curtis. I'd gotten it from Tubby's before we left. "I thought you might like a cup," I said. The creamer and a couple of sugar packets were on top.

Curtis smiled at me. With his bushy eyebrows and nose that looked as though it had been broken at least once, he was an imposing man—a good trait for a security guard—but when he smiled his expression was transformed.

"Thank you, Ms. Paulson," he said. "I was a bit late getting started this morning, so I'm like my old truck that leaks oil; I'm down a quart."

Hercules was still prowling around, checking every-thing out. Marcus was doing the same, I realized, mi-nus the whisker twitching.

"What are you looking for?" I asked. Marcus turned to look at me. Hercules kept nosing around.

"Are you talking to me or him?" Marcus asked, ges-turing to the cat, who was sniffing the edge of one of the metal pylons that was restricting access to the ex-hibit area.

"You," I said.

He shrugged. "I don't know, exactly. Something, anything that we might have missed."

"You'll figure this out," I said. "You always do."

Hercules was still sniffing the pylon. His pink tongue came out and he gave the shiny metal surface a tentative lick. "Leave that alone," I called to him.

He gave a sharp meow but otherwise ignored me.

I walked over to the cat. "Don't lick that," I said firmly. "You don't know what's on it."

Of the two cats, Owen was the one who had finicky little quirks about his food, but I'd never seen Hercules do something as undignified as lick a metal post.

He looked up at me, put a paw on the base of the metal pylon, and meowed again. I knew that insistent tone. It meant, "Look at this."

I leaned over to look at the spot he'd licked. "Move your foot," I said.

He obligingly lifted his white-tipped paw. There was a tiny smear of what looked like blue paint on the shiny metal.

Curtis joined me. "That's paint," he said.

"Don't eat that," I said to Hercules.

His green eyes met mine and he licked his lips.

"What is it?" Marcus asked. He'd walked over and was standing behind Hercules. The cat looked up at him and then back at the pylon. As far-fetched as it seemed, I knew there was some connection he was waiting for me to make.

"I'm not sure," I said slowly. I scraped a tiny speck of the paint off the pylon with a nail and then sniffed the end of my finger, hoping that I wasn't inhaling some obscure, drug-resistant bacteria.

"What are you doing?" Marcus said, pulling a face like I'd just scraped a piece of gum off my shoe and started chewing it.

Herc's green gaze was fixed on my face, and even though no one else would have believed it, I could see a gleam of expectation in his eyes.

"It smells like egg," I said, more to the cat than to Marcus, wondering at the same time if it was just my imagination at work.

Hercules sat back on his haunches then, seemingly satisfied that he'd made his point.

"No one was in here eating eggs," Curtis said.

The cat shot him a look of disdain as only a cat could do.

Hercules had been having a sardine and a slice of hard-boiled egg every Sunday since the weather got warmer. We'd sit in the backyard and I'd have coffee while the boys had their Sunday treat. Hercules had developed a fondness for the hard-boiled egg. It really wasn't that big a surprise that his nose had discovered the small splotch of paint.

"Egg tempera," I said slowly.

"Paint," Marcus said.

I nodded. "It's a mixture of pigment, egg and something to keep the egg from drying out too fast; water, vinegar, Maggie says some artists even use wine."

He crouched down beside me and studied the pale blue dab on the pylon base. Then he looked at me.

"That's fresh paint, not a flake of old paint that fell off something and stuck," I said.

"So one of the artists had wet paint on a shoe or a pants leg and brushed against this at some point. You said yourself that Maggie and the others were in and out a lot in the days before the art from the museum arrived."

I shook my head. "No. These are brand-new pylons. I helped take them out of the box and set them up right after we closed the library on Thursday."

"Was Maggie here after that?" he asked. "Or any of the others?"

"No," I said. "Just Margo and Gavin and the staff from the museum who came with the artwork."

He looked at Curtis. "Did Mr. Solomon bring anyone else in here while you've been here?"

Curtis shook his head. "Every time he's been here, he's been alone, except for Detective Lind."

"Okay, thanks," Marcus said.

The guard went back to his chair.

Hercules was watching us intently, head turning from side to side as we talked.

"Rena Adler paints with egg tempera," I said, getting to my feet. I remembered seeing a dab of blue paint on her finger. "She's the only local artist in the exhibit who does."

Marcus stood up as well. He looked at me and shook

his head. "I see where you're going with this, Kathleen, but it's a pretty big leap from someone paints with a particular kind of paint to saying they killed someone." He pulled his hand back through his hair and as he did I remembered Harry Junior making the same gesture as he stood in my porch Friday morning . . . talking about his brother . . . and Rena Adler.

I looked at Marcus. "Harry said she was asking Larry a lot of questions. He thought she was flirting with him and so did I, but what if she was fishing for information? She took him coffee." I pointed at the floor. "When he was working downstairs. Where the setup is for the temporary security system."

He stared at me for a long moment. Then he pulled his phone out.

"What are you doing?" I asked. I glanced at Hercules, who was washing his face. Clearly he figured his work was done.

"Bringing the crime scene techs back to take a closer look at that pylon and the others."

"I thought you said it was too big a leap," I said.

"Maybe it is," he said, "but I don't have anything else." He gave me a half smile. "So I may as well jump."

16

I took Hercules out to the truck while Marcus called in the crime scene team.

"Good job," I told him. "I promise you a sardine when we get home."

He licked his whiskers and then nuzzled my chin.

"Please stay here," I said.

"Mrrr," he replied obligingly as he curled up on the driver's seat.

"I won't be long," I promised.

I had just enough time to clear out the book drop and stack the books and magazines on several carts before Hope arrived.

"Hi, Kathleen," she said with a wry smile. "Looks like it's déjà vu all over again." She turned to Marcus. "Crime scene is right behind me."

"I'm going to get out of here," I said. I touched Marcus's arm. "Call me later."

He nodded. "I will."

Owen was sitting on the back steps when Hercules

and I got home. He looked from Hercules to me and narrowed his eyes.

"Yes, I took your brother with me," I said as I unlocked the door.

He made a grumbling noise almost under his breath. I leaned down to scratch behind his ear and he turned his face to one side, making it clear I was on ignore. "Next time come home when I call you," I said.

Owen stalked into the kitchen. He walked over to the basement door, pawed it open and disappeared down the stairs.

"Did you ever figure out what he's doing down there?" I asked Hercules as I put things away.

He gave me a blank look.

I gave Hercules a little piece of a sardine as a thank-you for his sleuthing. He ate it, washed his face and paws and followed me into the living room, curling up in a patch of sunshine on the rug for a nap while I returned e-mails and phone calls. Marcus didn't call until after supper.

"Any luck?" I asked.

"I can't really answer that," he said.

It was as good as a no. "What about the paint?" I asked. "Can you at least tell me if it's egg tempera?"

"It is," he said. I heard the squeak of his desk chair and knew from the sound that he was still at the station. "It proves nothing, Kathleen," he said, lowering his voice.

"It proves Rena Adler was at the library when she shouldn't have been," I said.

"No, it doesn't. All it proves it that someone got a bit of paint on that metal pylon at some point. It's not like it's her fingerprint in paint."

"I'm sorry," I said.

"Me too," he said. "It looks like you'll be able to get the building back on Tuesday. Hope will let you know for sure."

Hercules had raised his head and was listening to my side of the conversation.

"Are we still on for dinner tomorrow?" I asked.

"Absolutely," Marcus said, and I swear I could hear a smile creep into his voice. It made me smile as well. "I'm making my famed turkey Provençal."

"Sounds very fancy."

"Micah was impressed when I tried the recipe out on her."

I was grinning now. "Well, if Micah gave it two paws, I'm sure it'll be delicious," I said.

We said good night and I hung up the phone. Hercules was still watching me. "The paint isn't enough," I said.

He made a sour face.

"I know," I said.

I looked at the laptop sitting on the footstool. "Do you want to see if we can find out anything about Rena?" I asked.

Hercules got up, came over to my chair and meowed at the computer. I patted my legs. He jumped up and settled himself. I reached for the laptop.

There was very little to find online about Rena Adler. She had no online presence—no Web site, no Facebook page, no Twitter account. Since I didn't have any of those myself, it didn't strike me as odd, but what did was the fact that prior to two years ago Rena Adler hadn't seemed to exist. No matter what search terms or search engine I used, there was nothing to find about the woman back more than a couple of years.

I leaned back in the big wing chair. "It's as though she just appeared out of nowhere," I said to Hercules. "It doesn't make sense."

He looked at the phone.

I sighed. "Marcus will just say this doesn't mean anything." I looked at the name in the search box and scrolled down through the results again. There were more selections that had nothing to do with Rena Adler the artist than there were ones that did. There was even a link to a fan site for the Irene Adler character from the Sherlock Holmes world.

Irene Adler. Rena Adler.

"Is it really that simple?" I asked the cat.

I didn't wait for him to answer, assuming he was even going to. I typed the name "Rena" and "name meaning" in the search engine.

It seemed it really *was* as simple as that. The name Rena was of Hebrew origin. It meant joyful song. It was also a variation of the name Irene.

Rena Adler. It was a play on the name Irene Adler, the woman who bested Sherlock Holmes.

"The name's a fake," I said to Hercules. "That's why we couldn't find anything about her beyond two years ago. Rena Adler didn't exist before that."

I chewed my lip. Marcus would think I was crazy. Hercules was eyeing me as though maybe he was having the same thought.

"So let's just say, for the sake of argument, that Rena Adler used to have a different name. Who was she and why did she change it?"

My cell phone, on top of a stack of papers next to the chair, buzzed then. I leaned sideways for a look, one hand on the computer, the other holding Hercules. It was Gavin. I let it go to voice mail. I hadn't spoken to Gavin since we'd gotten back from Minneapolis and he'd shared his other alibi.

I thought about the conversation with Julian McCrea. Would I ever hear from the art dealer? I wondered. When Gavin had first mentioned the man, I'd had high hopes that talking to him would give us some kind of clue. I remembered how dismissive Marcus had been. I sighed. It looked like he was going to be right.

"Maybe Gavin had just been angling for a way to spend some time alone with me," I said.

Hercules narrowed his green eyes as though he was considering the possibility.

"After all, his other suggestion had been that the drawing had been stolen by some art thief/cat burglar."

"Merow!" Hercules said.

"No, not someone who steals cats. Someone who's stealthy like a cat."

I rubbed my right shoulder. I was having a conversation with a cat about cat burglars. No wonder the idea that Rena Adler had changed her name and was somehow connected to what had happened at the library seemed to make sense to me.

"She dropped out of sight about two years ago. It was like she just disappeared." That's what Gavin had said about Devin Rossi. Two years ago art thief Devin Rossi had disappeared and artist Rena Adler had suddenly appeared.

"Just because it's far-fetched doesn't mean it's not true," I told Hercules.

"Murp," he agreed.

I reached for the phone and called Gavin.

"Hi, Kathleen," he said. "I was just talking to Hope Lind. It looks like they're going to let you open the library on Tuesday. I just wanted to let you know it'll be next Thursday or Friday before the museum can retrieve the exhibit. They're still making space."

"Why?" I asked. I was beginning to think there was a metaphorical black cloud hovering over the library.

"I'm not sure, but I think the problem with the sprinkler system was worse than they're letting on."

I closed my eyes for a moment. "It's all right," I said. "We can make things work for a few days."

"I'll help any way I can," Gavin said. I realized from the background noise I could hear that he was probably in the bar at the St. James.

Hercules jumped down from my lap and started nosing around the pile of papers next to the chair. I shook my head. He shook his back at me and nudged the pile with his shoulder.

"Gavin, do you have a phone number for Julian McCrea?" I asked. I knew he did. He'd set up our luncheon, after all.

"I do," he said. "Why?"

The stack of papers Hercules had been poking at fell over then. He jumped backward and then looked guiltily up at me. I glared at him.

I couldn't exactly say I wanted to call the art dealer to find out what Devin Rossi looked like. Well, I could have, but I didn't want to.

"Kathleen, are you still there?" Gavin asked.

I switched the phone to my other hand. Hercules was wisely still out of my reach. "I'm sorry, Gavin. One of my cats just knocked a pile of papers over."

I could see my photo album on the bottom of the stack, the cover flipped open. Maggie had been looking at it the last time she'd been over, teasing me about my teenage tartan skirts and neon tights, and I hadn't put the book away.

Suddenly, I knew how to answer Gavin's question. "I have a photo of my mom onstage as Adelaide in *Guys and Dolls*. I thought maybe if Julian would like it, I'd send it to him as a thank-you for talking to us."

"I know what you're trying to do, Kathleen," Gavin said, a knowing edge to his voice.

"You do?" I said.

"You think if you offer to send the picture it might motivate him to ask around, see if he can learn anything about the Weston drawing."

"Something like that," I said.

"All right, fine," he finally said.

I reached down, grabbed a pad of paper from the floor and wrote down the number he gave me.

"Good luck, Kathleen," Gavin said. I heard a woman's voice in the background. "I have to go."

"I'll call you in the morning," I said. "Good night."

I set the phone down and looked at Hercules. He looked at me.

"I should be mad at you," I said.

The cat didn't so much as twitch a whisker.

"Between you and your brother I feel like all I do is pick up paper."

Still no reaction.

I glanced down at the photo album on the floor. Thanks to Hercules knocking things over I'd come up with a plausible reason to call Julian McCrea. And I would send him the photo if he wanted it. In a moment of levity my mother had signed it before she'd given it to me.

"Well," I said slowly. "You did help me. Indirectly. So I guess you're off the hook."

He blinked, turned and headed for the kitchen. He stopped in the doorway and looked expectantly back over his shoulder.

"Indirectly," I repeated. "That doesn't warrant a treat."

"Murp," he said, disappearing—not literally—around the doorway.

I padded out to the kitchen and gave Hercules a second tiny bite of sardine, because who was I kidding? We both knew I was going to. Owen wandered in, looked at his brother eating and then looked at me.

"What did you do to warrant a treat?" I asked.

He seemed to think for a minute, then tipped his head to one side and gave me his "I'm so adorable" look. "Oh, for heaven's sake," I said. Then I got him a chunk of the little fish.

"You're both spoiled," I said, leaning against the counter. "Your character has been weakened."

They looked at each other. Something passed wordlessly between them and then they dropped their heads and went back to eating.

Since Owen and Hercules were having a treat I decided I'd have one as well. I made a cup of hot chocolate and took it to the table with the last cinnamon roll.

"Am I crazy?" I said.

Neither cat even bothered to look up at me.

My cell phone was sitting in the middle of the table. I had Julian McCrea's number now. There was nothing to stop me from calling him and asking about Devin Rossi. Nothing except the fact that the more I thought about it, the more preposterous my idea seemed. An art thief who had been stealing from museums and galleries all over North America changes her name, retires to Red Wing, Minnesota, to live the quiet life of an artist, then comes out of retirement to steal a drawing from an exhibit in my library.

"I think it might have been an episode of *Murder, She Wrote*," I muttered, mostly to myself.

On the other hand . . . *"It's better to do something and know than not do it and wonder."* How many times had I heard my mother say those words?

I got up and retrieved the piece of paper with Julian McCrea's phone number. When I came back to the kitchen, both cats were sitting next to my chair and two furry faces were pointed in my direction. I took it as a vote of support.

Julian McCrea answered his phone on the fourth ring. "Good evening, Kathleen," he said smoothly. He must have had caller ID.

I smiled, hoping it would come through in my voice. "Good evening, Julian," I said. "I hope I haven't taken you from anything important."

"You haven't," he replied. "What can I do for you?"

"I have a photograph of my mother in character as Adelaide. It's even signed. You mentioned you were a bit of a fan. I'd like to send it to you as a small thank-you for meeting with me. Is there an address I could use?"

"That's very thoughtful," he said. "Do you have a pen?"

I did. He gave me a post office box address and I wrote it underneath his phone number.

"I'm sorry that I don't have any more information for you," Julian said.

"It's all right," I said. "I understand. I don't think this is going to be an easy case to solve."

"The police aren't any closer to figuring out who took the Weston drawing?"

I shifted in my chair, pulling one foot up underneath me. "Or who killed Margo Walsh. No." I hesitated. "Do you remember we spoke about Devin Rossi?"

"Let me guess," Julian said. "Gavin still thinks that perhaps she was the thief." I could hear the amusement in his voice.

I tried to match his tone. "I know it's kind of silly to think an art thief came to a small town in Minnesota to steal a drawing that isn't even worth that much money."

"No offense, Kathleen, but, yes, a little."

"We're all kind of grasping at straws," I said. "So I hope you won't think less of me if I ask if you know what Devin Rossi looks like. Is she possibly quite tall—over six feet, with an athletic frame? There was a woman like that in the library the day before the picture was stolen and Margo was killed."

Rena Adler was probably a couple of inches shorter than I was. The person I'd described *had* been in the library the day before Margo's murder. She was the women's basketball coach at the high school.

I didn't know if Julian McCrea's business dealings were legitimate or not. I didn't want anyone to know what I suspected, just in case.

"I'm sorry," Julian said. "I met a woman I believe was Devin Rossi once at a party for the Antony Williams exhibit about three years ago at the Weyman Gallery in Chicago. Without heels I don't think she's as tall as you are. She had blond hair and, I think, blue eyes. I'm sorry, that's all I can tell you."

"I guess that would just be too easy an answer," I said. "Again, thank you for talking to me. I'll get the photo in the mail to you."

"It was my pleasure, Kathleen," he said. "Good night."

I ended the call and set the phone back on the table. Then I got up and went into the living room for my laptop. Rena Adler had blue eyes. Except for the hair color—which could easily be changed—Julian's description of Devin Rossi could easily have been Rena, or, I had to admit, a million other women. Julian had said he'd met Devin Rossi at a party in Chicago. Was it possible there were photos from that party online? There were. But I couldn't find Rena Adler in any of them.

"It's her," I told the boys. "I know I'm right. So how am I going to convince Marcus?"

The cats exchanged glances. Then they looked at the refrigerator. Clearly this was going to take more thought. And more sardines.

I warmed up my cocoa and went back to the table. I still had half a cinnamon roll on my plate. The idea of an art thief living in Red Wing and coming to Mayville Heights to steal the Sam Weston drawing might sound far-fetched, but I was starting to think it was possible.

But how was I going to prove that Rena Adler was that art thief? And, as much as it made me uncomfortable to think about, Margo's killer?

Owen came over to my chair. Without waiting for an invitation he launched himself onto my lap.

"Hello," I said.

He nuzzled my cheek, then leaned around me and tried to lick my cup.

"Forget it," I said. "Hot chocolate is not for cats." I set the cup on the table and realized that it hadn't been the hot chocolate Owen had been trying to get at. There was a smudge of icing from the roll on the side of the blue porcelain. I swiped it with my finger and licked off the icing.

Owen grumbled in protest.

"Cinnamon rolls are definitely not cat food," I told him.

His expression said he wasn't convinced.

I reached for my cup. I'd left a smear of icing behind on the blue porcelain. And my fingerprint in sugar, butter and vanilla.

I shook my finger at Owen. He followed it, looking almost cross-eyed. "That's how we can prove who Rena Adler really is."

Owen shook his head and focused on my face instead.

"Marcus said that there was one partial print from one of her robberies. All we need to do is get Rena's fingerprints."

The cat looked at me, almost as though he was wondering how I was going to do that. I looked over at the mixer sitting on the counter.

"Don't worry," I said. "I have a plan."

17

Marcus liked to tease that I thought pretty much any problem could be solved with a plate of brownies. That wasn't true. I thought a blueberry muffin or a nice coffee cake would also work.

"This problem calls for a coffee cake," I told Owen. He licked his whiskers.

I reached for my phone and called Maggie. "I didn't take you away from some romantic moment, did I?" I asked.

She gave a snort of laughter. "Not unless you think snaking the toilets at the shop is romantic. What's up?"

"It doesn't look like the library is going to open for a few more days. I was thinking of making a coffee cake tomorrow and wondered if you were up for a coffee break Monday morning. You're going to be in your studio, aren't you?"

"Uh-huh," she said. "I'd love some of your coffee cake."

"Are Ruby and Rena going to be around?" I asked. "Maybe they could join us."

"What are you up to?" Maggie said.

"I'm not up to anything." I was glad that she couldn't see my face.

Somehow Owen knew it was Maggie on the other end of the phone. He was trying to push his face in against it. "Owen's trying to say hello," I said.

"Hey fur ball," she said.

He heard her. He leaned his head against my hand and started to purr.

"He's purring," I said.

"And you're not being straight with me, Kath."

I exhaled softly. "I just want to talk to Rena and I don't want to make a big deal out of it."

"Does this have to do with what happened at the library?" Maggie lowered her voice. That told me that someone probably was with her, most likely Brady Chapman.

I hesitated. I didn't want Maggie mixed up in the middle of this.

"I won't help you if you don't tell me what you're up to," she said. I was surprised by the determination in her voice. "We could have lost you in that fire before Christmas." She stopped and I heard her swallow.

Maggie, Owen and I had been caught in a burning building back in December in a fire started by the person who had killed Brady Chapman's mother. Maggie had managed to get out, but Owen and I had been trapped for a while. Maggie still blamed herself for not being able to get us out.

"Mags, I'm fine. I'm not going to do anything dangerous or stupid." I knew I had to tell her more. "I want to talk to Rena because I think maybe . . . maybe she hasn't been completely honest about her background. Remember that art dealer Gavin and I went to Minneapolis to talk to?"

"Yes," she said slowly.

"Not all of his business is legitimate, and I think Rena may know him."

"Does Marcus know what you're doing?" she asked.

For a moment I thought about lying. "No," I said.

"Are you going to tell him?"

"If there's anything to tell, I will." I shifted Owen sideways a little so I could reach my cup. That meant he couldn't keep his head next to the phone. He made a face at me.

"All right," Maggie said. "It had better be a really good coffee cake."

"Rhubarb streusel."

"Give the furry one a kiss from me," she said.

"Thanks, Mags," I said.

I put the phone on the table. Then I picked up Owen and kissed the top of his head. "From Maggie," I said. I knew he understood what I'd said because he started purring again.

I got to Riverarts at about five minutes to ten on Monday morning. I carried the coffee cake up to Maggie's top-floor studio. She was standing in front of a large piece of particleboard propped on her easel. I tapped on the open door. "Good morning," I said.

She turned around. "Hi, Kathleen," she said. "Is it ten already?"

I nodded. "Uh-huh."

She rolled her eyes. "That means I've been standing

here staring at this for the last twenty minutes and I'm still no closer to figuring out what color I want to use on the background."

"What are you working on?" I asked.

The piece of wood was at least two feet wide by three feet high.

"It's a collage for Riverwatch, all things I found washed up on shore. They're starting a public information campaign to make people aware of what's ending up in the water." She moved over to her sink and reached for the kettle. "And you wouldn't believe what ends up in the water."

"I hope it helps," I said.

"Me too," she said. "Sometimes it's easier if people see what goes into the river instead of just hearing about it."

She filled the kettle and plugged it in. I set my cake keeper on the counter. I knew Maggie had plates and forks, but I'd brought napkins.

She picked one up. "I like these," she said with a grin. The design was cartoon cats on a dark blue background. "That one looks like Owen," she said, pointing to a cat in the upper left corner. "Where did you get these?"

"My mother found them somewhere," I said. "She thought that cat looked like Owen and the one just to the right of the middle could be Hercules."

Maggie squinted at the paper square. "She's right," she said. "I forgot to tell you, she e-mailed me on Friday."

I took off my heavy sweater and draped it over one of the stools at the work island in the middle of the room.

"My mother e-mailed you?"

Maggie nodded. "You know that she's taking one of her classes to New York for a theater weekend."

I nodded.

"She said she's going to join the crowd outside the *Today* show and see if she can get Matt Lauer's autograph for me." Maggie's blue eyes were sparkling.

"If anyone can do it, my mother can," I said.

Ruby poked her head around the doorway then. "Are we having cake?" she asked. Her hair was mint green with a black streak at the front.

"Rhubarb streusel coffee cake," I said, grinning at her.

"Is Rena around?" Maggie asked.

"She's downstairs," Ruby said. "I saw her about fifteen minutes ago. You want me to ask her to join us?"

Maggie nodded. "I've been wanting to ask her about maybe doing a workshop when we get the new space finished at the shop."

"Be right back," Ruby said.

Maggie gave me a look and then went to get plates and forks from her storage cabinet. "Tea or hot chocolate?" she asked.

"Hot chocolate, please," I said. Despite Maggie's efforts, I wasn't a big fan of herbal tea, but I liked cocoa almost as much as coffee.

Rena Adler paused in the doorway of the studio when Ruby returned with her. "Are you sure I'm not intruding on anything?" she asked. She was wearing gray yoga pants with her hair pulled back in a low ponytail.

"You're not intruding on anything," Maggie said. "Kathleen brought coffee cake."

I turned from where I was slicing the cake and smiled. "Hi, Rena," I said.

"Hi, Kathleen," she said.

"Tea or cocoa?" Maggie asked.

"Cocoa, if it's not too much trouble," Rena said.

Ruby was already perched on a stool at the center workspace. "Hey, Kathleen, when is the library going to reopen?" she asked.

"It looks like the end of the week," I said, handing her a piece of cake.

Rena took the seat beside her and I gave her the other plate I was holding.

"Does Marcus have any leads?" Maggie asked as she brought mugs to the table. She gave Rena a sideways glance. "Kathleen's boyfriend is a detective."

I turned to pick up the other two plates. "Nothing he's telling me about," I said.

"What happens to the rest of the artwork?" Rena asked. She ate a forkful of cake and then smiled. "Oh, Kathleen, this is good!"

"Thank you," I said. I reached for the container of marshmallows Maggie had set in the middle of the table and dropped two into my cup. "The artwork is all going back to the museum. The rest of the stops for the exhibit have been called off."

"That bites," Ruby said around a mouthful of cake.

"It does," I agreed. "And I'm sorry you all lost your chance to have your work be part of the exhibit here at the library."

Maggie smiled over the top of her tea. "It just wasn't meant to be. Something else will come along."

"Hey, Kathleen, any chance we could put together

an exhibit of local art at the library, maybe this summer?" Ruby asked. "I know it wouldn't pull in as many people as the museum artwork would have, but there are a lot of tourists in town then."

"I'll have to run it by the board, but I like the idea," I said. "Would you be willing to put together something in writing that I can take to them?"

Ruby shrugged. "Sure." She looked at Maggie. "That okay?"

"Yes," Maggie said. "And maybe we could coordinate some workshops at the store. Oren should have everything finished by summer." She turned to Rena and smiled. "Would you think about coming and doing a workshop in egg tempera?"

Rena nodded. "If I'm in town, absolutely."

"How did you start working in egg tempera, anyway?" Ruby asked, shifting sideways on her stool to look at Rena.

"I liked the effect," Rena said, brushing a loose tendril of hair back off her cheek. "I started playing around, but believe it or not, it was actually a weekend workshop that got me hooked."

"How did you end up in Red Wing?" I asked.

She smiled across the table. "Would you believe I saw a short video about Red Wing online and fell in love with the town?"

Maggie's mouth was full but she began to nod.

"The man with the springer spaniel?" I said.

Rena nodded.

"That's Morgan," Maggie said. "The dog, I mean. Tim, his owner, is a documentary filmmaker. He grew up in Red Wing."

"Where did you live before Red Wing?" Ruby asked as she speared another piece of cake. I wanted to hug her. She was asking most of the questions I'd been going to ask.

"Pretty much everywhere. My dad designs recycling plants. We'd spend a year or two somewhere and then move on. Living in Red Wing may be the longest I've ever stayed in one place." She looked at the three of us. "What about you? Did you all grow up here?"

"Ruby and I did," Maggie said. She slid off her stool and headed for the kettle. "Kathleen came here from Boston to supervise renovations at the library."

"And you fell in love with Mayville Heights," Rena said.

Ruby looked up from her plate. "More like with a certain police detective."

I felt my cheeks getting red. "That's not the only reason I decided to stay," I said. "I really do like living here. And there's Owen and Hercules."

Rena looked confused. "Owen and Hercules?"

"My cats," I said. "They kind of think they're people. I don't think they'd do well in the city." I looked over at Maggie, who had just put more water in the kettle and plugged it in again. "They're a bit spoiled."

"Owen and Hercules are not like other cats," Maggie said. "They're very intelligent."

That was an understatement, I thought.

"Wait a minute," Rena said, gesturing at Ruby with her fork. "I saw those paintings you did. Were those Kathleen's cats?"

Ruby grunted a yes because her mouth was full of

cake. She swallowed and began to tell Rena about the boys posing for her.

Rena Adler was very good at deflecting any conversation away from herself, I realized. I was even more convinced that she was hiding something. But was I right that she was really Devin Rossi? And even more important, had she killed Margo?

As I listened to her and Ruby talk, with occasional comments added by Maggie, I found myself hoping I was wrong. Rena was funny, kind in her comments about other artists' work without being fake or cloying. I could see both Maggie and Ruby liked her.

After about another ten minutes or so, Ruby got to her feet and stretched. "I need to get back to work," she said. She smiled across the table. "Thanks for the cake, Kathleen. And the tea, Maggie."

"You're welcome," I said.

"I'll put something together on that art exhibit idea and e-mail it to you if that's okay?" she said.

I nodded. "That's good."

Ruby looked at Maggie. "You'll be down at the shop this afternoon?"

"I'm meeting Oren there at one o'clock," she said.

Rena slid off her stool. "I should get back to work as well." She looked from me to Maggie. "This was fun. Thank you."

"I'm glad you joined us," Maggie said. She tipped her head in my direction. "Kathleen makes great brownies, too."

"Was that a hint?" I teased.

She nodded. "It was."

Rena smiled at us. "See you later," she said.

I watched her head down the hall, waving at Ruby as she passed her studio door. I closed Maggie's door and turned around to discover she'd taken all the cups and plates over to the sink. So much for my plan. I closed my eyes and blew out a breath.

"It's in a bag on the counter," Maggie said.

I opened my eyes. "What's on the counter?"

She turned from the sink. "Rena's cup. That's what you wanted, isn't it? Something with her fingerprints?" She gestured at the brown paper bag sitting next to the kettle.

"How did you know?" I asked walking over to her.

She turned off the tap. "Did you notice how Rena deflected any questions about herself? When Ruby asked where she'd lived before she moved to Red Wing she didn't name a place. She said 'everywhere.'"

I leaned against the wooden cabinet. "I noticed."

"That's not the first time she's done that," Maggie said, reaching for the small towel she kept on a hook next to the sink. "She did the same thing with Susan one of the times we were at the library." She dried her hands. "I think she's hiding something."

I nodded. "I think you're right."

Maggie raked a hand through her blonde curls. "She didn't kill Margo Walsh."

"I like her too, Mags," I said, gently.

"I'm not saying that just because I like her. She doesn't give off that kind of energy." She shook her head. "I'm not saying she's not keeping secrets, because it's pretty obvious she is. I just don't think killing Margo is one of them."

I looked over at the paper bag. "I hope you're right."

I left Riverarts and walked over to Eric's. I'd left the truck in the library parking lot. It was too early for lunch, but a large cup of coffee sounded pretty good.

Nic Sutton was working. "Hi, Kathleen," he said. "What can I get you?"

"Two large coffees to go," I said.

"I just put a new pot on," he said. "If you can wait for a couple of minutes you can have a fresh cup."

"Sounds good," I said. "Thanks."

I dropped onto one of the padded stools at the counter and pulled out my phone, hoping I'd get Marcus and not his voice mail. I couldn't help smiling when I heard his voice.

"Do you have time for a break?" I asked.

"I'd love one," he said. I imagined him leaning back at his desk and stretching his arms over his head. "Where are you?"

"I'm at Eric's," I said.

"I'll be there in about five minutes."

I was just snapping lids on the paper take-out cups when Marcus walked in to the café. I walked over to meet him. "How about a walk along the trail?" I asked.

"Fine with me," he said.

I handed him his coffee and we left the restaurant, crossing the street to walk along the path that curved along the water's edge.

"How was your morning?" I asked.

"Too much paperwork," he said. He took a sip of his coffee and made a little murmur of happiness. "Why is Eric's coffee so much better than the coffee at the station?"

"Because they don't buy the coffee beans at the Dollar Store. Because no one pounds on the top of the coffeemaker when they think it's not making coffee fast enough. Because they actually wash the carafe once in a while." I ticked off the reasons on my fingers.

He shot me a sidelong glance. "That was a rhetorical question," he said, taking another sip.

"Marcus, did you or Hope talk to an artist named Rena Adler?" I asked.

He frowned at the change of subject and stared off into the distance for a moment. "She's one of the local artists, isn't she? Hope talked to her." He stopped walking. "Why?"

I took a drink to buy a moment. "Because I don't think Rena Adler is her real name." I held up one hand. "Hear me out before you say anything."

He caught the hand in his own and gave it a squeeze. "I will," he said. Then he smiled. "I will," he repeated.

I took a deep breath. "Do you remember Gavin telling us about Devin Rossi, the art thief?"

Marcus nodded. "Yes." He gave my hand another squeeze before he let go of it. We started walking again.

"Devin Rossi seemed to disappear two years ago. At the same time Rena Adler seemed to appear out of nowhere." I took a sip from my cup. "I called Julian McCrea. He met Devin Rossi once at a museum gala. Except for the hair color, his description of her could have been a description of Rena. And . . ." I paused.

"And what?" Marcus asked. He gave the take-out cup a shake and took another drink.

"And she's evasive about her past. She manages to deflect any questions anyone asks about where she lived or what she used to do." I waited for Marcus to tell me this was a police investigation and I should stay out of it.

"I know," is what he did say.

"What do you mean, you know?" I said.

"She was evasive with Hope as well, and Hope couldn't find any more about the woman than you did."

I brushed my hair back off my face. "Do you remember telling me that there was a partial fingerprint from an art heist that was probably Devin Rossi's?"

His blue eyes narrowed. "I remember," he said, slowly.

I held up the paper bag. "Rena Adler's fingerprints are on the mug in this bag."

"I can't use that in court."

We'd stopped walking again.

"I know," I said. "But Rena or Devin or whoever she is doesn't know that."

Marcus shifted from one foot to the other. "If—*if* for the sake of argument Rena Adler is Devin Rossi, she probably does know that."

I exhaled loudly. "Okay, but if the fingerprints tell you that Rena isn't, well, Rena, you can at least talk to her again. You don't have to tell her how you know."

He may have been frustrated, but I could see a gleam of interest in his blue eyes.

I laid a hand on his arm. "Marcus, Rena Adler is Devin Rossi. I'm certain of it."

"Because she doesn't like talking about her past? Or because she looks like the woman Julian McCrea described to you?"

"Because of her name."

He looked surprised and his eyes shifted uncertainly from side to side. Obviously that hadn't been the answer he was expecting. "I don't understand."

"The name Rena. It can be a variation of Irene."

"Irene Adler." I watched as the name registered with him. "The woman," he said slowly. "Sherlock Holmes."

I nodded.

"It could just be a coincidence."

"But it's not," I said. "We have a reciprocal agreement with the library in Red Wing. People with library cards from their library can use them in ours and vice versa. Rena borrowed a couple of books from this library: *A Coffin for Dimitrios* and *The Murder of Roger Ackroyd*. Eric Ambler and Agatha Christie. Mystery classics." I exhaled slowly. "Marcus, I'm not wrong about this."

He looked out across the water for a long moment, as if somehow the answers might be bobbing on the water. Then he turned back to me. "All right," he said, holding out his hand.

I gave him the bag.

"You know it's a long shot," he warned.

"Not to me," I said. I smiled up at him. "Anyway, we were a long shot."

"Point taken," he said, and the look he gave me made my insides feel as wobbly as a bowl of Jell-O salad at a Fourth of July picnic.

We turned around then and walked back to Eric's.

"Where's the truck?" Marcus asked, looking around.

"I left it at the library. It was such a nice day I decided to walk over to Riverarts."

"I can drop you," he said.

I shook my head. "Thanks, but I think I'll walk."

He reached for my free hand and gave it a squeeze. "I'll talk to you later," he said.

My coffee wasn't that hot anymore, but I finished it as I walked to the library. I wasn't going to waste a perfectly good cup just because of the temperature. Marshall Holmes was coming toward me on the sidewalk as I came level with the building. He raised a hand in greeting.

"Good morning," I said as he got closer.

"Good morning, Kathleen," he said. He glanced at the building. "Are you reopening?"

I shook my head. "Not for a few more days."

"I guess it's a good thing I have my e-reader, then." He smiled. "I admit I like a paper book better, though."

I smiled back at him. "If people didn't like paper books I'd be out of a job."

Marshall looked over at the building again. "I'm sorry if I'm being intrusive, but are there any leads in Margo Walsh's death?"

"I'm not really sure," I said. "The police are still investigating."

"I didn't know Margo very well," he said. "But I hope they find whoever killed her."

"So do I," I said. "And I hope you get your drawing back as well."

"It's not what's important," Marshall said. "But thank you." He glanced at his watch. "It was good to see you, Kathleen. I'm going to be in town for a few more days. I'll be in for some 'real' books."

"I'll see you then," I said.

Marcus arrived just before suppertime.

"So?" I said, turning from the stove to look at him.

"So you were right."

"I knew it," I said. Hercules and Owen were sitting at my feet and I would have high-fived them both if they'd known how. And if they'd had hands. "Are you going to ask her to come in to answer more questions?"

"I'm not sure that's the best way to go about things," he said, peeling off his jacket. He paused for a moment. "What happened to the local pieces that were part of the exhibit? Are they still at the library?"

Owen looked at me, yawned and headed for the basement door. Bored with the conversation or heading for his lair in the cellar, I wasn't sure.

"They are," I said. "Gavin and I were going to see if we could return them to the artists sometime in the next few days." Hercules leaned against my leg.

"Could you return Rena Adler's artwork, say, tomorrow? And without Solomon?"

"I don't see why not," I said. "What are you thinking? You don't want to question Rena at the police station?"

"No, I don't," he said. "I don't want to question her in any kind of official way at all. If I do that, she's likely to request a lawyer."

"You're having second thoughts."

"I don't want to do anything to jeopardize the investigation. Like I told you, I can't use those fingerprints as evidence."

"But if you have a conversation with her at the library, anything you learn is evidence," I said.

"It's a fine line, but yes," he said.

"Okay. How about this? Gavin has a meeting in Minneapolis with the insurance company. He won't be back until after lunch. I'll call Rena and see if I can set something up for midmorning. Then when Gavin gets back he and I can return everyone else's pieces."

"Sounds good," Marcus said.

I called Rena after supper. Marcus had gone back to work. She was happy to hear she could get her paintings back. I felt a twinge of guilt as I set a time for her to meet me at the library the next morning. Owen cocked his head to one side and eyed me as I hung up the phone.

"I hate this part," I said to him with a sigh. "I like Rena."

"Merow," he said.

There really wasn't anything else to say.

18

The sun was shining in the morning and the sky was slash of blue overhead as though Mother Nature had taken a wide paintbrush to the sky, so I walked down Mountain Road to meet Marcus at the library. As soon as we were inside the building I headed for the book drop. There weren't nearly as many books and magazines as there had been in the past few days. I had enough time to take care of them before Rena showed up.

"I like her," I said to Marcus as I sorted the books onto carts.

"Any special reason?" he asked. He was leaning against the circulation desk, handing books and magazines to me.

I looked up at him. "I told you how she managed to change the subject anytime the conversation turned to anything personal?"

He nodded.

"Well, Ruby and I were talking about possibly having an exhibit of local artwork at the library this summer and maybe tying it into a workshop at the co-op. Maggie asked Rena if she'd been willing to do something with egg tempera. I was watching her."

"And?"

"She said yes and I believed her. I watched her body language." I held up a hand before he could say anything. "She could have said no. She could have made an excuse. For that matter, why did she stay in Mayville Heights at all once the show was canceled? If she killed Margo, why didn't she leave town? I know she's been working at the high school with Ruby, but she could have gotten out of that."

He ran his hand over the cover of a children's picture book. "I think there's jam on this one," he said.

I took the book and set it aside in a pile I was keeping for Abigail to repair.

"Maybe she stayed so she wouldn't look guilty," Marcus said. "Maybe she stayed to keep an eye on our investigation. Right now, I don't know."

I took the last magazine he handed me, set it on top of the others and got to my feet. I glanced at my watch. "Rena should be here soon," I said. "I'll go watch for her."

Marcus straightened up. "I'll do that," he said. He went to wait between the double doors and I wandered over to stand in the entrance to the exhibit area. Marcus had sent Curtis out for coffee. I looked around the space. I remembered Margo working with Larry Taylor to make sure the lighting was absolutely perfect.

I felt a lump in my throat. It seemed that her passing hadn't really left a hole in anyone's life.

I had my crazy family as well as Lise and my other

friends back in Boston. I had Marcus and Maggie and Rebecca and Harrison and so many special people here in Mayville Heights. I liked Rena Adler, but I had also liked Margo, for all her perfectionism, and I wanted whoever had killed her brought to justice. Somebody had to fight for Margo, and it looked like that was going to be me.

I heard voices behind me. Rena had arrived and Marcus was letting her in.

"Hi, Kathleen," she said as she stepped into the main part of the building. She'd brought cardboard to wrap around her paintings and I could see a roll of bubble wrap poking out of the top of her canvas tote. Marcus took the cardboard from her.

I reminded myself that if Rena hadn't done anything wrong there was nothing to worry about and forced myself to smile at her. "Good morning," I said.

"Am I the first one here?" she asked, looking around.

"You're the only one, actually," I said, taking the cardboard from Marcus and leaning it against the desk. "Ruby said you'll be at the high school all day for the next couple of days. I thought it might be easier for you to get your paintings today."

"It is. Thanks," she said. She glanced at Marcus. "Thank you, too, Detective."

"You're welcome," Marcus said. He looked around. "Tell me which pieces are yours and I'll lift them down for you."

Rena pointed at her two paintings, one of a small mouse and the other of a turtle near the edge of a pool of water.

Marcus lifted down the turtle painting and carried it

over to the checkout desk. I slid the card with Rena's name and the name of the painting out of its holder on the wall and handed it to her.

She ran a hand along the side of the frame. "I like this frame," she said. "When Margo chose it I wasn't so sure, but now I can see she was right."

"You can keep it," I said, running my own finger over the smooth pale wood.

Rena looked uncertainly at me. In jeans and a long-sleeved black T-shirt, with her black hair in a loose side braid, she looked a lot younger than I knew she had to be.

"Margo wanted you all to have professionally framed pieces. She arranged it through the museum." I smiled at the memory of Margo, walking the length of the upstairs hallway, having an animated conversation with someone from the museum. "She was hoping these pieces would be part of other shows."

"What happened to her was horrible," Rena said softly, her expression a mix of sadness and gravity.

The emotion looked genuine. The energy coming off her felt genuine. A knot of uncertainty twisted in my stomach.

"The last time you saw Margo Walsh was right after lunch on Thursday?" Marcus asked.

Rena shook her head. "No. Before lunch." She looked at me and I nodded my head in confirmation. "We were all here. All the local artists, I mean."

His gaze had been drawn to the picture on the counter. "That's the turtle preserve isn't it?"

Rena smiled. "It is. How did you know?"

"I've hiked all through that area, though not for a

while." He narrowed his blue eyes at her. "It's very good. Have you been painting your whole life?"

She nodded and reached for the roll of plastic wrap in the bag at her feet. I was surprised that she was wrapping the painting so carefully. Maybe it was going somewhere other than back to Red Wing with her. "If you count finger painting in kindergarten, then, yes," she said.

"I didn't like finger painting," I said with a sheepish smile.

Rena turned to look at me. "Why?"

"I didn't like getting my hands dirty because we could only go to the reading corner with clean hands and that was my favorite place in the classroom."

"It sounds like our destinies were already set," she said.

I laughed, remembering having this same conversation with Maggie and Ruby. "If our destinies are set in kindergarten, then my brother's destiny is to burp for a living."

"Burp?" Rena asked.

The edge of the plastic refused to tear. I reached over the counter and retrieved a pair of scissors for her.

"Ethan's big accomplishment in kindergarten was learning to burp the entire alphabet."

"You're not really serious," Rena said as she cut the plastic and then reached for one of the large pieces of cardboard that she'd brought with her.

"Give Ethan a big bottle of root beer and he can still do it."

She laughed as she held up one sheet of cardboard, looking from it to the painting. She gave Marcus a sidelong glance. "What about you, Detective?" she asked. "What were you into in kindergarten?"

A smile played at the corners of his mouth. "I was coatroom monitor."

"What's a coatroom monitor?" I asked.

He brushed something off the sleeve of his sport coat. "I made sure everyone hung up their coat and put their boots underneath their hook."

I looked at Rena. "I think we may just have proved your theory."

She laughed again. Rena was guarded, careful, but it seemed to me that she had relaxed, just a little.

I looked back over my shoulder. "The pond with the turtle is beautiful, but the mouse is my favorite," I said. "The detail is incredible."

Rena lifted the painting and slid the cardboard underneath. Marcus reached over and helped hold the frame, edging the scissors out of the way. "Thank you," she said. "I did that one all from photographs." She made a face. "It's hard to get a mouse to pose for very long."

"Is there really egg in egg tempera paint?" Marcus asked.

Rena nodded, shifting the placement of the painting a little to the left. "Yes. Egg yolk for the most part, along with the pigment and something to keep the mixture from drying out too quickly. Water usually, but not always. I think the final effect is more like watercolor. You don't get the intense colors you would with, say, oil paint, but you can create some incredible detail." She folded the cardboard along a line she'd already scored, bringing one side up over the front of the painting. "The technique goes back to the Egyptians."

I remembered what Julian had said about having likely seen Devin at the gallery party. "You must be a fan of Antony Williams, then," I said.

"I am." She lifted her head and looked at me, surprised. "How do you know his work?"

"I used to live in Boston. My family is still there. His portrait of Queen Elizabeth was part of an exhibit marking her Diamond Jubilee." I reached for the tape roller at her feet and handed it to her. "I was so taken with his work I came home and looked up his other paintings online."

Rena folded the cardboard over the plastic-wrapped painting. "Do you have a favorite?" she asked.

"Eleanor on Her 87th Birthday," I said. "He captured every line on her face, every single strand of her hair."

"It's even more incredible in person," she said.

"Could I hold that?" I said, gesturing at the cardboard.

"Oh yeah, thanks," Rena said. I held the folded cardboard in place as she secured it with several wide pieces of tape.

"So you were at the Weyman Gallery party, what, three years ago?" Marcus said.

"Uh, no," Rena said. She glanced up at Marcus, frowning just a little. She was good. Her voice didn't falter. Her hands didn't so much as twitch. The only thing that gave her away was looking away just a fraction too soon.

"That painting is part of a private collection," Marcus continued. "It's only been shown in public once in the past thirty years. At that party."

Rena recovered well. "I guess I must have been

there, then," she said with a small smile. "People give me tickets to things." She looked at me and shrugged. "It's like collecting a few sets of salt and pepper shakers. Suddenly everyone you know is bringing you a pair when they go on vacation."

"A very valuable watercolor painting was stolen from that gallery the day after the party closed," Marcus said. "The only thing the police found was part of a fingerprint that they weren't able to identify."

Rena smiled at him. "So you think that I went to the opening gala and did what? Hid in a bathroom stall for twenty-four hours so I could steal a painting?"

"Your name wasn't on the guest list."

Rena still wasn't rattled. "Like I said, people *give* me tickets to things all the time." She stressed the word "give." "I'm not a thief. I'm a starving artist."

Marcus took a pen out of his pocket. He hooked one of the handle loops of the scissors and held them up. "Then you won't mind coming down to the police station with me."

"For what?" she said. "You think I killed Margo Walsh? You're crazy. Why would I do that?"

"Your real name is Devin Rossi." I said the words as a statement, not a question.

Rena looked at me. "No. My real name is *not* Devin Rossi. And I didn't kill Margo. Why would I?" She looked from me to Marcus. A shadow passed across her face and she sighed. "Look, talk to the insurance company," she said, gesturing with both hands. "I didn't kill Margo. She hired me to disable the security system and steal the Weston drawing."

19

For a moment there was silence; then Marcus said, "Rena Adler, you have the right to remain silent. Do you understand?"

Rena set down the tape dispenser and folded her arms over her chest. "Yes."

He continued reading her the rest of her rights. When he finished she nodded. "I understand, Detective. But I don't need a lawyer. Go ahead and ask your questions."

I touched her arm. "Rena, are you sure about that?" I asked.

"I'm sure," she said. Her gaze never left Marcus's face.

"What did you do with the artwork?" he asked.

"Nothing. When I got here the security system was already turned off and the drawing wasn't in the display case."

"Let me get this straight; Margo Walsh hired you to steal the Weston drawing, but when you broke in it was already gone?" Marcus didn't try to hide the skepticism in his voice.

"Yes. She wanted to prove that the security system wasn't enough to protect the artwork so the tour would be canceled."

Rena turned her head to look at me then. "The first meeting we all had with Margo." She pointed across the library to one of our meeting rooms. "You were there, Kathleen. You heard what she said about the pieces belonging in a museum."

I glanced at Marcus and nodded. "Margo thought the artwork was too old and too fragile to be out of a controlled setting." I turned to Rena. "I don't understand; you said your name isn't Devin Rossi."

"My real name isn't Devin Rossi," she said. "My real name is Rena Adler, and, yes, it's a variation on Irene Adler, but I'm guessing you already figured that out. My father was a mystery lover. I got the name Devin Rossi from a movie."

So even though Rena's name had made me think she might be Devin Rossi, I was wrong about which of her names was a fake.

"Can you prove Margo hired you to break in to the library?" Marcus asked Rena.

"You mean did I sign a contract or write a receipt? No." There was nothing defensive in her body language, but there was an edge of sarcasm in her voice. If anything she looked . . . angry. "Talk to the insurance company. They were involved in this."

"I already have talked to them. They didn't say anything about some plan to test the security system."

It was impossible to miss the surprise that flashed across Rena's face. She closed her eyes for a moment. When she opened them again she focused totally on

Marcus. "Then check Margo's bank accounts or her credit cards. She transferred ten thousand dollars to an account in Turks and Caicos just after one a.m. Thursday morning."

"Do you have a routing number?" Marcus asked.

"If it comes to that," Rena said. She took a deep breath and let it out slowly. "I didn't kill Margo. You must have her cell phone. There should be a text from Doyle's Art Supplies telling her her order isn't ready. That's me letting her know there was a problem. She sent a text back saying she'd call to change her order. But she didn't call. I was at Eric's Place for about an hour. The waiter was flirting. He'll remember me."

"You were flirting with Larry Taylor to find out how the security system worked," I said. "You were trying to figure out how to disable it."

Rena looked away for a moment. "I'm sorry about Larry. He's a nice guy. And, no, he didn't do anything to compromise the library's security, if that's what you're thinking."

Marcus glanced over at the main doors. "You couldn't have tampered with the keypad. It's set up to call the police if there's a security breach."

For a long moment Rena just looked at him. Then she shrugged. "In theory it is possible to redirect the keypad, send it to a rogue cell phone network. Or so I've heard. But like I told you. The system was off. "

"You'll need to come down to the police station," Marcus said, pulling his keys out of his pocket. "And you really should find a lawyer. There's still that fingerprint from Chicago you need to explain."

I saw a hint of a smile cross Rena's face. "I don't

think that's going to be that big a problem," she said. "I don't think the alleged owner really wants to explain how she ended up with that painting in the first place."

"Where's the Weston drawing?" Marcus asked again.

Rena brushed her hair back impatiently from her face. "I didn't take it. I told you. It wasn't in the case."

"You're asking me to take a lot of things on faith, Ms. Adler," Marcus said.

Rena actually smiled at him. "You know I didn't take the drawing, Detective," she repeated.

Marcus held up a hand. "Hang on a second," he said. He frowned at Rena. "What do you mean, *I* know you didn't take it?"

"I know the police have the drawing, Detective. I'm assuming you're saying you don't to throw whoever killed Margo off base."

"We don't have the drawing," Marcus said, flatly.

Rena shook her head. "You mean all this time this building's been closed and you still haven't found it?"

"Wait a minute," I said, pointing with one finger. "You think the Weston drawing is here? In the library?"

She looked from me to Marcus and back to me again. "It has to be. It was dotted, so there's no way it can leave the building with the alarm system still in place. I assumed Margo put it somewhere for safekeeping." She was looking at us both as though we were incredibly dense—which is how I felt. I had no idea what she was talking about and, judging from Marcus's face, neither did he.

I looked blankly at Rena. "What do you mean the drawing was dotted?"

"I mean there was a computer chip—a very tiny

computer chip—attached to the back of it," she said. "If anyone tried to take it out of the building the chip would trigger the security system and—"

I shook my head. "No," I interrupted. "We weren't using that aspect of the system here. It was too expensive and both the museum board and the insurance company thought the risk of anything happening was small. That was Gavin's recommendation as well." I did see the irony in that.

Rena ran a hand over the cardboard encasing her painting. "Margo went over his head. She convinced the insurance company that the extra security was needed and there wasn't much the board could do at the last minute. She wanted them to see that no matter what security procedures were in place, the artwork wasn't safe."

I rubbed the back of my neck with one hand. A knot of frustration made it feel as though a giant hand was squeezing the back of my head.

Marcus shook his head. "No, she didn't. There was no extra security. No computer chips on the back of any of the artwork."

Rena looked like someone had just punched her in the stomach. "I don't understand," she said. "Why would Margo tell me that?"

I didn't have an answer. I couldn't understand why Margo had wanted to sabotage the exhibit at all.

"So if the drawing had a computer chip attached to it, what were you supposed to do with it?" Marcus asked.

Rena pointed across the library. "I was supposed to hide it in the fourth book from the left in that case over there." She was indicating one of the special cabinets that held our rare book collection.

Marcus's phone rang then. He pulled it out of his pocket and held up his hand. "I need to take this; give me a minute."

He walked a few steps away from us.

"Kathleen, I didn't kill Margo," Rena said. "I had no reason to. Because of her, my paintings were going to be on display; my first real exhibit."

I held out both hands. "You seriously thought the exhibit would continue after you stole the drawing?" It was hard to believe Rena could have been that dense.

She shook her head. "No, I knew there wouldn't be an exhibit here, but Margo was going to add all the Mayville Heights artists to the next stop on the tour."

I didn't know what to say. I knew that Margo had already spent time at the other five stops on the tour. The layout of the artwork had already been planned. There was no way the artists from Mayville Heights would be part of the exhibit in some other place.

Marcus put his phone back in his pocket and walked back over to us. He gave Rena a look, narrowing his eyes, and I realized something in his attitude had changed. I wondered who had been on the other end of the phone.

"Do you know anything about the history of the Weston drawing, Detective?" Rena asked. She was still fingering the cardboard wrapped around her painting.

"I know there's some dispute about whether or not Weston himself is the artist," Marcus said.

"Margo believed, very strongly, that he wasn't. She did a lot of research on Sam Weston and on that drawing in particular. She went to talk to his first wife's great-great-grandson. I don't know what she found out, but whatever it was, she was convinced that that particular drawing wasn't done by Weston and that several others weren't, either."

"She told you all that?" Marcus didn't even try to keep the skepticism from his voice.

Rena smiled, not particularly warmly. "Uh-huh. It'll probably surprise you, but I agree . . . agreed with her." She gestured in the direction of the computer area turned exhibit space. "These pieces should be in a controlled environment with proper security. They're part of this country's heritage—part of our heritage."

"We should get going, Ms. Adler," Marcus said.

Rena nodded. "I understand." She turned to me, indicating the wrapped painting as she did. "Is it all right if I leave this here?"

"Of course it is," I said. "I'll put it upstairs in my office." I looked at Marcus. "Is that all right?"

He nodded. "It's fine." He looked around. "I'm sorry, Kathleen," he began.

"I can't stay here," I finished. Once again I was shut out of my own library.

Marcus took me by the arm and led me over to the main doors. Rena was putting a bit more tape on the cardboard-wrapped painting.

"You don't think she killed Margo," I said.

He shook his head. "How do you do that?"

"That was Hope on the phone and she told you something that convinced you that Rena isn't the killer." I was only guessing, but his expression told me I was correct.

He pulled a hand over his mouth. "Rena is left-handed," he said.

I glanced over at her. "I noticed that, too."

He didn't say anything.

I turned back to him. "The killer wasn't," I said slowly. Then I gave my head a slight shake before he could speak. "I know. You can't tell me that."

He shrugged. "I'm sorry." He looked around. "There was no computer chip on that drawing," he began.

"But you want to search again."

"I do."

Another thought had just occurred to me. "Marcus, if Rena didn't kill Margo, that means someone else got in here and did."

He nodded.

"But if it wasn't about the drawing, if she didn't walk in on the thief, on Rena, then why would anyone want to kill her?"

Marcus shook his head. "I don't know."

I took Rena's painting up to my office. While I was gone Marcus opened the cabinet and checked to make sure the drawing wasn't inside.

It wasn't.

"Is it all right if I let Lita and Everett know we're going to be closed a bit longer?" I asked as we headed for the front door.

"It's all right," he said. "But for now, everything else stays between us."

I nodded, then reached for his hand to give it a squeeze. He smiled and the gleam that flashed in his blue eyes sent a warm feeling flooding through my chest.

I turned and walked back to Rena. "Think about a lawyer," I said softly.

All she did was smile at me.

Curtis Holt was at the front doors. I realized Marcus had worked out the timing of that in advance. He and Rena headed for the police station and I walked over to Henderson Holdings and brought Lita up to date on what was going on. Then I headed home.

Hercules was sitting in the blue Adirondack chair in the backyard when I got home. I scooped him onto my lap and sat down. "What are you doing out here?" I asked.

He looked over at the big maple tree and meowed. Hercules had a love-hate relationship with a grackle that spent a lot of time in that tree. I thought of their perverse connection as love-hate because while Hercules had managed to snag one of the bird's feathers, he'd never come any closer to the bird—something he was quite capable of doing. And the grackle, in turn, had dive-bombed the cat, but never, as far as I had seen, touched a single strand of fur on his head.

"Where's your friend?" I said, stroking his fur. It was warm from the morning sun.

He responded with a sharp meow.

"I'm sorry," I said. "I meant your archnemesis."

Hercules made a grumbling sound low in his throat, shook off my hand, then jumped to the grass and headed for the house. He didn't bother waiting for me; he just walked through the door into the porch.

I watched him, thinking how much easier it would be if I could do that instead of stopping to fish out my keys all the time and unlock things. I couldn't help laughing as I let myself into the porch the normal way. When had I gotten so blasé about the cats' abilities?

I spent the afternoon catching up on what work I could from home. Lita called with a message from Everett that in essence promised any resources I needed to get things back to normal at the library as quickly as possible. I called Maggie to let her know we'd need her space for a few more days if that was okay. I told her that Rena was answering some questions for the police, but it didn't look like she'd killed Margo. I didn't think that violated Marcus's request not to talk about what had happened at the library. Gavin didn't call and I didn't call him, either.

I couldn't get Rena's story out of my head. Margo had hired her to break in to the library and take the Weston drawing out of its case and hide it? That made no sense. The case we kept the rare books in would make a good temporary hiding place, but I couldn't believe that Margo would do anything that might put the fragile piece of artwork at risk of damage. This whole thing was so out of character for the person I'd gotten to know.

But why would Rena make up a story like that? Even though Margo was dead, there were parts of her tale Marcus and Hope would be able to check on.

When I got to tai chi, Maggie took me aside to tell me that Rena was out on bail and had to stay in town, but she didn't seem concerned about the time she'd spent at the police station. "Did Marcus say anything?" she asked.

"I haven't talked to him," I said, wondering if he hadn't called so I wouldn't have to be evasive with Maggie—or anyone else.

I was restless when I got home. Roma had an early surgery at the clinic so I was driving out to Wisteria Hill to feed the cats in the morning. Now that Roma lived in the old farmhouse full-time, I fed the feral cats only when she was out of town or tied up with a patient. I hung my old jacket on the doorknob and went down to the basement for my heavy rubber boots. Roma had warned me that the path around the side of the old carriage house was wet and muddy.

While I was down there I decided to try to figure out why Owen was spending so much time in the basement. A waist-high workbench took up almost half of the back wall of the cellar. Harry Taylor had told me it had been built by the previous owner of the little farmhouse. Owen had taken over part of the knee-level shelf. It looked like the stash of a hoarder. He'd dragged down the old sweatshirt I'd told Maggie he'd swiped from me. There was a mitten that I recognized as belonging to her, several catnip chicken body parts and three black feathers. They looked like they might have come from a grackle.

I leaned against the bench holding the feathers, trying to make sense of how and why Owen had them. The little "war" between Hercules and the large bird was exactly that: between the two of them only. The bird hadn't so much as lifted a wingtip in Owen's direction, probably because it was Hercules who liked to hang around the maple tree the grackle considered to be its territory. Owen was generally prowling the yard or rooting in Rebecca's recycling bin.

So how had Owen gotten those feathers? From another bird? I didn't think so. From what I'd seen, the big black grackle kept all other similar birds at bay.

Could Owen have taken a run at the bird? I thought about the various squabbles he and Hercules had been having the past several months. There was an element of tit for tat in all of it.

I blew out a breath. No, it was just too preposterous to think Owen and Hercules were fighting because Owen had gone after the bird Hercules had been jousting with for the past year. They were cats, after all, not people.

I took my boots and the three feathers and went upstairs.

Owen wandered into the kitchen from somewhere carrying the disembodied head of a yellow funky chicken. He dropped it next to his water dish.

"Why do you have these?" I asked, holding out the black feathers.

He blinked at me.

I leaned forward, one hand on my knee. "If you've been after that bird, you have to stop."

"Mrr," he said, dropping his head to study a spot on the floor.

"Hercules and the bird are like . . . like Austin Powers and Dr. Evil."

I shook my head. What *was* I doing? Trying to explain to one cat that he had to stay away from the so-called archenemy of another cat by referencing a movie from the 1990s, albeit one both cats had watched with Maggie and me.

I straightened up. No, this was crazy. I held up the feathers. "Bad," I said sternly. "Very bad." Then I dropped them in the garbage can.

Owen gave a snippy meow and turned his head so he wasn't looking at me.

"Don't do that again," I warned, glaring at him. I wondered if as far as he was concerned all I'd been saying was "blah, blah, blah," for the last minute.

I went to the sink and washed my hands. When I turned around again Owen was studying my things by the door.

"Mrrr?" he asked.

"I'm going out to feed the cats in the morning," I said in answer to what I was assuming was his question. "And before you ask, no, Marcus isn't going with me."

He cocked his head to one side.

"He's working. Some new information in the case." I blew out a breath. "I'm starting to think we're never going to find Margo's killer."

"Mrr," Owen said again.

"It's not Rena and I'm glad about that. I don't know her very well, but I like what I know." I checked the back door, making sure it was locked.

Owen was still watching me.

If anyone heard me having a one-sided conversation with a cat, they probably would have thought I was more than a little delusional, but the fact was, saying it all out loud helped me make sense of things. And the conversation didn't usually feel so one-sided, although I wasn't going to admit *that* to anyone.

I made myself a cup of cocoa, put three marshmallows on top and sat at the table with my cup, quickly giving myself a marshmallow mustache. As much as I enjoyed a cup of coffee, you couldn't put marshmallows on top.

"Everything seems to be tied to that picture," I said. "Everything comes back to that."

Owen launched himself onto my lap and sniffed in the direction of my mug. "Freeze, mister," I warned, putting one arm around him.

He looked up at me, all furry gray tabby innocence.

"Marshmallows are not cat food," I said, frowning at him. "Not in this life or any other."

He made a sound a lot like a sigh.

"Yes, I know, your life is so hard." I leaned down and kissed the top of his head. "And I meant what I said before: Stay away from that grackle or your brother is going to destroy every chicken you have. Think of it this way: Maggie is your friend and the grackle is Hercules's friend . . . sort of."

Owen made a face, which could have meant he was considering my words or that he was wondering when I was going to stop talking.

I picked up my mug and took another drink.

My computer was still on the table. With both of my hands occupied, Owen took the opportunity to stretch out a paw and touch the keyboard, waking the laptop up. He looked at me again, expectantly, it seemed to me.

"Okay, maybe we should see what we can find out about the history of that drawing," I said, pushing my mug to one side and pulling the computer closer.

Owen immediately turned to look at the counter. He meowed softly.

"Yes, I suppose the research would go better with a couple of stinky crackers," I said. I got up, set him on the chair and got the crackers for him. When I turned back around he was up on his hind legs, looking at the computer screen with one paw on the edge of the keyboard.

I swept him onto my lap again and held out a cracker. He took it from me and murped a thank-you.

I opened my Web browser and typed in my favorite search engine. "You have marshmallow on your whisker," I said, keeping my eyes on the screen.

He dropped his head and took a couple of furtive swipes at his furry face.

The history of the Weston drawing was, I discovered, a little murky. It had turned up almost fifty years ago in the private collection of a New York businessman, although there was no provenance with the piece and no record of where or when he'd purchased it. It had been believed that the drawing was part of a collection of Weston's work housed at the Butler Institute of American Art. Since there were photographs of the drawing from more than one exhibit at the museum, some people believed the piece had been stolen, but the institute had no paperwork to back up the claim.

"Interesting," I said to Owen, raising an eyebrow, Mr. Spock style.

His response was to paw at the touch pad and bring up another site.

Charles Holmes had purchased the drawing for his private collection, although he had been generous about lending it and other artwork in his collection for exhibit as long as the displays were accessible to as much of the general public as possible. Before his death, Holmes had agreed to loan the Weston drawing and two other watercolors for this tour because it was taking the artwork to an audience that didn't usually get to see such pieces.

There had been rumblings about the authenticity of the drawing for decades, I discovered, but if Charles Holmes had been aware of it—and it was hard to believe he hadn't—I couldn't find any public comments he'd made on the subject.

I leaned back in my chair and picked up my mug. My cocoa was cold. I got up to warm it up and set Owen on the seat again. "What do you think?" I said as I waited for the microwave. "Should we look up this generation?"

"Merow!" he exclaimed with great enthusiasm, which was probably more for the jar of peanut butter I'd just taken down from the cupboard than for my idea.

Once I had a cup of hot chocolate that was actually hot and a piece of peanut butter toast, I went back to the computer to see what I could find about Marshall and Diana Holmes.

Marshall Holmes was Charles's only child. He'd taken over his father's grocery store chain and managed to make the business even more successful, something that often didn't happen when a business was handed down from parent to child.

Diana Holmes was the senior Holmes's stepdaughter, the only child of his second wife, Catherine. Charles Holmes had raised Diana from the time she was eight years old and by all accounts considered her to be his child in every way. Diana Holmes ran the Charles and Catherine Holmes Charitable Foundation and had increased its endowment by almost thirty percent in the five years she'd been in charge.

There were so many photos of both Marshall and Diana online. Marshall sweaty and beaming after a marathon, cutting a ribbon at the opening of a new store, and giving the eulogy at his father's funeral wearing a dark suit and somber expression. There was Diana in a short sequined dress with a ventriloquist's dummy in a variety show for charity, and serving at a downtown Chicago soup kitchen.

"So we know both Diana and Marshall Holmes are successful," I said to the cat, letting him lick a dab of peanut butter from my finger. "But what are they like as people?"

He was too busy getting every bit of peanut butter to have an opinion.

I thought about my encounters with Marshall and Diana. They had both been very pleasant and well spoken, but something about the way they had interacted had made me wonder if they were in agreement on how to handle Charles Holmes's art collection. According to what I was reading online, it had been left equally to both of them.

I lifted my hair and let it fall against my neck. "So. Any ideas?" I said to Owen.

His response was to hop down off my lap and head for the back door. It was a warm evening so I'd left it open. He headed purposefully into the porch. After a moment I heard him meow. Clearly he wanted out and didn't really care if I learned any more about the Holmes siblings.

"I'm coming," I said.

Owen was sitting in front of the outside door. I opened it for him, but instead of going outside he just poked his head out, looked across the back lawn and meowed.

"Go if you're going, please," I said.

He didn't move.

"Owen," I said sharply. "I'm not you're doorman . . . doorwoman, doorperson, whatever the politically correct term is. In or out."

He looked up at me, his tail whipping across the floor in annoyance. Then he looked across the yard again and meowed once more.

And then I got it. "I could call Rebecca," I said slowly. "She might know something about Diana and Marshall Holmes. It's possible Everett knew Charles Holmes."

Owen turned and headed back to the kitchen, making muttering sounds all the way. Trust a cat to want to have the last word.

I sat down on the bench by the window in the porch and took my cell out of my pocket.

"Hello, my dear, how are you?" Rebecca asked when she answered the phone.

"I'm well, Rebecca," I said. "How are you?" Hearing her voice automatically made me smile.

"Well, at the moment I'm beating the pants off Everett at Texas Hold'em," she said.

"She cheats," I heard Everett call in the background.

Rebecca laughed. "He's not losing graciously."

"That's because you're cheating," he countered.

"I won't keep you," I said. "I was hoping you might be able to get a little information for me."

"Does this have something to do with everything

that's happened at the library?" she asked, lowering her voice a little.

"Yes," I said, wondering if this was such a good idea after all. I didn't want to put her in any kind of conflict with Everett.

"I'd love to help, my dear. What do you need? And don't worry about Everett."

"How do you manage to read my mind?" I asked.

"It's my secret power," she said. I could imagine her smiling as she said the words.

"Well I'm glad you're using it for good and not for evil," I teased.

"So how can I help?"

"Do you know anything about Marshall or Diana Holmes?" Owen was sitting at my feet, intently watching my face.

"I know Everett did some business with their father, Charles. That's how the exhibit ended up coming to the library. I can certainly find out more about them."

I pulled my free hand down over the back of my head. "I don't want to put you in a difficult position, Rebecca."

She laughed, and somehow the warmth of the sound came through the phone at me. "Oh, Kathleen, there's nothing difficult about playing a nosy old lady. Give me a day and I'll see what I can find out for you."

"Thank you," I said.

"I'm happy to help."

We said good night and I hung up the phone.

I went back into the kitchen to discover a guilty-looking Owen under the table and the garbage can tipped over on the floor.

"Owen!" I exclaimed.

This wasn't the first time Owen had tipped over the trash, although he hadn't done it in a while. The last time, he'd leapt on the can in an ill-advised effort to snag a scarf from the hooks by the door.

He hung his head, but I could see one eye watching to gauge how mad I was.

I set the can upright and sent a stern look in the cat's direction. "Don't do that again," I warned. "Or it won't be Hercules who's making your chickens disappear."

I cleaned up the mess and then went to the sink to wash my hands. I felt a furry body wind around my ankles. I bent down and picked Owen up.

"Merow?" he said, cocking his head to one side.

"I'm still mad at you," I said.

He leaned forward and nuzzled the side of my face.

"I am," I insisted. "You can't jump up onto the garbage can. You're not one of the Flying Wallendas. Next time I go to the thrift store I'll get you a scarf."

His response was to lick my chin. I couldn't help feeling that somehow I'd just been had.

I set Owen back on the floor and he walked over to the back door and looked in the direction of Rebecca's little house. Then he turned his wide golden eyes on me.

"She's in," I told him. "The game is afoot."

20

I was just coming around the side of the carriage house in the morning, heading back to my truck and feeling very grateful for my boots because it had rained overnight and it looked like it was going to start again, when Marcus called.

"Hi," he said. "Where are you?"

"I'm up at Wisteria Hill," I said, wiping my feet on the grass by the front of the old building before walking back to the truck. "I just fed Lucy and the others."

"Roma's out of town?" he said. "Where did she go? When did that happen?" He'd suddenly switched into what I thought of as cop mode, for some reason.

"She's not out of town," I said, opening the truck door and tossing the bag with the food dishes onto the floor on the passenger side. "She had an early surgery so I volunteered to come up."

I brushed off my jeans and slid behind the wheel. "Did you need Roma for something? Is Micah okay?"

"She's fine," he said. "She swiped part of a piece of

toast off my plate this morning, but other than her possible criminal bent, she's fine."

It had taken a little persuasion from Roma and me to get Marcus to adopt the small ginger tabby, but they made a good pair. She brought out the softer side of him that a lot of people didn't always get to see.

"It's nothing," Marcus continued. "I'm just a bit surprised you're out there without me."

I smiled. I had good memories of feeding the cat colony with him as we'd gotten to know each other. "Roma asked me at tai chi last night," I said. "I figured you'd be tied up with the case. Has anything changed?"

He exhaled loudly. "We're going to start searching the library, book by book, this morning, but it's going to take some time. Do you know how many items we'll have to go through?"

"Forty-one thousand eight hundred and fifteen, counting DVDs and CDs," I said. I paused for a moment. "Give or take."

He laughed. "Okay, I deserved that."

"Are we still on for tonight?" I asked as I fished my keys out of the pocket of my jeans.

"Yes," he said. "I was planning on picking you up at about six thirty, if that works."

Mayville Heights was experimenting with offering some outdoor concerts on the Riverwalk during the spring and summer. The senior high band was kicking things off with a concert planned for seven fifteen on the grassy area in front of the St. James Hotel.

"That's fine, but I think it's a safe bet that we'll be in the community center, not outside, judging by how it looks overhead." I leaned forward to look through the windshield. Gray clouds were rolling across the sky.

"That's okay," he said. "That'll work."

I heard voices in the background. "I have to go. I'll see you at six thirty and then we'll pick up Roma."

Marcus had suggested we invite Roma to go to the concert with us. "You and I are together and Maggie is seeing Brady Chapman." He'd managed not to roll his eyes at the last part. "I know Roma has Eddie, but he's not here."

I knew Roma was still struggling with the idea that Eddie wanted to marry her. I thought it might be a good idea to get her out of the house for a while, so I'd enlisted Maggie to help me convince Roma to join us all at the concert. What I really wanted was to tell her to trust that Eddie loved her and to marry him. I agreed with Maggie: There was more than one way to make a family. I also wanted to tell her not to waste any time with him, but I hadn't exactly listened when she and Maggie had tried to tell me that about Marcus, so when she talked about Eddie I listened and tried not to judge.

I spent a large part of the day at Maggie's studio, trying to keep the various groups that had relocated from the library working in their temporary space. Abigail came to help me and I was very glad to have her unflappable presence beside me.

Marcus pulled up to the house at twenty-five minutes after six. He was wearing jeans and a gray V-neck pullover with a navy T-shirt underneath and a black rain slicker. He'd shaved again and he smelled like a combination of spicy aftershave and Juicy Fruit gum.

"There's something I really need to tell you before we go get Roma," he said. He suddenly looked very serious. "I should have told you days ago and I'm sorry."

My cell phone rang then. I held up a hand. "Hold on a sec," I said.

It was Harry Taylor.

"Hi, Kathleen," he said. "I was at the library and it's raining."

"I noticed," I said.

"Well, the police took down the rain chain and a section of gutter. I'm pretty sure we've got some water going into the loading-dock area. I need to get in there and turn on the pump. Do I need to call Marcus Gordon?"

"Hang on, Harry," I said. "Marcus is here with me." I quickly explained what was going on. "Can I go let Harry into the loading dock? Please? We won't be going in to the library proper."

He nodded. "Go ahead."

"I'm on my way," I told Harry.

"No need," he said. "I'm almost at your place."

"Okay," I said. I dropped my phone into my pocket. "You go get Roma, save me a seat. I'll meet you at the concert," I said to Marcus.

"Kathleen, we really need to talk," he said.

"After the concert. I promise." I gave him a quick kiss that landed on his chin instead of his mouth, and then I dashed out into the rain.

Harry was waiting in his truck. At the library, we walked around to the loading dock and he gave me a boost up. I'd already called the evening security guard to let him know we'd be banging around at the back of the building. I didn't want him to think someone was trying to break in.

There was just a small amount of water inside. Harry got the pump working while I walked around to make sure everywhere else was dry.

"We're good for now," Harry said, "but we need to get that gutter and chain back up as soon as we can."

I nodded. "I'll talk to Marcus."

I made it to the community center with five minutes to spare.

I could see Marcus four rows from the front. Roma was on the aisle and there was an empty seat next to Maggie and Brady with Maggie's coat across the back.

"Thanks, Mags," I said, dropping into the folding chair next to her and handing back her coat.

She smiled. "Don't thank me. It was Brady's idea."

I leaned around her and smiled at Burtis Chapman's oldest son. He may have been a lawyer and his dad may have been a businessman who danced around the edges of the law, but father and son were a lot alike and I liked them both. "Thank you for saving seats for us," I told him.

"Anytime, Kathleen," he said with a smile that was just like his father's, too.

"Everything okay at the library?" Marcus asked.

I nodded. "Harry got the pump working." I leaned across him and smiled at Roma.

"Marcus said you had to go to the library. Is everything all right?" Roma asked.

"Harry saved the day, as usual," I said.

"How were the cats this morning?"

"They all looked fine. Smokey ate well and he doesn't seem to be limping as much."

Smokey was the oldest of the feral cat colony as far as Roma knew. He'd injured his leg just before Christmas and had had a slow recuperation, but in the past month he'd seemed to be doing a lot better.

"How did your surgery go?" I asked.

"Better than I hoped," Roma said, tucking her dark hair behind one ear.

She gave me a brief rundown on the operation to stabilize the hip of a black lab that had been hit by a car. I liked to listen to Roma talk about her work. I found it fascinating. The librarian in me loved to learn about pretty much everything. The members of the band began to take their places then, and I straightened up.

The concert began with a selection of classical pieces. The senior band was very, very good, one of the top school bands in the state, mostly because of their music director, Tony Morrow. He was short and stocky, built like an MMA fighter, with a deep love of music. I knew from his borrowing habits that he had eclectic taste in music, and I'd come to enjoy seeing him come into the library and being able to talk to him about what he was listening to in a given week.

Tony's enthusiasm for music was contagious, and when he'd mentioned the upcoming concert to me, I'd promised to be there.

Marcus put a hand on my arm. "I need to tell you something," he whispered.

Before he could say another word, Maggie leaned forward and glared at him. I smiled and mouthed the word "later." Marcus looked . . . troubled. Whatever he was going to say had to have something to do with the case. It could wait.

The second part of the program was more contemporary music, and the kids all looked a little less serious. They launched into Journey's "Don't Stop Believin'," and Tony's grin stretched from ear to ear as he conducted. He shot a look in my direction and winked.

Roma was in the aisle seat. She smiled and leaned around Marcus. "Kathleen, did you do this?" she whispered. It was her favorite song.

"Not me. I swear," I said, smiling back at her. Maggie poked me in the ribs with her elbow. I pressed my lips together and tried to look contrite.

Marcus still looked uncomfortable. Brady, on the other side of Maggie, was grinning like a fool. A bad feeling began to buzz at the base of my skull.

"No," I said softly.

Maggie looked back over her shoulder, then grabbed my arm. "Kath," she said, her voice low and tight.

I glanced back. Eddie had just walked in. The buzzing in my head got louder. He was wearing a suit and carrying a single red rose.

I met Maggie's eyes. "No," I said again.

He looked so damn happy. I had a Walter Mitty–esque fantasy in which I jumped up and tackled Eddie before he made it to us. But given that I was a five-foot six-inch librarian and he was six foot four inches of NHL hockey player, it wasn't going to happen.

The song ended with a flourish just as Eddie made it to us. He dropped to one knee and held out the rose. Roma looked at Eddie and then back at Maggie and me. She didn't look panicked or even surprised. She just looked . . . sad. She got to her feet and took the flower he was holding out.

There was so much love shining on Eddie's face that my chest tightened. I didn't know who to hurt more for: him or Roma.

"Roma Davidson, I love you," Eddie said, his voice edged with emotion. "Will you marry me?"

She didn't answer. She just looked at him while what seemed like half the town watched and waited.

I looked in Tony's direction, trying to get his attention. "Play!" I mouthed urgently, shaking my hand in the air.

He looked surprised, but something in my expression compelled him to lift his baton and start the next song. It was Donna Summer's "She Works Hard for the Money." I knew that wasn't a coincidence. It was another of Roma's favorites.

Eddie's smile faded. He was still holding Roma's hand and she still hadn't said a word. Slowly he got to his feet.

I tipped my head in the direction of the door to the hallway. "Go," I whispered at him. I touched Roma's arm. "Go with Eddie," I said softly.

She didn't turn to look at me or say a word, but she went with him, still holding hands, and the whole room applauded.

I looked at Maggie and tried to swallow down the lump in my throat. It wouldn't go.

"She needs us," Maggie said.

I nodded. "I know."

Everyone's attention was back on the music. Two

girls and a boy, all in black-framed shades, were rock-
ing their sax solo. Beside me Marcus looked . . . guilty.
Suddenly everything made sense. He'd been in on this.
That's what he'd been trying to tell me. By the look on
Brady's face, him, too.

Why on earth hadn't Marcus said something sooner?

He caught my hand as I started to slip past him. "I'm
sorry," he whispered.

I felt a surge of frustration. I yanked my hand away.
"You're such a guy!" I hissed.

Eddie was standing in the hallway.

Alone.

He turned to look at us, sadness etched in every line
on his handsome face. "She left," he said.

"I'm sorry," I said. It didn't seem like enough, but I
didn't have any other words.

"I thought she'd say yes." He tugged at the knot in
his tie. "I don't care about the age difference or kids or
anything." He blew out a breath. "Will you two please
just . . . be with her?" He made a helpless gesture toward the outside door with one hand.

I nodded.

Maggie hesitated. Then she put a hand on Eddie's
shoulder. "She loves you," she said. "That hasn't changed."

He nodded, barely, in response.

Maggie turned to me, zipping up her jacket as she
did. "We should go find Roma," she said.

I touched Eddie's arm for a brief moment and then
followed her out.

"Which way?" Maggie asked once we were out on
the sidewalk. She looked up and down the empty
street. There was no sign of Roma in either direction.

I pointed left. "That way," I said and started walking.

"Are you sure?" Maggie said, easily catching up with me with her long legs.

"Yes," I said. My bangs were hanging in my face. I brushed them back with one hand. "No. I don't know. Roma came with Marcus. If she's walking home, she'll go this way."

The street curved and there was no sign of Roma in the block ahead of us. We'd come out the back door, so I pulled Maggie down a block, jaywalking in the middle of the street. Up ahead I caught sight of Roma, walking rapidly down the sidewalk, shoulders hunched, the hood of her jacket pulled up against the light rain.

"Can you run in those?" Mags asked, looking down at my high-heeled boots. She was wearing her red high-tops.

"I hope so," I said.

Maggie darted a quick look for traffic and we ran down the street after Roma. We caught her at the corner, Maggie sprinting ahead to put a hand on Roma's shoulder and stop her.

She turned, held out a hand and let it drop to her side. "I couldn't say yes," she said.

Maggie wrapped both her arms around Roma's shoulders. "It's okay," she said.

I caught Maggie's eye and then looked down the street in the general direction of Eric's Place. "C'mon. Let's go get out of the rain," I said.

We started walking again. Maggie kept one arm around Roma's shoulders.

"Why did he do that?" Roma asked. "The music.

The rose. In front of everyone. He knew I . . . he knew I wasn't sure."

"He loves you," Maggie said. "I think he wanted to do something big to show you how much."

"I didn't want to make a fool of him," Roma said quietly.

"It's okay. You didn't," I assured her.

She looked at me. "Then everyone thinks I said yes."

"What everyone thinks isn't important."

Maggie nodded. "We'll figure that out later."

It was quiet at Eric's. Nic was behind the counter. I guessed that Eric was in the kitchen.

Nic turned and smiled at us. "You can sit anywhere," he called, gesturing to the room with one hand.

"Thanks," I said. "Would you bring us a pot of hot chocolate?"

He nodded.

Maggie chose a table against the end wall. Roma took off her jacket, sat down and slumped against the back of the chair. She looked at both of us. "What am I going to do?" she asked, pain evident in her eyes.

"Nothing," Maggie said. Her blond curls were damp and she shook her head. "Leave the universe to its own devices for a little while."

I hung my jacket on the back of my chair and took a seat. "Maggie's right," I said. "You don't have to do anything right now."

"What do I say to Eddie?" She looked stricken at the idea that she'd hurt him. The way she felt about the man was all over her face. Anyone could see it. The proverbial blind man could see it.

"You tell him you need more time," I said. "And then you take as much as you need."

Roma twisted the silver ring she always wore around her finger. "Time is the problem. There's too much of it between Eddie and me."

"He doesn't care about that," Maggie said.

"'Love is not love which alters when it alteration finds,'" I said softly. I'd been thinking the words and had said them out loud before I realized it.

"Shakespeare?" Roma asked.

I nodded.

"The words are beautiful, but it doesn't change anything." She looked past me out to the rain-soaked street.

Nic came over with three mugs and a couple of stainless steel carafes. He filled the mugs from one jug and set the other in the middle of the table.

"If you need anything else, let me know," he said.

Roma looked at her cup, ran a finger around the rim and then picked it up. She looked at us. "I know you're both right," she said. "I know Eddie doesn't care that I'm older than he is. He even says he doesn't care about more children. But I care."

I leaned forward. "What can we do?" I asked.

She almost smiled. "You're already doing it."

Marcus walked in about five minutes later. He stood just inside the door and looked in our direction.

"I'll get this," I said.

I walked over to him. He looked contrite.

"You mad?" he asked.

I shook my head. "No. Well, maybe I was for about thirty seconds. That's what you were trying to tell me earlier, wasn't it?"

He nodded. "Eddie wanted it to be a surprise. But the more I thought about it, I didn't want to keep secrets from you."

I smiled at him. "I'm sorry I called you a guy."

"I am a guy," he said. "I thought Eddie's idea was romantic."

"Maybe in different circumstances," I said.

"How's Roma?" he asked.

I glanced over at her. "Upset. Worried about Eddie."

Marcus shook his head. "He loves her, Kathleen. I'm certain about that."

"It doesn't have anything to do with that," I said.

"He's not going to give up."

"I didn't think he would."

"Okay," he said. "Okay." He held out the keys to the SUV. "Here. Take Roma home."

"How are you going to get home?"

"I can get a ride with someone. Don't worry. I'll pick up the car in the morning." He leaned down and kissed my forehead. "I'll talk to you tomorrow."

He looked over at Maggie. "Brady's outside."

"I'll tell Maggie," I said. I caught his arm and gave it a squeeze before I walked back to the table.

"Mags, Brady is outside," I said.

Roma looked up at her. "Go," she said. "I'm all right."

Maggie smiled at her. "No," she said. "I'm going to go talk to him for a minute but I'll be right back."

"Maggie," Roma began.

Maggie shook her head and smiled again. "No," she repeated. Then she got up and headed for the door.

"I should go find Eddie," Roma said.

I shook my head as I reached for my mug. "Eddie's fine. You should have a bowl of pudding cake."

"Pudding cake?" she said, frowning at me.

I took a sip of my cocoa. It was still hot. " 'Duct tape or chocolate can fix pretty much anything,' is what you say, and I don't think this is a duct tape kind of problem."

That got me a small smile. "You're right about that."

I leaned back in my chair and caught Nic's attention. He came around the counter and headed in our direction. "What can I get you, Kathleen?" he asked.

"Is there any of Eric's pudding cake in the kitchen?" I asked.

He smiled. "There might be. I can check."

"Would you, please?" I asked.

"Sure thing," he said. "Three bowls if there is?"

"Please," I said. I knew Maggie would never say no to Eric's pudding cake.

Nic headed for the kitchen.

"Do you understand why I can't say yes to Eddie?" Roma asked. "He was playing in the minor leagues when Sydney was little and he missed so much of that time with her. He told me once that he wished he could have a do-over. I'm just too old for that."

"There are other options," I said gently.

"I know. But they're expensive and they take time."

"And?" I nudged.

She twisted the silver ring she wore around and around her index finger. "I've seen what the stress of those other options can do to people. I don't want that to happen to Eddie and me." She looked at me. "Do you think I'm wrong?"

"It doesn't matter," I said. "I'm on your side no matter what. I'm your friend. When Marcus and I finally got together, which both you and Maggie had thought should happen from the beginning, did you say I told you so?"

"Yes, I did," she said. "At least twice. Maybe three times."

"All right. Bad example. My point is, even though you thought I was wrong about Marcus, you and Maggie were always there for me."

"I don't want either of you to take sides," she said, wrapping her fingers around her cup.

"I don't think we have to," I said. "But if it comes to that, your side is the one we're on."

Maggie came in the door then, shaking herself before she walked over to us. Nic stepped out of the kitchen then, carrying a tray with three bowls of Eric's chocolate pudding cake.

"You ordered pudding cake?" Maggie said, slipping off her jacket and dropping back onto her seat.

"You did want some, didn't you?" I asked.

"Absolutely. Chocolate is like a good painting."

I frowned at her.

"Good for the soul," she said as Nic set a steaming bowl in front of her.

Once we all had a dish, Maggie stretched out her arm and put her hand, palm down, in the middle of the table. "We're the three musketeers," she said.

"We're not the three musketeers," Roma said. "That's just something you made up when you and Kathleen carjacked me so you could follow Will Redfern and find out why he was taking so long to finish the renovations at the library."

"And we did," Maggie said, picking up her spoon with her other hand and trying the pudding cake. "Umm, this is good," she sighed. Then she slapped her hand against the table. I reached over and put my hand on top of hers.

"All for one," I said.

"Stop trying to make me feel better," Roma said.

I shook my head. "Sorry. I can't do that. All for one."

She looked from me to Mags and her lower lip trembled. "You're the best friends I've ever had," she said. Then she swallowed hard and laid her hand on top of mine. "And one for all."

21

I drove Maggie home first. She reached forward from the back and hugged Roma in the passenger seat. "'All shall be well, and all shall be well, and all manner of things shall be well,'" she said softly.

"Julian of Norwich," I said. It had been a long time since I'd heard the quote generally attributed to the Christian mystic.

"If you want to talk or just be quiet, call me," Maggie added.

Roma nodded. "I will."

I waited until I saw Maggie go inside her apartment building; then I turned to Roma. "Come home with me," I said. "I'll loan you a pair of fuzzy pajamas and I promise that Owen and Hercules won't ask you any annoying questions."

"I should go home," she said.

"Why?" I asked.

She pulled a hand back through her dark hair. "I don't know."

"So come with me."

"All right," she finally said with a shrug.

"We're home," I called as Roma and I stepped into the kitchen.

After a moment a furry black-and-white head peered around the living room doorway. A moment later a gray tabby head looked around the doorframe on the other side. The cats exchanged a look.

"Merow!" Owen said. Then he disappeared. Luckily, not literally.

Hercules padded into the kitchen.

I took Roma's jacket, hanging it on one of the hooks by the back door.

"How about some tea?" I asked.

"Is it that the herbal tea Maggie likes?" she asked, pulling out one of the kitchen chairs and sitting down.

I nodded. "It is."

"Then no, not really."

I smiled. It was good to see Roma's sense of humor. "How about another cup of hot chocolate?"

She thought for a moment. "I think that would be good." She tucked one leg up underneath her and folded her arms over her midsection.

Hercules came and sat next to her chair. He looked up at her, his green eyes narrowed almost as though he was wondering why she was here.

"How was your night?" Roma said to him.

"Mrrr," he said.

When the milk was heated and the cocoa made, I joined Roma at the table. She stirred her hot chocolate, watching the little whirlpool she made in her cup. "Don't be mad at Marcus, Kathleen," she said finally, looking up at me. She almost smiled. "I know he was part of all this. Eddie had to have had someone helping him. They probably did some male version of a pinkie swear."

"I'm not mad," I said, dropping a marshmallow in my cup and dunking it with my finger. "You're right. He did help. And he did try to tell me, right before Harry called about the library."

We sat in silence for a moment, Hercules watching both of us but keeping his own counsel; then Roma said softly, "He's a good person."

I wasn't sure if she meant Marcus or Eddie.

We sat and talked for a while about everything but Eddie's proposal. There wasn't really anything else to say about that.

Roma yawned and covered her mouth with one hand. "I'm sorry," she said. "It's not the company."

"It's okay," I said. "The spare room bed is made up. I'll find you a pair of pajamas."

Hercules went ahead of us up the stairs and turned in to the bathroom. He stopped under the wooden cupboard on the wall, looked up and meowed.

"Good idea," I said. Roma was used to me talking to the boys, but she raised her eyebrows at me this time.

"I have some of Rebecca and Maggie's bath infusions," I said. "Would you like one for the tub?"

Rebecca's mother had used a lot of herbal remedies and had acted as an informal nurse in the town when Rebecca was young. Rebecca in turn had learned a lot of her mother's herbal secrets and had been teaching them to Maggie. They'd made poultices and wraps several times for me, and their tub infusions seemed to help everything from sore muscles to an overloaded mind.

I fished in the cupboard and held out two wraps of cheesecloth tied with string. "What do you think?" I said to Hercules.

His nose twitched as he sniffed at one and then the other.

"Meow!" he said, pawing the air in the direction of the one in my left hand.

"This one gets the paw of approval," I said. I put two fluffy towels on the wicker stool underneath the cupboard and set the sachet of herbs and flowers on top.

"Thank you, Hercules," Roma said.

I got her a pair of soft flannel pajamas from my bedroom. They were hot pink, decorated with little gray-and-white images of Bigfoot.

"A present from Ethan," I said.

"Why did your brother buy you a pair of pajamas with Bigfoot on them?" she asked.

"Because he used to razz me about dating Bigfoot since I was living in the wilderness, according to him."

Roma smiled.

"I just remind him that I used to change his diapers," I said. "That always shuts him up."

"You and Ethan and Sara are still close," she said, taking the pajamas from me. "Even with you here and them in Boston."

"I miss them," I said, "but even if I were still in Boston I probably wouldn't see them any more than I do now. Ethan's band has been on the road most of the last six months and Sara has worked on two films."

"I wanted siblings when I was younger," Roma said. "Then I'd spend a month with my cousins in the summertime and being an only child didn't seem so bad."

"When I found out I was going to have a baby brother and sister, all I felt was mortified. My parents were divorced and there was the undeniable proof that they'd been having sex." I smiled at the memory of my melodramatic teenage self, deciding that I could never be seen in public again with my mother and father. "And then they brought Ethan and Sara home from the hospital and my mother let me hold them for the first time," I said.

"And you bonded with them," Roma said, holding the Bigfoot pajamas to her chest and folding her arms over them.

"Not even close," I said. "Ethan spit up all over the front of my favorite shirt and at the exact same time Sara did the same on the back of it." I grinned and raised my eyebrows. "They've always been competitive."

It was good to see Roma laugh. "So what changed?" she asked.

"I'd get up in the middle of the night and sneak in to look at them. I was convinced they'd ruined my life, but I couldn't stay away from them, either. One night Ethan was awake and I just started talking to him. Then Sara woke up, too. As long as I was talking they didn't cry. About a week later Mom got up to check on them and found the three of us downstairs watching one of those really bad Japanese Godzilla movies with subtitles on TV."

I smiled at her. "And I'm going to stop talking," I said. "Toothbrush and toothpaste in the cupboard on the second shelf. If you need anything else, just yell."

She nodded. "I will."

I cleaned up the kitchen while Roma was in the bathtub; then I had a bath myself, sinking down in the water until it was up to my chin. I wondered how Eddie was. I wondered if there was any way Roma would change her mind.

I was sitting on the edge of the bed brushing my hair when my cell phone buzzed. It was Marcus.

"Hi," he said. "You weren't sleeping, were you?"

"No," I said.

"How's Roma?" he asked.

"Sad, mostly," I said, standing up and walking over to set the brush on my dresser. "I convinced her to stay here for tonight."

"I thought you might."

"How's Eddie?"

Marcus exhaled softly. "Pretty much the same as Roma. He's already on his way back to St. Paul. He left about an hour ago."

I yawned. "I'm sorry," I said. "It's been a long day."

"Go to bed. I'll talk to you in the morning." I could hear the smile in his voice. "Good night."

"Good night," I said.

I woke up at five minutes after two, unsure of why I was awake. I padded out into the hallway in bare feet. The door to the spare bedroom was open. Roma wasn't in bed.

I was halfway down the stairs when I heard voices. Then I realized it was just one voice, Roma's. I crept silently to the bottom of the steps and moved across the living room floor until I could see into the kitchen. Roma was at the table, her back to the doorway, one foot up on her chair with her chin resting on her bent knee and her arms wrapped around her leg. Hercules was sitting at her feet.

She was talking to him. And he was listening, his head tilted a bit to one side. It occurred to me that maybe Roma had found exactly the right "person" to talk to who would listen without judgment. I took several steps backward and then I went silently back upstairs.

I drove Roma home after breakfast, moving Marcus's SUV out onto the street so I could back the truck out of my driveway. When I got back it was gone and there was a brown paper bag propped on the doorknob of the back door. There was a smiley face drawn on the front with a black marker and one of Eric's cinnamon rolls inside.

Rebecca called a few minutes after nine o'clock. "I have some information for you," she said. "Do you have a few minutes?"

"I do," I said. "Would you like to come over and tell me in person? I have coffee, tea and"—I leaned sideways to look at the counter, realizing as I did that Roma and I had eaten the last of the blueberry scones and I'd demolished Marcus's cinnamon roll—"sardine cat crackers."

Rebecca laughed. "As . . . tempting as that sounds, I'm not home. I'm actually downtown in Everett's pied-à-terre."

"Ahh, romantic," I teased.

"Yes, it was," she said a saucy lilt to her voice.

I could imagine her smile and the twinkle in her eyes. Rebecca and Everett could make the most cynical person out there believe in love and happily ever after.

"So what did you find out?" I asked, pulling my feet up so I was sitting cross-legged on the chair.

"The Holmeses are not the happy family they seemed to be on the outside," she said.

"All happy families are alike; each unhappy family is unhappy in its own way," I said.

"Exactly," Rebecca said. "I think Tolstoy had that right, although I think the unhappy families are that way for the same few reasons."

"What do you think the reasons were in this case?"

"I think there was only one: money."

I reached for my coffee. "Charles Holmes's art collection."

"Yes. I talked to the wife of one of Everett's business associates. Clara told me that Marshall Holmes tried to sue his sister over the collection. He thought Diana had used undue influence on their father."

"You said, 'tried to sue,' " I said.

"The case was dismissed," she said. "It seems that before he died Charles had decided to have all the artwork appraised with the idea that he'd divide the collection equally between Marshall and Diana. He died before anything really got started, so the way his will was written, they shared the whole collection."

"I can see how that caused problems," I said. I took a sip of my coffee.

"It seems there was enough evidence to show what Charles's intentions had been," she said. "Even though Marshall's lawsuit was dismissed, the judge ordered a complete appraisal of the art at the estate's expense with the goal being to divide the collection as fairly as possible."

"So shouldn't that have solved the problem?"

"Well, dear, you'd think it would," Rebecca said. "But from what I could gather, it hasn't. First of all, the appraisal process takes time, not to mention, some of the artwork is out on loan in various exhibits at the moment. And both Marshall and Diana have some limited veto over who's going to do the actual assessment."

I took another sip of my coffee and set the cup on the table. "They haven't started yet, have they?" I asked.

"The only piece that's been valued is the Weston drawing," she said. "Charles had that evaluated right before his death." She made a sound of annoyance. "Both of those young people are very childish in their behavior. On the other hand, this really is something Charles should have settled long before he died."

I sensed there was a similarity between Marshall and Diana Holmes wrangling over the Weston drawing and Owen and Hercules bickering about the grackle. Nobody wanted to give in first.

"Rebecca, do you think either one of them could have been involved in what happened at the library?" I said.

She sighed softly. "I hate to think it, Kathleen," she said. "But, yes, it's possible. Clara told me that both Marshall and Diana are having some—as she put it— cash-flow problems."

"They're broke," I said, stretching sideways and snagging the handle of the coffeepot with two fingers.

"As the proverbial church mouse," Rebecca countered. "The business and the foundation are doing quite well, but both children have been living way beyond their means for some time."

"I just have one more question," I said. "Did your friend happen to mention who did the appraisal of the Weston drawing?" Mentally, I crossed my fingers, remembering Lise's comment about Edward Mato and the Weston drawing: *I think he actually might have appraised it at some point.*

"I think she said his last name was Mato. I'm sorry. I don't remember his first name. I'm not sure Clara even said."

I did a little fist pump in the air. "It doesn't matter," I said. "Thank you for doing all this for me."

"Oh, my dear, you're very welcome," Rebecca said. "I quite enjoyed it. I think I would have made a very good spy."

I laughed. "I think you would, too. I'm glad we're on the same side."

Rebecca laughed and promised she'd be over soon for tea, and we said good-bye.

I got up and stretched. I didn't have anything I could really share with Marcus, but I felt confident I was on the right track.

I looked at my watch. Lise should be in her office in Boston. I punched in her number.

"Hey, Kath, what's up?" she said when she answered.

"I need your help with something," I said.

"Name it. It's yours."

"Your friend, Edward Mato. Do you think he'd talk to me?"

"I don't see why not," she said. "Are you looking for more information about that missing drawing?"

"I have a couple of questions about its history," I said.

"Let me call him and see what he says. Is it okay if I give him your number?"

"Yes," I said.

"Okay," she said. "I'll see if I can track him down."

"I owe you," I said.

"Umm, I know," she said with a laugh. "I'll put it on your tab."

I knew it could be hours or days before I heard from Edward Mato, if he even agreed at all to talk to me about the Weston drawing, so I was surprised when my phone rang about ten minutes later and it was him.

Edward Mato had a smooth, deep voice and a slightly formal manner of speaking.

"Lise told me it was your library that *Below the Falls* was stolen from," he said.

"*Below the Falls*, that's the name of the Weston drawing?" I said. I hadn't heard the drawing called by that name.

"That's the title the artist gave it, yes."

"Mr. Mato, you appraised that drawing for Charles Holmes before he died. If it turns out that it was actually the work of his first wife, what would that do to its value?"

"Please, call me Edward," he said.

"I will," I said. "If you'll call me Kathleen."

"You've heard the rumors about the drawing's origins, then, Kathleen," Edward Mato said, phrasing the sentence as a statement, not a question.

"Yes, I have. And I know it's not the only piece by Weston that's in question."

"You do your homework." I thought I heard a note of approval in his voice.

"I like to know what I'm talking about, where I can," I said.

"Even without incontrovertible proof, a collector could conceivably be willing to pay two, two and a half million dollars for *Below the Falls*."

Two and a half million dollars. Two and a half million reasons to steal the drawing and replace it with a fake. Two and a half million reasons to kill Margo Walsh.

"You told Charles Holmes that you believed his drawing hadn't been done by Sam Weston."

"That's correct. Based on my knowledge of Native American art and techniques from that time period as well as what I know about Weston's work, I told Mr. Holmes I believed *Below the Falls* was created by his first wife, not Weston himself."

"You said *Below the Falls* is the title the artist gave the drawing. You meant Stands Sacred," I said.

"Very good," he said. I could hear the smile in his voice.

"Would your appraisal be enough for a court to give the drawing to the Dakota Sioux people? I know they've returned land and other property based on treaty agreements."

"It's possible," he said. "I've been an expert witness twice in legal actions."

So if someone was going to sell *Below the Falls* to a collector, now was the time.

I thanked Edward Mato for his time and ended the call.

"Now we're getting somewhere," I said. There were no cats around and I felt a little silly just talking to myself.

So if Marshall and Diana Holmes were both having financial problems and they were co-owners of a drawing worth more than two million dollars, did it mean that one of them was involved in Margo's murder?

I walked outside and sat on the steps, hoping that somehow the fresh air would clear my head. I saw movement at the edge of the grass where my yard joined Rebecca's. Owen came stalking across the lawn. He climbed the steps and sat down beside me. There was a scrap of newspaper hanging cock-eyed from one of his ears.

I snagged the bit of paper and held it up. "Stay out of Rebecca's recycling bin," I said, glaring at him.

"Murp," Owen said.

"You think I don't know you're over there all the time," I said, setting the corner of newsprint on my leg and smoothing it flat with a finger. "You pretend you're over there to do rodent patrol when really you're just nosy. It's classic misdirection."

He looked at me unblinkingly. Then he lifted a paw and nonchalantly began washing his face.

"Misdirection," I repeated slowly. Maybe it *was* the fresh air. Or Owen's penchant for rooting around in Rebecca's recycling bin. Or maybe my little gray cells had finally put the pieces together.

22

I called Maggie, and when I explained what I was thinking, she gave me Rena's phone number. It was looking like she would be able to make a plea deal with respect to the charges against her.

I wasn't even sure Rena would answer her phone when she saw it was me calling—after all, I had been part of that ambush at the library—but she did pick up on the fifth ring.

"I have one question I'm hoping you'll answer for me," I said.

"I've already answered a lot more than that for the police," she said.

I wasn't exactly surprised by her reaction. She had no reason to help me. "Fair enough," I said. "I still have your paintings in my office. I can give them to Maggie if that's better for you."

There was silence for a moment; then she said, "If I answer your question, will it help catch the person who killed Margo?"

"It might."

"What is it?"

"Did you and Margo ever talk face-to-face about stealing the drawing?"

"No," Rena said. "We were never alone face-to-face. All of our conversations were either by e-mail or cell phone. She called herself Madame X."

"How did you know it was Margo, then?"

"I didn't at first. But I knew her voice sounded familiar the first time we all met at the library; that and the last-minute invitation to be part of the exhibit are what twigged for me."

I was on the right track. "Thank you," I said.

"That's it?" Rena asked. "That's going to help somehow?"

"I think so."

"Well . . . good luck," she said.

I ended the call and looked down at two furry faces. "We're right," I said. "Now all we have to do is prove it."

I turned my computer back on and began scrolling through the archives for the Lifestyle section of the *Minneapolis Star-Tribune*. Now that I knew what I was looking for, it wasn't that hard to find.

After about an hour I stood up and stretched. Owen had wandered off, but Hercules was sitting by my chair. "I know who did it, how they did it and why they did it," I told him, scooping him up into my arms. I swung around in a circle, holding the cat to my chest, and then did a little victory dance.

Hercules gave me a loopy eyes-crossed look. "We're going to catch some bad guys!" I said.

Catching bad guys wasn't that simple, it turned out.

I'd talked to Marcus three times by the time it was time for tai chi, and I was tired and frustrated. My form was wonky and I wanted to stop in the middle and go home, but I made myself keep going.

Ruby gave me a hug after class. "You're just having an off night," she said.

She didn't know the half of it, I thought.

Maggie walked over to us. "The St. James?" she asked, raising an eyebrow.

I nodded. "Yes."

The hotel bar was quiet, not surprising for a Tuesday night. Gavin Solomon and Marshall Holmes were at a table in the center of the room. Gavin looked up when we walked in. "Hi, Kathleen," he said, getting to his feet. "I was just going over the insurance company's plan for returning the artwork to the museum with Marshall. Can you join us? I can bring you up to date."

Marshall smiled up at us. "Please," he said, gesturing at the table.

"Thank you," I said. I looked at Gavin. "Could we do that in the morning? It's been long day."

"Sure," he said, frowning slightly. "I'll call you."

"Good to see you," I said to Marshall.

"Good to see both of you," he replied.

Maggie had already taken a seat at a nearby table. We each ordered a glass of red wine. Maggie propped both elbows on the table. "Okay, what's going on?" she said.

I rubbed the back of my neck with one hand. "You know how Abigail and Susan have been helping out keeping the different groups running in your studio?" I asked.

Maggie nodded. "They've been great. It wouldn't have worked without them."

"Everett said the board would pay them for that time if I could get the paperwork in before the board meeting tomorrow."

"That's good, isn't it?" Maggie asked.

"It would be if I could get into my office to get the actual paperwork." I sighed loudly.

"So, get Marcus to let you in."

The waiter came back with our wine. Maggie smiled at him. He was so captivated with her smile he tripped over his own feet on the way back to the bar.

"He won't," I said playing with the little coaster my wineglass had come with.

Maggie held up her glass, studied its contents and then took a sip. "Why not?" she asked.

"My office is sealed until they finish searching the building."

"So get the paperwork from Lita."

It was hard to keep my feelings from showing. Out of the corner of my eye I saw Gavin put away his cell phone, stand up and shake hands with Marshall Holmes. "I can't. She's out of town on some kind of family emergency."

"So you'll get the money approved at the next board meeting," Maggie said with a shrug.

"Both Abigail and Susan could use the money now. The library has been closed," I said. "They aren't getting paid." I folded one arm up over my head. "Why does Marcus have to be so unreasonable?"

Maggie raised an eyebrow at me. "C'mon, Kath. It's

a police investigation. I thought you wanted them to catch whoever killed Margo."

I took a deep breath and let it out slowly before I answered her. "I do. But how is me getting a couple of forms from my office going to interfere with that? It's not like he hasn't let me into the building before this. I thought now that we're together things were going to be different, but Marcus is just sliding back into his same old rigid ways."

Maggie set her glass down. "That's not fair. He's just doing his job. And it's not like you to expect some kind of special favors."

"I'm not asking for 'special favors,'" I said. I could feel the tightness in my jaw and hear it in my voice. "I'm just trying to make sure Susan and Abigail get paid for doing their jobs—actually, for doing more than their jobs." There was a knot of anxiety gnawing at my stomach. "It's not like you to take someone else's side, Mags."

Maggie sat up very straight in her chair. "I'm not taking any side, Kathleen," she said. "I think this whole business at the library has been really difficult and I think you may have lost your perspective." She looked at me for a long moment. Then she pushed her chair back. "I think it would be better if I left."

I looked down at the table. "I think you're right," I said. Maggie walked away. I could feel my heart pounding in my chest. When I looked up, Marshall Holmes was standing by the table.

"Kathleen, are you all right?" he asked. "I'm sorry if I'm intruding."

"You're not," I said. "I, uh, it's been a difficult day."

Marshall smiled. "I've had a few of those." He gestured at Maggie's empty chair. "May I sit down?"

"Please," I said. I picked up my glass and set it back down again. "You had to have heard me arguing with Maggie. I'm sorry about that."

"There's no need to apologize," he said, pulling out the chair and sitting down. "The theft of the Weston drawing and Margo Walsh's death have put a lot of people on edge, myself included. I know it's easy to get overwhelmed."

I sighed softly. "I'm beginning to think the police are never going to solve this."

"I thought they were searching the library again," Marshall said.

He was wearing jeans and a jade green sweater over a pale blue shirt with the sleeves pushed back. I thought about how many picture books I could have bought for Reading Buddies with the money he'd probably paid for that sweater.

"I don't think they're going to find anything," I said. Then I shook my head. "I'm sorry, Marshall. That was petty of me. It's just that I need to get into my office and I can't."

He tipped his head to one side and raised his eyebrows slightly. "Can't you persuade your detective friend to bend the rules just a little for you?"

I shook my head, wondering if I looked embarrassed. "I don't know if you've noticed, but he can be a little"—I hesitated, looking for the right word—"rigid. He's not the type to bend the rules. It's come between us before."

Marshall leaned toward me. "I understand a lot better than you'd think, Kathleen," he said. "My father was that kind of person. I loved him but he was a very black-and-white man. I can't tell you how many times we butted heads." Then he laughed. "Well, I could, but I won't because you'd wonder why I kept doing it."

I took a drink of my wine and got to my feet. "I think I should just go home," I said.

Marshall walked outside with me.

"Thank you for the conversation," I said. "Good night." I turned to head down the sidewalk and Marshall fell into step beside me.

"I'll walk you to the library," he said. He held up a hand before I could say anything. "I know you said you're going home, but I know you're not. And I'm not trying to imply you're helpless in any way, but it is getting dark."

"I'll think I'll just say, 'no comment,' " I said.

He smiled. "Good answer."

When we got to the library I turned to face Marshall. He was at least as tall as Marcus. Without heels I felt small standing next to him. "Thank you," I said. "But I think you really should go now."

He stuffed his hands in his pockets. "I'm going to wait out here for you. Whoever killed Margo is still on the loose and I'll feel better if I stick around." He shrugged. "My father was also big on being a gentleman."

I looked up at the sky. "Come inside, Marshall," I said. "It's going to rain by the look of those clouds, and it would probably be better for both of us if you weren't lurking around out here."

I pulled my spare set of keys out of my pocket, let us into the building and shut off both alarm systems. There was no security guard on duty anymore. After their initial panic, the insurance company had decided they only needed a live person in the library during the daytime. Gavin had laughed when he told me, saying that maybe they thought art thieves were afraid of the dark.

I turned on only one set of overhead lights. Marshall followed me up the stairs. I tried not to look at the piles of books on the main floor.

At least my office was untouched. I found the forms I needed in my filing cabinet. "I just need to go next door and copy these," I said to Marshall, holding up the papers. "I'll only be a minute."

"Do you mind if I borrow your phone book again?" he asked, a bit sheepishly, pulling his flip phone out of his pocket.

"Sure, go ahead," I said. I pointed to the bookshelf behind him. "It's in the same place. I'll be right back."

I walked down the hallway and picked up a plastic bag from the table in the lunchroom. I counted to twenty and stepped back into the office.

23

Marshall Holmes was standing in the middle of the room, holding the phone book upside down by its spine.

I held up the plastic bag. "Are you looking for this?" I asked. *Below the Falls* was inside the bag.

"Oh, my word, you found the drawing," Marshall said. "Where was it?"

"In that phone book," I said. I exhaled slowly. "Where you put it."

His eyes darted to my desk.

"I'm sorry," I said. "I don't have another paperweight for you to hit me over the head the way you did to Margo."

He was good. He frowned, shaking his head. "You think I killed Margo? You think I'm the one who hit her over the head with that brass cat?"

I swallowed the lump in my throat. "How did you know the paperweight was a brass cat?"

He wasn't at all rattled. "Because I was here. I used your phone book." He held it up. "Remember?"

"The paperweight wasn't here when you were in my office," I said. "It was a gift from a friend in Boston. I got it in the mail the day Margo was killed. By you."

Marshall rubbed a hand over his mouth. "It was an accident," he said, changing tack. He swallowed hard. His hands were shaking. "Margo and I had gotten to be friends putting this tour together. She felt the same way that I did, that the drawing was too fragile and potentially too valuable to be part of the exhibit."

"So you took it, so the whole tour would be canceled." My knees were trembling. I hoped he couldn't tell.

Marshall clenched his teeth and tight lines formed around his mouth. He gestured at the bag holding the drawing that I was still holding. "I took the drawing to keep it safe. That's not a crime. It belongs to me."

"Half of it belongs to you," I said.

"All of it *should* belong to me." His eyes flashed. "I'm a real Holmes. Diana isn't."

"Why did you kill Margo?" I said.

"I didn't mean for it to happen. You have to believe me," he said. "You know she didn't want the artwork out of the museum, especially the Weston drawing."

I nodded.

"She said more than once that no one seemed to understand what a bad idea it was. I thought . . . I thought it meant we were on the same page."

He cleared his throat. "I was here. Just Margo and I. Ownership has its privileges. The drawing was sitting there in its case. I thought, what if I took it? What if we made it look as though there had been a break-in? That would be the end of the exhibit."

"So it was a spur-of-the-moment thing?"

"It was. It was an accident, I swear." He sucked in a breath and looked up at the ceiling for a moment. "I made the mistake of telling Margo I was going to sell the drawing to a private collector who had the resources to make sure it was preserved properly."

He looked at me again, his expression pleading with me to understand. "Margo wanted the drawing to stay in a museum, where it could be examined and analyzed by art historians and anthropologists. They'd pick at it and pick at it until it was damaged. Until it wasn't worth anything anymore. I said no." He looked away again, running his left thumb over and over his fingers like he was trying to wipe something away.

"I walked away from her. I came in here," he said. "She followed me. She put her hands on my chest and she kept pushing me." He swallowed again. "I just reached blindly behind me. I didn't mean to hurt her."

I took a couple of steps closer to him. "Well then, tell that to the police," I said.

He looked at me, opened his mouth as though he was going to say something, and then closed it without speaking. His hand snaked out and snatched the bag holding the drawing from me. His entire expression changed. He shook his head, a condescending smile on his face. "I can't believe you fell for that," he said.

Behind him a voice said, "Funny. I was just thinking the same thing about you."

Marcus was standing in the doorway.

"How did you know?" Marshall asked after he'd been read his rights and the handcuffs had been snapped on.

"You switched phones to have an excuse to use the phone book here in my office."

He shook his head but didn't say anything.

"You have a smartphone," I continued. "I found photos of you online taking a call with a smartphone outside the opera. And how could a businessman manage without one these days? Which means you planned it all."

I remembered what Rena had said about the security system being off when she'd gotten to the library. "I think you shut off the alarm system somehow—it can be done and money buys a lot of information—took the Weston drawing, and it was Margo's bad luck to walk in on you. I found a photograph of Diana online from a charity talent show. When I did a little more digging, I found out you were in the same show, part of a magic act. You picked the lock." I gestured at my office door. "You hid the drawing here just in case the police considered you to be a suspect. You didn't count on the library being closed for so long."

Marshall didn't say anything, but a tiny nerve next to his eye began to twitch.

"You and Margo weren't friends. She wasn't helping you." I moved a step closer to him. "She wasn't the type of person to fall for your charm, but she was the type of person who would have come back here to make sure everything was perfect."

"And that got her killed," Marcus said.

Marshall's expression darkened. "I want my lawyer," he said.

Diana Holmes arrived just as the police were taking her stepbrother away. Neither one of them bothered with their public faces this time, and the animosity they felt for each other was obvious.

"The drawing will have to stay in police custody for now," Marcus told her. "It's evidence."

"I understand," she said giving him a cool, business-like smile. "It won't be a problem. My lawyer will be in touch with you. The drawing won't be going back to the museum." One eyebrow went up. "Under the circumstances."

"A judge won't give the drawing to you," I said.

Marshall might not have been her biological brother, but the condescending smile Diana gave me was identical to the one her brother had given me. "My brother tried to steal it," she said. "That's not going to work in his favor."

"You tried to steal it, too," I said.

She didn't flinch. "Excuse me?" she said, looking at me like I was something she'd found stuck to the sole of her very expensive shoes.

"It was a nice touch, mimicking Margo's voice so the person you hired to steal the drawing thought it was her," I said. "I would never have guessed except I saw that photo of you in the variety show for the children's hospital with your dummy. I understand you were very good."

She gave an offhand shrug. "I have no idea what you're talking about," she said.

"But I do," Hope said. "You transferred money to an account in Turks and Caicos recently. You didn't do a very good job of covering your tracks." She gave Diana a cool smile. "And by the way, you're under arrest."

Just like it had for her brother, the public face slipped

away, showing something a lot more ugly underneath as Diana Holmes was led away.

Marcus had to go to the station, but Maggie came out to the house to celebrate with me. She'd played her part to perfection. We talked for about an hour over tea and cupcakes I'd gotten from Sweet Thing.

Mags stretched her arms up over her head and yawned. "Sorry," she said. She smiled down at Owen, who, as usual, was settled beside her chair. "It's not the company."

He made a little murp as if saying he understood.

I walked out into the porch with Maggie. "Thank you," I said, wrapping her in a hug. "You were great."

"I'm glad I could help," she said. "I'm glad Margo's killer was caught."

I nodded. "Me too."

When I went back into the kitchen, Hercules was alone, sitting by the table. "Where's your brother?" I asked.

The little tuxedo cat gave me a blank look.

The basement door opened then, pushed, I could see, by a furry gray paw. Owen came across the floor, three black feathers in his mouth, the same three feathers, I realized, that I'd taken away from him and tossed in the garbage can. Now I realized why he'd tipped it over.

He dropped the feathers in front of his brother, shook his head and made a hacking sound before pushing them toward Herc.

Was this a peacemaking gesture? Had Owen actually understood everything I'd said to him the other day?

Hercules stretched out one white-tipped paw and pulled the feathers toward him. His eyes never left his brother's face. Then he bent his head, picked up the feathers in his mouth, turned and headed for the living room. Just before he got to the door he stopped and looked back over his shoulder. He gave a strangled "meow" because his mouth was full, and then he was gone.

After a moment I heard a sneeze, followed by another one. Clearly he'd spit out the feathers. I really hoped not on my footstool.

Harrison Taylor was sitting at a booth when I walked into Fern's Diner late Saturday afternoon. Harry Junior and Elizabeth were both at the counter, each with a cup of coffee. Elizabeth wasn't even trying to pretend she was there for any other reason than to watch her father. She was turned on her stool with her back to the counter so she could see the entire restaurant.

I slid into the booth across from Harrison.

"She's not exactly subtle, is she?" he said, pointing a finger in his daughter's direction.

"The apple doesn't fall far from the tree," I said with a smile.

The old man laughed. "Touché, Kathleen," he said.

Across the room he caught Peggy Sue's eye. He pointed to his own cup and then gestured at me. She nodded and in a moment came over with the coffeepot and a mug for me.

"How're things at the library, Kathleen?" Harrison asked, smiling a thank-you at Peggy, who smiled back at him.

"We reopened this morning," I said, adding cream and sugar to my cup.

"You must have been happy."

"I did a little dance by the circulation desk before we opened up," I said, grinning across the table at him.

"I'm sorry I missed that," he said.

We spent the next ten minutes talking about the library. Several times from the corner of my eye I saw Elizabeth look at her watch and then glance at the front door of the diner.

Finally, she slid off her stool and walked over to us. Harry followed. "Hi, Kathleen," she said.

"Hi," I said. I leaned around her and smiled at Harry.

Elizabeth had turned her attention to her father. "So where is she?"

The old man made a show of looking at his watch. "Is she late?"

"You know she is," Elizabeth said. "I'm sorry. She stood you up."

Harry gave a snort of derision. "You're not sorry, child."

She crossed her arms over her chest and gave him a defiant look. "No, I'm not. I told you this woman, whoever she is, was just trying to take advantage of you, and it turns out I was right."

Harrison smiled up at her. "It turns out the joke's on you," he said. "This meeting was a setup."

Elizabeth's eyes widened and Harry shook his head, a wry smile spreading across his face.

The old man pointed from his daughter to his son. "You all need to butt out. I can manage my own love life on my own, thank you very much."

I expected Elizabeth to be angry with her father, but all she did was lean down and kiss him on the cheek. "If you think you've won then you've forgotten whose daughter I am," she said. She smiled at me. "Good to see you, Kathleen." She looked at her brother. "I'll wait for you in the truck."

Harrison looked as though someone had just pulled the rug out from under him. Harry Junior was grinning broadly. He leaned over, patted his father on the shoulder and said, "I think you've finally met your match, old man." Then he left.

"I'll be damned," Harrison said.

I laughed. "Apples and trees," I said.

Peggy came back to top up our cups. I looked from her to Harrison. "So, how long has this relationship between you two been going on?" I asked, bouncing my crossed leg slowly in the air. Their guilty expressions told me I'd called it correctly.

"Are you going to tell on me?" Harrison asked. I noticed he'd covered Peggy Sue's hand with his own.

"It's not my story to tell."

He narrowed his blue eyes at me. "How did you know?"

I reached for my coffee. "Peggy is the only other person in town who's read every Mickey Spillane book we have. That and the fact that the two of you grinned at each other like a couple of sixteen-year-olds when she brought the coffee over."

Harrison smiled. "I'll remember that."

Peggy set the carafe on the edge of the table. "Kathleen, my intentions toward Harrison are honorable, despite our age difference."

"I don't doubt that," I said.

Harrison squeezed her hand and let it go. "I'm not stupid, Kathleen," he said. "I know there's a lot of water under the bridge when it comes to Peggy and me. We're friends and we're taking things real slow, but for the record, just because I'm old doesn't mean I'm not still in working order."

I shook my head and put my hands over my ears. "That's way more information than I need to have."

Harrison laughed. Peggy blushed and I was very glad he didn't say anything more.

When I got home Marcus was in the kitchen making dinner with two furry assistants looking on.

"Everything all right?" he asked, looking up from the stove.

"Everything's fine," I said.

"How serious is this new relationship of Harrison's?"

I laughed. "I don't know and I'm not sure I really want to."

The table was set with a blue tablecloth. There were candles and a small vase of daisies in the center.

"What's all this?" I asked.

Marcus turned down the heat under a pot and stepped away from the stove. "I talked to Eddie. He isn't giving up on Roma."

"I'm glad," I said.

Marcus put his hands on my shoulders. "I'm sorry that I almost ruined things between us last year," he said. "If there was a chance to go back in time and relive just one moment, I would relive that moment down on the Riverwalk when I accused you of not trusting me."

He was so serious.

"It's okay," I said. "We got to where we are in the end, and that's what matters."

"I trust you with my life, Kathleen. I trust you with more than my life. I trust you with my heart." He hesitated, and I felt my own heart begin to hammer in my chest.

Both cats were looking up at him.

"Merow!" Hercules said loudly.

"Merow!" Owen echoed even more insistently.

Marcus glanced down at them. "Okay," he said.

Then he put his arms around me and kissed me. "I love you," he said.

If you love Sofie Kelly's Magical Cats series,
read on for a sample of the first book in
Sofie Ryan's *New York Times* bestselling
Second Chance Cat Mystery series!

THE WHOLE CAT AND CABOODLE

is available from Obsidian
wherever books are sold.

Elvis was sitting in the middle of my desk when I opened the door to my office. The cat, not the King of Rock and Roll, although the cat had an air of entitlement about him sometimes, as though he thought he was royalty. He had one jet-black paw on top of a small cardboard box—my new business cards, I was hoping.

"How did you get in here?" I asked.

His ears twitched but he didn't look at me. His green eyes were fixed on the vintage Wonder Woman lunch box in my hand. I was having an early lunch, and Elvis seemed to want one as well.

"No," I said firmly. I dropped onto the retro red womb chair I'd brought up from the shop downstairs, kicked off my sneakers, and propped my feet on the matching footstool. The chair was so comfortable. To me, the round shape was like being cupped in a soft, warm giant hand. I knew the chair had to go back down to the shop, but I was still trying to figure out a way to keep it for myself.

Before I could get my sandwich out of the yellow

vinyl lunch box, the big black cat landed on my lap. He wiggled his back end, curled his tail around his feet and looked from the bag to me.

"No," I said again. Like that was going to stop him.

He tipped his head to one side and gave me a pitiful look made all the sadder because he had a fairly awesome scar cutting across the bridge of his nose.

I took my sandwich out of the lunch can. It was roast beef on a hard roll with mustard, tomatoes and dill pickles. The cat's whiskers quivered. "One bite," I said sternly. "Cats eat cat food. People eat people food. Do you want to end up looking like the real Elvis in his chunky days?"

He shook his head, as if to say, "Don't be ridiculous."

I pulled a tiny bit of meat out of the roll and held it out. Elvis ate it from my hand, licked two of my fingers and then made a rumbly noise in his throat that sounded a lot like a sigh of satisfaction. He jumped over to the footstool, settled himself next to my feet and began to wash his face. After a couple of passes over his fur with one paw he paused and looked at me, eyes narrowed— his way of saying, "Are you going to eat that or what?"

I ate.

By the time I'd finished my sandwich Elvis had finished his meticulous grooming of his face, paws and chest. I patted my legs. "C'mon over," I said.

He swiped a paw at my jeans. There was no way he was going to hop onto my lap if he thought he might get a crumb on his inky black fur. I made an elaborate show of brushing off both legs. "Better?" I asked.

Elvis meowed his approval and walked his way up

my legs, poking my thighs with his front paws—no claws, thankfully—and wiggling his back end until he was comfortable.

I reached for the box on my desk, keeping one hand on the cat. I'd guessed correctly. My new business cards were inside. I pulled one out and Elvis leaned sideways for a look. The cards were thick brown recycled card stock, with SECOND CHANCE, THE REPURPOSE SHOP, angled across the top in heavy red letters, and SARAH GRAYSON and my contact information, all in black, in the bottom right corner.

Second Chance was a cross between an antiques store and a thrift shop. We sold furniture and housewares—many things repurposed from their original use, like the tub chair that in its previous life had actually been a tub. As for the name, the business was sort of a second chance—for the cat and for me. We'd been open only a few months and I was amazed at how busy we already were.

The shop was in a redbrick building from the late 1800s on Mill Street, in downtown North Harbor, Maine, just where the street curved and began to climb uphill. We were about a twenty-minute walk from the harbor front and easily accessed from the highway—the best of both worlds. My grandmother held the mortgage on the property and I wanted to pay her back as quickly as I could.

"What do you think?" I said, scratching behind Elvis's right ear. He made a murping sound, cat-speak for "good," and lifted his chin. I switched to stroking the fur on his chest.

He started to purr, eyes closed. It sounded a lot like there was a gas-powered generator running in the room.

"Mac and I went to look at the Harrington house," I said to him. "I have to put together an offer, but there are some pieces I want to buy, and you're definitely going with me next time." Eighty-year-old Mabel Harrington was on a cruise with her new beau, a ninety-one-year-old retired doctor with a bad toupee and lots of money. They were moving to Florida when the cruise was over.

One green eye winked open and fixed on my face. Elvis's unofficial job at Second Chance was rodent wrangler.

"Given all the squeaks and scrambling sounds I heard when I poked my head through the trapdoor to the attic, I'm pretty sure the place is the hotel for some kind of mouse convention."

Elvis straightened up, opened his other eye, and licked his lips. Chasing mice, birds, bats and the occasional bug was his idea of a very good time.

I'd had Elvis for about four months. As far as I could find out, the cat had spent several weeks on his own, scrounging around downtown North Harbor.

The town sits on the midcoast of Maine. "Where the hills touch the sea" is the way it's been described for the past 250 years. North Harbor stretches from the Swift Hills in the north to the Atlantic Ocean in the south. It was settled by Alexander Swift in the late 1760s. It's full of beautiful historic buildings, award-winning restaurants and quirky little shops. Where else could you buy a blueberry muffin, a rare book and fishing gear all on the same street?

The town's population is about thirteen thousand,

but that more than triples in the summer with tourists and summer residents. It grew by one black cat one evening in late May. Elvis just appeared at The Black Bear. Sam, who owns the pub, and his pickup band, The Hairy Bananas—long story on the name—were doing their Elvis Presley medley when Sam noticed a black cat sitting just inside the front door. He swore the cat stayed put through the entire set and left only when they launched into their version of the Stones' "Satisfaction."

The cat was back the next morning, in the narrow alley beside the shop, watching Sam as he took a pile of cardboard boxes to the recycling bin. "Hey, Elvis. Want some breakfast?" Sam had asked after tossing the last flattened box in the bin. To his surprise, the cat walked up to him and meowed a loud yes.

He showed up at the pub about every third day for the next couple of weeks. The cat clearly wasn't wild—he didn't run from people—but no one seemed to know whom Elvis (the name had stuck) belonged to. The scar on his nose wasn't new; neither were a couple of others on his back, hidden by his fur. Then someone remembered a guy in a van who had stayed two nights at the campgrounds up on Mount Batten. He'd had a cat with him. It was black. Or black and white. Or possibly gray. But it definitely had had a scar on its nose. Or it had been missing an ear. Or maybe part of a tail.

Elvis was still perched on my lap, staring off into space, thinking about stalking rodents out at the old Harrington house, I was guessing.

I glanced over at the carton sitting on the walnut sideboard that I used for storage in the office. The fact that it was still there meant that Arthur Fenety hadn't come in while Mac and I had been gone. I was glad. I was hoping I'd be at the shop when Fenety came back for the silver tea service that was packed in the box.

A couple of days prior he had brought the tea set into my shop. Fenety had a charming story about the ornate pieces that he said had belonged to his mother. A bit too charming for my taste, like the man himself. Arthur Fenety was somewhere in his seventies, tall with a full head of white hair, a matching mustache and an engaging smile to go with his polished demeanor. He could have gotten a lot more for the tea set at an antiques store or an auction. Something about the whole transaction felt off.

Elvis had been sitting on the counter by the cash register and Fenety had reached over to stroke his fur. The cat didn't so much as twitch a whisker, but his ears had flattened and he'd looked at the older man with his green eyes half-lidded, pupils narrowed. He was the picture of skepticism.

The day after he'd brought the pieces in, Fenety had called to ask if he could buy them back. The more I thought about it, the more suspicious the whole thing felt. The tea set hadn't been on the list of stolen items from the most recent police update, but I still had a niggling feeling about it and Arthur Fenety.

"Time to do some work," I said to Elvis. "Let's go downstairs and see what's happening in the store."

ABOUT THE AUTHOR

Sofie Kelly is an author and mixed-media artist who lives on the East Coast with her husband and daughter. In her spare time she practices Wu-style tai chi and likes to prowl around thrift stores. And she admits to having a small crush on Matt Lauer.

CONNECT ONLINE

sofiekelly.com